# Blood Lust

## A Dhampir Action Thriller

by

Bernard Lee DeLeo

# Blood Lust

## A Dhampir Action Thriller

by

Bernard Lee DeLeo

*****

PUBLISHED BY:

Bernard Lee DeLeo and RJ Parker Publishing Inc.

**ISBN-13: 978-1523641437**

**ISBN-10: 1523641436**

# Blood Lust

*****

## License Notes

This eBook is licensed for your personal enjoyment only. This eBook may not be resold or given away to other people. Please respect the author's work. This is a work of fiction. Any resemblance to real life persons, events, or places is purely coincidental.

*****

The unauthorized reproduction or distribution of a copyrighted work is illegal. Criminal copyright infringement, including infringement without monetary gain, is investigated by the FBI and is punishable by fines and federal imprisonment.

# DEDICATION

As it will be with every novel I write from now until my own End of Days, I dedicate this novel to my deceased angel, wife, and best friend: Joyce Lynn Whitney DeLeo.

# Chapter One

# Dhampir

I raced through the densely wooded area in a split second's rush from hiding to pounce on the doe leading her fawns to water. With her body yanked into a position where sharp hooves meant little, my fangs sank deeply through rough hide to the elixir of existence for me: blood. I drank deeply, the doe's life flitting behind my eyes in a shutter storm of forested images. I released her, leaping far into the clear. The doe immediately retreated to her two stunned fawns, watching me with unblinking eyes, making movements of defense with lifted hooves. When I saw her wound would not continue to bleed out, I turned away, hiking toward the trailhead parking lot miles away, practicing my woodcraft with concentration on making no sound. If needed, I could mask my scent as I had done today, and become a creature unthreatening to the other woodland inhabitants. I acquired what I needed to survive, but avoided killing.

I'm a Dhampir. For the uninitiated, I have all the strengths and cravings of a vampire, but none of the weaknesses. No, I don't know how I came into existence. My Mom went to college in Sacramento, California, an only child whom my Grandparents doted on. They reluctantly agreed to her moving into an apartment near Sacramento State College. Mom went to a party off campus with some friends on Halloween with a Goth theme. An intense looking young man took an interest in her. Although slender, Mom told me he was very tall, and when she danced with him he felt made of steel. One thing led to another of which Mom kept to herself. She awoke in her apartment. The man who had spent the night with her was gone. Nine months later, Mom lived with my Grandparents again, and I came along. The pregnancy nearly killed Mom because I fed in the womb on her. Imagine her surprise when she tried to breast feed me. Instead of milk, my tiny needle sharp fangs fed on her blood. My Mom is iron willed. She was then, and she is now. My bite heals, so after she figured out what I needed, she would clasp me to her neck for feeding. To say I grew in strange ways would be an understatement – a story for another time. Bottom line is I have the greatest Mom and Grandparents on earth. They still live in Placerville. I have a place further into the mountains in Pollack Pines.

I am also what they call a prodigy. I completed college at sixteen in computer and engineering technology. If I lived in many other countries, I would have been enslaved for the greater good. I'm twenty-four now. I create apps for computers and mobile technology. My monetary worth makes even thinking about it unnecessary. There is also a bit of consulting in my life on the down low as it were. See, I have a childhood friend named Erin. She lived next door to me. We did everything together, because I think Erin sensed I might not be like other kids. My Mom instilled in me a moral code from the moment I could understand the concept. She taught me I could not drink from people. She also made sure I practiced daily to control my strength. Mom called it raising the dark superman. When Erin and I were ten, we played by one of the many streams running through Placerville from the Lake Tahoe basin. We pretended to be everything a kid's imagination can envision. Then she found out what I was.

We decided to hike along the stream. Erin claimed we trekked in darkest Africa along the shore of the Congo River.

"Hey kids," a man's voice called out from behind us.

We turned to see a clean shaven, tall, lean guy dressed in slacks, tennis shoes, and black windbreaker. His brown hair looked fashionably long and unmoving in the breeze, so probably sprayed. He carried a dog leash in his hands with an engaging smile. "Hi kids, have either of you seen my dog. He's a black lab, named Sparky."

Erin also wanted to be a detective when she became an adult. From the time I first remembered watching TV with her, she absorbed every cop and CSI show available. That did not bode well for our lost dog guy. "Please leave us alone, mister. If you lost your dog, you didn't lose him around here. We're a long way from any park or street."

The man's smile disappeared, to be replaced with a sinister smirk. "Smart girl. What's your name?"

Erin had outed the guy. I knew we were in trouble. I could smell it: Erin's fear, the man's excitement, even the dampness in the air. She was right to be afraid.

"He's going to kill us, Jed," Erin whispered sideways at me through clenched teeth.

My full name is Jedidiah Israel Blake and I didn't take my eyes off him. "I won't let him. Walk toward the road, Erin. I'll follow in a few moments."

"I'm not leaving you!" Erin tried to resist me moving her behind me, but she could do nothing except be swept in the direction I intended.

"No one's going anywhere." He moved closer, reaching under the back of his windbreaker.

I couldn't worry about secrets. I ran him down, gripping and breaking the wrist of his hand reaching as we hit the ground. He screamed out as I buried my fangs in his neck. He quieted instantly. I drank with lust, a magnificent feeling so primal I probably growled while doing it. The taste of human blood, hot from its unwilling donor, invigorated me, but brought visions from his past foul life flooding through my brain. I sucked the life out of him in a fury I had never felt before. Only Erin's cool hand shaking my bare arm where it clutched the man's broken wrist, and her hushed pleadings stopped me.

When I stood, letting his body drop down, Erin pulled me over to the stream, only the gasps for breath hinting at anything changed within her. "You have to wash your face and hands, Jed."

No screams, no accusations of being a monster. Erin simply helped me wash and then we went home, leaving the predator where he lay. We returned home the way we had come, because he had reached our position at the stream from a road over the ridge nearby. Erin kept glancing at me with a curious look as if she had not witnessed me maul and suck a man's essence from him. We were bonded for life.

"How long before your eyes return to normal?"

"Uh... I don't know. Do they look funny?"

"They're black. Can I see your fangs?" Erin slowed to grip the sides of my face as she peered upwards.

By that time in my life I could extend and retract at will, so I did it for her.

"Wow... your mouth widens there. They aren't even visible, and they have a hollow pin hole away from the fang point," She observed clinically. Erin released my face and took my hand as we walked. "Thank you."

"You didn't even scream. You're tough... like my Mom. She and my Grandparents can see anything, and you know... they accept it now."

"We're walkin' around in daylight, so you're like Blade the Vampire Hunter: a day-walker," Erin said. "We have to keep your powers secret."

"That would be best. My Mom's going to freak when she finds out what happened."

"I'll tell her. It won't be a big deal. That guy deserved it, and now she has someone else to help keep your secret. I'll be your Igor."

I laughed even after all these years thinking about that line. My Igor and I had many adventures growing into adulthood. I needed a lot of help not killing people who thought they could pick on the kid genius. Erin, to my Mom's relief, took over some of the surveillance chores when I was out of her sight. My Igor created the four step SUCK program for me. It meant 'Stay Under Control Killer'. When I reached six and a half feet by sixteen, nearly all incidents of people baiting me disappeared. She's still finishing college, because she became a cop at twenty-one, but by then had finished her BA degree in Criminology. Erin works toward her graduate degree now. She's been on the Sacramento Police Force for three years, and aims at being the youngest female detective ever with my help.

My help means I can smell or taste what has happened. If there's blood at the crime scene I can taste it, drawing visions of what has happened. I can also smell small hints of anything connected to the murder. She's only been the first on scene with her partner four times where someone was murdered. We collaborated on two she was able to sneak me on scene for after the CSI people and detectives left. Then we recreated how the murder happened so she could make a persuasive report to the detectives. They laughed at her first, but she pushed past their derision, hammering points home they could not ignore. The detectives listen to anything she springs on them now, so Erin does mostly her own detective work, allowing anything she finds to be credited to them.

I love computers and tech work building apps. I don't mind helping Igor, but she knows I don't enjoy it like she does. We've been confidants and lovers, but Igor said I was too intense. She said I killed her ambition when we made love, whatever the hell that means. Now, unfortunately, we're not even friends with benefits. Erin dates other guys, and I do what I do. My Mom's retired at forty-four, and my Grandparents travel all over the world which was what they wanted. I have so much money, I'm able to do anything, including owning my own blood bank like all the vampires do in the movies. I have to hunt once in a while though. I had to meet Erin at a crime scene in a half hour. She and her partner had duty keeping the public away from a particularly horrific crime scene. I have a computer cover now. I built an app for CSI which revolutionized crime-scene investigation. Once the CSI people finish, Erin's allowed to let me do supposed research for updating my app, which they already use.

Erin met me outside the apartment building. She's a gorgeous, auburn haired, five and a half foot tall minx, who loves yanking my chain. She wants to be a detective so bad I think she'd even start sleeping with me again if it would speed the promotion. God, Erin looked hot in that uniform. I must need therapy. I think I have either a cop fetish or an Erin fetish.

"Officer Constanza," I began, "How may I be of service?"

She peered at me with an annoyed look. "You've fed. Your eyes are still black. Put on your sunglasses. I told you this could be my big break, you dork."

I did as ordered. "Your continued disrespect for my position in this partnership leaves much to be desired, Officer Constanza."

"Come on, Jed." Erin yanked me toward the apartment building, but when I don't want to be yanked, I don't move. "Hey... did you just Donkey-Kong me?"

Donkey-Kong is a term she uses when on multiple occasions I've not moved when yanked. It irritates her which was the main reason I did it. "What's in it for me?"

She looked startled for a second. I always perform as ordered without question. "You get to improve on your thing-a-jig-it for CSI people."

"I have more money than I know what to do with, even though I'm giving away more to charity than the budgets of small countries. I invented an app for CSI already-"

"Can we walk while you motor mouth? Tony will be back from dinner break soon."

"I guess." I let Igor drag me to someone's doom. "My CSI app performs hundreds of checks including preliminary DNA trace now. I can rest on my laurels for the next decade without a single improvement."

Erin kept dragging, but I could see the squirrel in her head, speeding inside the thought wheel, reaching for nuts. "What's with you? You're helping me make detective. That's what's in it for you. Haven't I been your Igor all these years?"

Oh no you don't. You do not get to pull the Igor card on me. "Haven't I saved your life on multiple occasions, tutored you on an accelerated course through school, and ended the stalker that scared the crap out of you?"

"He did not scare the crap out of me. I was only sixteen. Quick Mart was the only job I could get at night after school. I didn't know the perp stalking me home was an ex-con out on parole. I had it handled."

"By had it handled do you mean you had a plan for your clothes being ripped off and you bitch slapped to the ground? He had you half into his van when I arrived on scene."

Erin snuffed back laughter. "Okay... okay, but I had him surrounded. Where the hell were you when I was getting mugged?"

"You ordered me not to get involved unless it was life and death. I was merely following orders."

Erin gasped, stopped in her tracks, and punched me in the chest. Then she yelped and held her hand for a few moments. "You did get there earlier! You were on his tail the whole time, and you let me get mangled. You claimed you just happened to come by when you did."

"So what's your point?"

"Oh I see. I got schooled because I issued too many orders. That's mean. Then I was right. You followed me home all the time."

I shrugged. "I love the dark. Mom knew nothing could hurt me. So, I used to stalk everyone at night, including you when I knew where you were. I wasn't the only one following you, but luckily I was one of the ones following you."

"You ripped that poor guy apart. Without your Igor, you would have been plant food." She began dragging me again.

"No, but many innocents may have perished. Back to my original question, what's in it for me?"

"This is because I dumped you, isn't it. That was years ago and it still hurts. I get that, but it was too much. You ruin me. I can't even think straight when I'm with you that way. We're past that now. You're obsessing. It's affecting our friendship. Get over it."

"I am over it," I lied.

"Okay, what'll it take to get you to help me?" We reached the yellow crime scene tape across the door. Erin faced me.

"Show me the scene." What's the use? "Let's do this."

Erin took a deep breath and ducked under the crime scene tape. "You're pouting now."

I broke the crime scene tape and walked in. I smelled death, fear, horror, and the worst of all the embers of dying life – regret. That last moment when helpless agony passes, leaving behind eternity. Erin led the way to a coagulating pool of blood. The body of course was gone.

"She was alive when he cut her apart. How many pieces?"

"How… never mind. Six. We don't know if it was a man that-"

"It was a man." I knelt next to the pool of blood, slipping on the Nitrile gloves Erin handed me.

It would not be like a fine aged wine. I didn't say anything to Erin about why I needed to feed before doing this. I scooped a bit of the coagulated blood, knowing my Igor hates this part. She could watch me suck a living man dry, but when I dip for old blood, hunting for clues, it's too much. She turns away. I tasted enough of the blood to confirm my assumptions about the smell. I closed my eyes, assaulted by images through the woman's eyes. I cannot move or speak, and yet I can feel each extremity being removed - the pain, beyond belief. I see the killer. I smell him. He smells of a chemical mix, like a laboratory. Lean, thick blonde hair to his neck, early thirties, cold blue eyes, no fear, no passion, no remorse – a monster at work. Erin shook my shoulder. I straightened from my revelry of mutilation and death. I peeled off the gloves, knowing Erin's partner Tony has returned. I turn with a welcoming smile.

I hold out my hand to the dark haired six footer. Tony's an affable pro with fifteen years on the force. He has a wife and two kids. Tony and I play basketball together on Sundays with a bunch of other guys I have to be very careful around, other police officers and lawyers. "Hi Tone, how's the ankle?"

He shook with me while giving Erin the fish eye. "It's all better, Jed. It was just a mild sprain. You two haven't been contaminating the crime scene with young wild animal DNA have you?"

"Very funny, meathead," Erin fired back. "Jed is researching as always, doing something useful besides retiring on the job."

Tony chuckled. "You always bring out the beast in my partner when you're around, Jed. What's with the sunglasses?"

"Mild eye irritation," I answered. "I think I see a few additions to be added to my CSI app. I'm not sure why I didn't think of it before, but the app should be able to measure the blood pool dimensions, estimating a number of unknowns."

Tony shrugged. "Whatever floats your boat, pal. You can go on dinner break, Eerie. Take blood man out and buy him something to eat. That coffee shop, Artie's, down the block is good."

"I told you to stop calling me Eerie." Erin started walking toward the door. "C'mon Jed, we'll go have a coffee. The old security guard will be fine until I get back."

I grinned at Tony and waved while Erin wasn't looking. Eerie? I like it. Why didn't I think of that nickname? "See ya', Tone."

"Don't let the man-eater drag you down, Jed."

Erin gave Tony the one finger salute without turning. Outside, Erin grabbed onto my arm as we walked. "Spill it. What did you see? I could tell you saw something."

"Don't be so pushy, Eerie."

"I'm going to shoot that prick Tony the moment I see him. If you call me that again, I'll stake you in the middle of the night."

"You'd have to sneak in on me, and you don't have the skills, Eerie."

Erin growled. "I'll seduce you again, and stake you while you're passed out from exhaustion."

I simply smiled at her. She blushed and turned away to walk toward the coffee shop down the block. When she 'seduced' me, I wasn't the one passed out. I caught up to her. "The killer drugged her with some form of curare to paralyze her, but it didn't kill her, or take away the pain. He's in his thirties, longish blonde hair, blue eyes, and about six feet tall. He smells of chemicals as if he works in a lab."

Erin spun on me. "Damn, Jed! The woman's name is Bonny Lassiter, and she works at Sutter Medical Center in the outpatient lab. We can go there now and get the guy! He probably works alongside of her."

"And the case, my dear Eerie? We have to create a case supporting my vision. It will do you no good at all to jump this guy without any proof. I agree we need to find him. Then I'll stalk the killer until we make your case to get the detectives interested."

With every word, Erin's facial expression turned from excitement to annoyance. Then she brightened suddenly as we walked into the coffee shop. "I know what we'll do. Sit down over here."

Erin led the way to a booth. After the waitress took our order, and returned with the coffees, Erin issued her orders for the day. "We'll go over there, find him, and I'll sweat him."

Oh boy, this doesn't sound like the Igor I've worked with in the past. "What exactly does it mean when you say you're going to sweat him?"

"I'll ask sharply worded questions about his whereabouts, his relationship with Bonny, how long they've worked together, and if they ever had a disagreement."

"Maybe we should think of another way to get the detectives interested in him. I don't think you're supposed to be interrogating anyone. What if this guy charges you with harassment?"

"I'm open to ideas, Jed."

"I like your idea of finding out his identity. Once we have that, I can stalk him. He cut Bonny apart without remorse. It wasn't an act of unrequited love. There has to be a back story to this, and we won't get it from him."

Erin took her time deciding, but I could tell she was warming to my idea. She nodded. "You're making sense. Do you think he's done this before?"

"Not here, and not recently anywhere. Think about it though. He uses a paralytic so he can saw pieces off while she's still alive. He did it for the pure unadulterated killing process. I doubt a murder like that has been committed in years, unless he did it overseas."

"I agree. I'm off in another hour. I'll change into civvies and we can check the lab for any sign of him. What did you feed on?"

"A doe."

Erin made her usual disgusted face. "You fed on Bambi's mother? That is sick."

17

"Yeah, and I did it in front of Bambi and his sister. I think I saw Thumper and Flower gawking at me too while I did the deed."

She made fake gagging noises, pretending she wasn't holding back laughter. The waitress arrived with our orders of tuna sandwiches and fries. "What are you going to do until I get off?"

"Find out if I'm right about this type of murder. It may give you a starting point with the detectives if I find a place where this has happened before, especially if we learn the killer's identity, and prove he was also in the same area as the other murders done in the same way.'

"You piss me off when you do the damn deductive reasoning better than I do. Maybe if they freeze me out of being a detective, we'll open our own place."

"You're only twenty-four. No one's freezing you out. Besides, I don't want to be a detective. I love what I do. Stay with the police force. You'll make it, and I'll help, even though you treat me like the creepy red haired cousin."

"Your hair's black, and you need guidance, which I've provided for you," Erin pointed out. "Your Mom depends on me to keep you in line."

"My Mom thinks you're a pushy bitch."

Erin gasped. She loves my Mom. I nailed her with that one, but I couldn't keep a straight face long enough to pull it off. Some Dhampir monster I am. "You snot!"

"Drop all that. I'll check for threads of other similar murders. You go be a good partner to long suffering Tony. Text me from the station when you're ready to go over to the Lab for a look at this guy. Then we'll update our plans."

"Take off your sunglasses, and let me see your eyes." I did as requested. Erin nodded. "You're good to go. I'm still mad at you."

"For what?"

"I'll think of something."

* * *

I traveled in my Batmobile, which is what I call my equipment SUV, especially when I'm roped into helping Erin. I have everything in it imaginable for doing field work. I also have it locked in such a way, even if a thief broke a window which is impossible, they couldn't get in and take anything out. There were no windows in the back. In the front I had unbreakable glass. The solid doors, with actual latches and security locks could not be broken into with anything less than a plasma cutting torch. I could afford to lose everything, but that didn't mean I wanted to. This part of town, not known as safe even in daylight hours, lived up to its dark potential. Two young men were seriously looking over my shiny black Batmobile. I knew they weren't admiring it, or thinking to buy it. I approached with a smile. Yeah, that would help.

"Hi guys."

They looked at my size and musculature with less than enthusiasm. I do not look like someone you ever want to mess with. They didn't. The two looked at each other, and reached for weapons. I may not have mentioned this, but I am hell of fast. I smashed into them with attitude, clotheslining the two at rapid speed. They hit the sidewalk as if run over by a car. I called Erin, and did a quick explanation.

"Shit, Jed… you didn't kill them, did you?" She whispered it all in very hushed voice Erin knew I could hear but not Tony."

19

"Are you stupid?"

She giggled. "I'll be right out."

By the time she arrived at the Batmobile, my two carjackers were only then beginning to move. "I didn't disarm them yet. I figured I'd watch them while you do it."

Erin put on gloves, and bagged their weapons as they mildly resisted her search. She didn't handcuff them right away because Erin knew they could do nothing but what I allowed them to do. She had the fancy plastic restraints. I stood each of them for restraining. They were not communicative yet. Erin read them their rights. In answer to her repeated questions of understanding, they muttered something unintelligible. She sighed.

"Did you have your camera security on too, Jed?"

"Yep. I'll e-mail the video to you. I'm not sure you can use it because of the way I ran them over, but maybe you can. If not, I'll testify. They were drawing weapons to carjack my precious Batmobile. I'll walk them over to your squad car. This should get you and Tony off early from your security guard work."

"You may be right. You did well, Jed."

"Their heads are still attached so I think I did damn well."

\* \* \*

Forty minutes later, I found a trail of similar murders across Europe, twelve up to present day. Interpol and the media called the killer 'The Paralizer'. He used a hybrid mixture of curare as I thought. If our police call overseas, they could get a breakdown on the chemical composition. I put that on the mental list for improving my app too. I received a text from Erin. Both carjacker weapons were used in other murders, so I was off the hook, but ordered to pick Erin up at the station. I know my mouth dropped open when I did. She wore a black micro miniskirt, black high heels, and a burgundy off shoulder top held in place by not much more than her nipples. That she walked away from the precinct building with a long light gray raincoat, and then stripped it off while approaching the Batmobile, meant part of this show was for me alone.

Erin slid into the seat next to me, unfortunately allowing the raincoat to drape over her lower half. "Get your head out of the gutter, Jed."

"Did you come to tell me you have to work for vice as a streetwalker?"

"I thought I'd stir our perp's brain a bit when we find him."

"I doubt it will be his brain stirring." I know it wasn't my brain stirring. I filled her in on what I found out about 'The Paralizer'. "All we need is an identity. The killings stopped a year and a half ago in Europe. If you give me a little time, I can hack into the hospital's employee records. We could then-"

"Yes! Then, we'll find out if the guy you saw came from Europe in the same time frame. You are a genius!" Erin slapped the back of my head. "Hit it. I want to get over there and skip the boring employee record hacks."

I did as ordered. "Real detectives do the boring research. They don't skip to the face off with the perp. Maybe you should consider getting into undercover vice work instead of homicide detective."

"Until you made that horrible observation I was thinking of giving you another chance at intimacy with me, but now I'm afraid friends without benefits will be your lot."

"You do understand, Igor, that I can tell when you're lying, right?" It was another of my annoying talents. Annoying to Erin anyway.

"Damn you, Dhampir! I can't even mess with your head."

I slipped a hand under her coat. "Let's go to my house in the mountains while I find out everything you need without confrontations. You can really mess with my mind then."

Her knees popped open involuntarily, accompanied by short gasping intakes of breath before she realized my intent. She slammed them shut and smacked my hand. "There will be no monster seduction. We do this my way."

I returned my errant hand to the steering wheel with a satisfied grin. I nearly had her on the ropes that time. It was a comfortable silence until we reached the medical center – comfortable in that Erin rode in a folded arms, eyes straight ahead posture, her only movement to glare at me every few minutes.

To say Erin received attention would be an understatement. We haunted the break areas and cafeterias near the lab facilities. I enjoyed Erin's company, or I would have been pointing out my earlier advice should have been followed. We had a coffee finally at a table instead of traipsing around the center when I saw him. He wore a set of those pale green lab outfits. We locked eyes as he sat at a table with his tray nearby. I smiled... one predator to another. He didn't smile back. Erin didn't turn, but she could tell I had him in sight.

"He's here?"

"Sitting alone two tables straight behind you, just as I told you: blonde hair, blue eyes, and lean. What now, Erin in charge?"

"I'm going back and sit with him. I'll introduce myself, and show him my ID. Then I'll ask him about knowing Bonny Lassiter, and if they worked together."

"In other words, you're going to sweat him just as you were going to do in uniform. Maybe you should have simply stayed in uniform."

"And maybe, Mr. Know-It-All, I'll perk something beyond what you imagine from him. Turn up your super hearing, Dracula. I'm going in."

"Oh, so now I'm a monster since I disagreed with you, instead of a hero like Blade."

"Exactly. Stay here, and don't move until I text you." Erin sashayed to the real monster's table without another word.

I took out my phone and pretended to be playing with it instead of listening to Erin's conversation. My glances at him revealed an instant interest in Erin's flirty, arrogant style policewoman role. He invited her to sit down, and answered all her questions with a slight smile. Yes, he worked with Bonny. Yes, he had seen her the day before. No, they had never been on a date or become involved. He even gave her his card voluntarily if she needed to ask him anything else. When she started to stand away from the chair, he covered her hand with his, asking her to dinner. I nearly crushed my phone when she agreed to it. She scribbled her address on a piece of notebook paper from her bag. She told him how nice it was to meet someone who didn't care if she was a cop.

After she left, I remained as ordered so as not to ruin her insanity. I know the monster had seen her at my table, but what was the use in second guessing my beauteous Igor. The monster had plans. Erin had plans. I had plans. I hoped the right plans worked. At that time, my only plan was somehow being with Erin when the miniskirt came off. Since I didn't see how I could make my plan work, I would have to let this other game play out. Erin texted me, so I left to join her. The monster watched me with his enigmatic smile.

"It took you long enough." Erin stood tapping her foot impatiently near the Batmobile.

I unlocked it, and opened her door. "You do realize you made a date with a monster who knows you were with me at my table, right? What, you don't think he suspects something?"

"Don't be jealous, Jed. I'm going to nail this guy. You wait and see. I'll catch him off guard." Erin held up the card he gave her. "I have his name now for you to work with. When he comes to my house, I'll invite him in for a drink before dinner, make nice, and fill in some more blanks. After dinner, I'll suggest having a nightcap at his place before he takes me home."

I shut her door. After getting in on my side, I considered all the things I could say, none of which she would listen to. Finally, I shrugged and drove toward her house. My silence bugged her. She kept giving me the cold eyed stare of retribution.

"I know what you're thinking!"

"No you don't."

"Don't you ruin this for me, Drac. I'm undercover. Don't be stalking me or any of your other monster tricks. I can take care of myself. By tomorrow, I'll have enough with what you find out in research, and I find out on the date, to give the detectives an impressive start. It will be my keyway to a gold shield."

I kept my mouth shut. When Igor gets like this, there's no talking her down off the plateau. I drove on without further comment. When we reached her house, a very nice place I bought for her, she turned, gave me the monster's card, and pointed at me. "I want your word you won't come near me tonight while I'm getting this guy set up on my own."

"You have Dracula's word on it. Good luck." For whatever Dracula's word was worth. I didn't know the guy.

Erin nodded at my unblinking stare. "Okay good. Get busy on the research. We'll go to the detectives tomorrow with everything I get on him."

"Okay, Erin. Good night."

After she went in, I drove around the block, parked, and tore into Anton Gronsky's life. I found everything we were hoping for. He was originally from Russia, worked all over Europe as a lab technician, and came to the United States on a visa at the same time the reports of dismemberment killings ended. I drove to his house in Citrus Heights, parked well away from his house, but within sight. I went into stalking preparation mentally. Anton came home for a while until it was time for his date with my Igor. He looked very nice. He left, and I followed on a different route which took me to Erin's house a few minutes before he arrived. When Anton went to her door, I sped over to her house in vampire mode, faster than the normal eye can see, and silently.

\* \* \*

"Hello, Anton." Erin held out her hand which Gronsky shook gently. "Come in and have a glass of wine before dinner."

"Thank you." Gronsky followed her in, taking the syringe out and injecting Erin with the curare serum the moment after he closed the door.

Erin slapped at the spot he injected her in, spinning in horror to face a smiling Gronsky, who caught her collapsing body. She could only stare at him, unable to speak or move. He carried her into the bedroom, placing her with care in the center of the bed. Anton patted Erin's face with fondness.

"Did you think to play me like a violin, little girl? I have played this game of deception far longer than you, all over the world. Did you think I would not break pattern. I wish I could have asked who the big guy was with you. I will eventually have to take care of him too if I am to stay in this area for a while longer. I bet you thought I would need a doctor's kit to fulfil my desire. I need only this." Anton opened his coat more, and extracted a surgeon's saw from the lining. "It is oh so very sharp, my dear."

He set aside the saw and retrieved a plastic bag from the coat lining with a full plastic body suit. Anton quickly stripped down with Erin watching in helpless anguish. After dressing in the plastic suit and gloves, Anton approached Erin with a chuckle of delight.

"I will start with your beautiful ankle. I will go slowly so we can enjoy the exquisite journey together."

Anton took his surgeon's saw in hand, gripping Erin's ankle. He smiled at the internally screaming Erin while placing the saw over the ankle. A split second before the saw reached Erin's skin, a blur shot by, and Gronsky's wrist snapped in two, the saw dropping to the floor. Anton gripped his broken appendage, starting to scream, but a measured chop to his throat shut off his voice. He fell to the floor gripping his throat with the uninjured hand. Suddenly, as if materializing from thin air, the big guy he had seen in the cafeteria stood over him, waving.

\* \* \*

It was kind of cool. Anton was surprised. Erin was surprised. I can't say I was surprised. I broke Anton into pieces, pulverizing bone so there was no bloody mess, but I would be able to fold him into form for disposal. I punished Erin by allowing her choices to catch up to her, and now she would not be able to make a case for the detectives. Anton Gronsky would have to disappear. I didn't taste Anton, because frankly, I wanted no part of the visions he had in his monster mind. After folding Anton, I went looking for a suitcase to put him in. Erin luckily had a big one that was perfect. Anton required a further adjustment or two, but fit very well. I closed him inside, and took my bag to the door. I then returned to my dear Igor, sitting next to her on the bed, and grasped her hand in both mine.

It was after midnight when Erin's lips began to move. "You...you bastard!"

Not exactly the thanks I thought I deserved, but word for word what I expected from my Igor. "Hi Eerie. How'd you like the date?"

Her eyes softened. She reached with trembling hand to my cheek. "Help me... get out of this skirt."

I had a plan after all that worked.

# Chapter Two

## No Benefits

A week later after it became apparent the killings were over but Anton Gronsky had disappeared, he became suspect number one because of working with one of the victims. Some genius in the police department decided to check him out overseas. They began to suspect his chilling past too. I added a little humor by putting his head on a pike outside the Sacramento Capitol Building with an electronic bulletin charting his guilt. Erin blew a gasket of course. She told my Mom everything. I would have told Mom anyway if she had given me a chance. Erin and I had a week of heaven after I folded Anton for disposal minus his head later. Wonderful moments between us always triggered Erin's guilt complex, which of course meant to her we were bad for each other.

My Grandparents came home the same week so they were all waiting for me when Mom called me over. Ralph and Mary Blake could not be shaken in any way, especially after helping Mom raise me. My Grandpa served in the Marines during the Vietnam War. Grandma was a nurse at one of the front line stations. G'pa fell in love with her the moment he saw her when he came to check on one of his buddies. G'ma told me he stared at her, so long she finally smiled at him and asked him if he was okay. She said he smiled back and said he was in love with her. They were married six months later after G'pa's time in country was up. They passed their toughness on to my Mom, Jillian Mary Blake.

On Monday morning after I deposited Anton's head at the Capitol Building, Mom called me to a meeting at the mansion I bought for her and my grandparents in Placerville on an acre of land. I arrived at 7am sharp, knowing Erin would be there to bring me to justice… so to speak. I knew she was working dayshift with Tony. Sure enough, Erin waited alongside my Mom and

Grandparents in the kitchen wearing her uniform. I greeted everyone with my happy go lucky wave of the hand. Yeah... because that always works in my favor.

"Damn Fang, what did you go and do that for?" G'ma calls me Fang when only family and Erin are present. I don't like it much. Everyone else does.

"I made a statement. Too many of these jackals think they can murder and mutilate without any worry about retribution. Gronsky made it on FaceBook, Twitter, and YouTube with all my trail of evidence outing him as a killer Interpol wanted overseas too."

"Did you check long enough to see what they're naming you now, Brainiac," Erin asked with annoyance. "Social media are calling you a vigilante killer they're nicknaming Headhunter."

Headhunter, huh? Cool. I knew better than to play this any other way than contrite remorse though. "Okay... maybe I went a little over the line."

"A little?" Erin began to puff out. Mom shut her down.

"That's enough, Erin. Jed saved your stupid ass. It's not really him we should be discussing, Officer Constanza!"

Erin gasped, spinning on Mom with mouth working but no words coming out. When she saw Mom smiling and holding back amusement along with my Grandparents, she shrugged it off. "Good one, Jill. I wasn't too smart with Gronsky. You don't approve of Jed putting his head on a pike at the Capitol Building though, do you? They're probably slowing the digital record of his super-speed delivery in ultraslow motion."

"I used a visual scrambler." I almost added dummy to the end of the statement but restrained the inner impulse.

"I like what Fang did," G'ma said. "I don't want him doing prison time though. Gronsky's dead with his head on a pike and Fang is free. Light a candle and move on."

"That's how I see it too," G'pa agreed. "No need dragging this out. It's obvious Jed took all the precautions necessary to keep his identity secret. He's not a robot."

"We all know Jed would be okay, but I am a bit worried about you, Erin," Jill said. "You were always the careful one in most instances, but you have a tendency once in a while of losing focus and doing something incredibly dumb. The Quick Mart job when you were sixteen and nearly getting killed is a clear illustration of what I mean. You've always had a tendency to take too many risks. It's not your job to die in the line of duty."

"You told Jill about the Quick Mart guy?"

"I tell her everything except personal stuff," I admitted. "I needed to ask her if she thought I should have let the guy live."

"Jed saved your teen butt that night," G'ma told her. "We understand how many times you've helped cover for him, dear. Fang's pretty sharp at staying out of trouble now. With his money he could probably buy his way out of most scrapes. You, on the other hand, have a career in law enforcement at stake along with your life."

Erin's features reflected the shock at becoming the target of conversation instead of me. "Jed put Gronsky's head on a pike at the Capitol Building, and I'm the one to worry about? I don't think so! What happened to the code?"

"I went along with you on this meeting because we needed to chat about changing times," Mom said. "You've been a real blessing, Erin. Jed loves you and we love you. Jed is no longer a child. I never could beat him into submission, but he listened to reason. He still does. At some point I knew we would all have to accept his decisions in life. Keep in mind if you hadn't taken Jed to the Gronsky crime scene neither of you would have crossed paths with the serial killer. You risked your life to capture him as an advancement ploy to be a detective. You could have chosen to go along with Jed's advice which would have worked risk free."

Erin spun on me again. "You told her everything."

"I think I already said that. Mom can't cover for me if she doesn't know the truth. I would have told her about Gronsky's head. You haven't considered the fact I've saved the FBI and menagerie of local law enforcement organizations hundreds of man hours searching for a suspect already dead."

"And Fang provided proof for them," G'ma added.

Erin stood from where she sat on Mom's couch. "I'm convinced it's time for me to step away from this partnership. Jed and I need a time out anyway. We're oil and water to each other on a personal basis. It's clear with the flack I'm taking from you folks my input is no longer appreciated. My Mom and Dad were never comfortable with Jed and I being together."

"You're being silly, Erin," Mom told her. "You're an adult too. We can't make decisions for you. Nor can your Mom and Dad. We'll respect your decision but your input was always appreciated. I know how strange living next to us was. Your help was wonderful. We have this new place now Jed gave us. Your folks were probably happy when we moved out of the neighborhood. Be careful out there, honey."

"I will. Bye everyone." Erin walked out of the house without a glance in my direction.

"Uh oh. That went well," G'pa commented.

"It needed to happen, Dad. I didn't mind Erin using Jed to earn her detective shield. I didn't know she planned to use him as a scapegoat when things don't happen the way she expects."

"What was all that stuff about oil and water," G'ma asked. "Has Erin been raking your coals, Fang? Is that what this is all about?"

"We've been intimate," I admitted. "We had a beautiful week together. Then she began doubting everything again: her work, her feelings, her place in the universe. I felt I had to do something about Gronsky other than let the whole department go on a manhunt for a guy I already knew was dead. I figured it might be an excuse for her to stop seeing me, but I had to do it. I didn't figure she would take offense at the facts amongst us and throw our friendship under the bus. I'll watch out for her."

"Erin wants the shield bad, kid," G'pa said. "She may have been a lot closer to getting it if she had followed your advice."

"She knows that too," I replied. "I have a mean streak. I knew I could stop Gronsky at any time. I waited until he was inches away from cutting her before I took him. Erin also deducted I let that Quick Mart stalker school her before I intervened. My sense of humor may no longer be to her liking. If she trusted me more and didn't get so impatient we'd make a great team like we were as kids."

G'ma gave me a hug. "You're a good kid, Jed. My advice is to give her space. Stalking her won't do any good with Erin. Letting Gronsky stick her was probably not the best of lessons though."

"I think Jed did the right thing, Mom. I'm not sure anything else would have gotten Erin's attention," Mom said. "She would have simply taken greater risks. I've been expecting this for a while. Take your Grandma's advice. Erin loves you but time apart will allow her to remember there's more to your friendship than getting her a detective shield."

I nodded in agreement. They were right. "On the plus side of this Gronsky case, I've made some improvements to my CSI app that I've extended my patent for. The police chief is really excited about it. After his CSI specialist looked it over, he said they would spread the word once it's been used in the field for a time. It's nice seeing you all in spite of the 'upbraid Jed' moment. That guy Gronsky deserved to be on a pike at the Capitol Building. Are there any more trips and travels planned since summer's nearly over besides staying in the air conditioned house?"

"Mansion, you mean," Mom said. "I'm not going anywhere until next February when my cruise date is planned. I wish this drought would end. If we don't get a decent snow pack in the mountains the whole state will be in trouble."

"Are you going with anyone on the cruise, Mom?"

"Maybe."

The grands chuckled amongst themselves. Apparently I was the last to know about Mom's personal life. That's okay, because my Mom's love life falls into the too much information category. She's been damn careful with whom she sees because of the money angle. She does usually mention anyone of special interest though.

"I'm happy for you, Mom. You usually let me meet your new friends though."

"He's a good guy, Jed," G'pa said. "George Canelo is an electrical contractor. We met him before we went overseas. Your Mom's having us all over for dinner tonight. Jill had more than an Erin smack-down on tap when she asked you over."

"Pop's right. Come to dinner tonight at six, Jed. George is looking forward to meeting you."

"Sure, Mom. I'd like that."

"You can't have him for dinner, Fang, so be on your best behavior."

"Very funny, G'ma. It probably would be hard to explain why my nickname is Fang, so could you maybe remember my real name for a change?"

"Sure, kid. I'll remember. What's in it for me?"

"You mean besides living in a mansion and being able to travel the world with VIP treatment?"

"Okay... fine... Jed, it is."

\* \* \*

I barely reached the Batmobile when my phone rang. Erin's picture beamed out from cell-phone land. "This seems like the shortest time out I've ever heard of, Eerie."

"Don't call me that."

"Or what... you'll give me a time out?"

Silence for a moment. "I need your help. Tony and I were called in for a murder scene. It's an assassination."

"Text me the address." What's the use in resisting? I'm a minion of the Dark Eerie.

"Thanks, Jed." She disconnected without a goodbye.

The address for Dignity Health Mercy General Hospital dinged onto my screen. Dignity Health receives blood from Blake Blood Bank, my personal supply center. I parked far down J Street as I saw the massive traffic jam ahead with many flashing lights. With equipment bag in hand I walked along the sidewalk until I reached the crime scene tape. A tall, lean black officer with Winters on his nametag smiled and lifted the tape.

"Hi Jed." He held out a hand and I shook it. "Long time, no see. CSI is creaming in their pants over your new app improvements. Were you called in to see how it's working?"

"I assumed Erin called me in for monitoring purposes or to speak with the CSI folks, Randy. When are you coming out to play ball again?"

Randy frowned. "My wife's on a gym workout program which means I'm on a gym workout program. When she gets sick of it, I'll be back at the park. We're getting too many lawyers playing anyway. What's that all about?"

"Ask Tone. His lawyer buddy sponsored them all. They're dropping out though to only a couple of regular shows. The rest took some hard lumps and decided to save it for the courtroom."

Randy enjoyed my basketball court report. He pointed ahead. "Straight down, Jed. The shooter zapped the victim in front of the Dig Health sign."

"Do you know who it is yet?"

Randy shook his head. "I know, but I can't speak."

"Understood. Have fun at the gym, brother. The wife comes first."

"Spoken like a true bachelor."

"Is Everett working the scene?" Everett Zanki led the Sacramento Sheriff's Department CSI Unit for all of Sacramento County. He and I were close friends since my CSI app had proven invaluable.

"He's there with an assistant, Kelly Lamb. She vented on your app's methodology for everyone to hear until Everett told her to shut up. Be careful around her."

"I will but the CSI app is merely a tool. It doesn't replace the tech in the field."

"I believe you, Jed. Good luck. This is a messy one."

"Thanks, Randy, but computer apps aren't lucky. They're just apps." He nodded, and I walked on to join the CSI team of Sacramento County Sheriff's Deputies gathering anything and everything they could find.

I saw Tony and Erin guarding the scene on the 39th Street front. I received a quick head shake in the negative from Erin. Tony grinned at me. I could tell they were too close to the head honcho gathering group at the murder scene for their comfort zone in greeting me. I recognized the Mayor, Police Chief, and the Chief of Detectives. I'd never met any of them, but I had been at the police station enough to see their pictures. The Sacramento Mayor Roy Haines, a politico you did not want to get between him and a camera, I knew very well from the media. I could smell the sweat, nervous fear, uneasiness, and blood to the point I toned down all my senses. Coupled with people smells of deodorant, body odor, perfumes, cologne, and arrogance, the scene was a miasma of what hell must be like… for a vampire or half vampire. I kept a low profile, waiting for Everett Zanki to notice me. He was bending over the victim.

The victim, a woman of lean stature in what looked to be expensive clothing, lie in a very large pool of blood with spatter expanding from where she was shot to many feet beyond. A few of the field agents collected everything of brain and skull matter. I could tell the brown haired woman shooting victim had been hit with a .50 caliber slug from a sniper rifle of some sort. I began to wonder what help I could render. They already knew time of death so my app would be good to confirm the known scene information, but that would be about it. I felt eyes watching me intently. I turned from perusing the Mayor's meeting which I listened to with heightened audio perception, directing my attention in the direction of the curiously hostile feeling flashing at me. A young blonde woman with CSI field gear on glared at me. She stood next to where Everett crouched, having joined him while I listened to the Mayor demanding results before the victim was cold.

She didn't look away when I met her gaze with a smile. Her lips tightened into a grimace with hands going to hips in an angry pose I seemed to be the cause of in some way. I had never seen her before. I would have remembered a woman who could make coveralls look erotically attractive. Everett straightened, saw me, and gestured impatiently for me to join them which I did while shouldering my bag. I slipped on black Nitrile gloves.

"I'm glad Erin could get you to consult, Jed. This is Kelly Lamb. She recently joined our department from New York. Kelly... this is the young man responsible for some of the most significant leaps in our tooling discovered in decades."

"Hi Kelly." I held out my hand. She wasn't having any.

"Yes... I've heard of you wonder boy. More money than you could spend in twenty lifetimes and still haunting crime scenes with your little gadgets."

"Did I offend you in some way without knowing it, Ms. Lamb? I don't believe I've ever met you." This woman intrigued me. Her attitude was beginning to bore me.

"I know what you are."

"No... you don't." I grinned. If she did, she'd be looking for a place to hide. "Go ahead though and tell me what I am."

"Kelly!" Apparently Everett was a bit tired of Ms. Lamb. "Extend to Jed the common courtesy of professionalism or get the hell away from my crime scene!"

Her boss startled Lamb out of the funk she descended into. Her face reverted to neutral. "I'm sorry, Mr. Blake."

"Apology accepted but I'd like to understand what it is about me that pissed you off."

"Kelly and half a dozen other CSI field agents were let go in her New York department related to the advancements in crime scene procedure due to your magnificent little app. The projections made because of your new software enhancements allowed us to process this heinous assassination within a nearly exact time frame by blood flow and temperature."

"I believe field agents can process a scene with powers of observation no gadget can replace," Lamb told me in a more reserved tone.

"I didn't create the app to replace people. It is a tool to be used like any other in your equipment bag. Surely you understand with new technology, agents must advance in their field along with the tools at their disposal. You are in a field of endeavor on the cusp of major techniques and changes. Embrace them or you'll be joining the buggy whip generation."

"You've certainly advanced in wealth due to the blood of others."

I laughed, making a calming gesture to Everett who was on the verge of throwing Lamb off scene. "A very dramatic and inherently stupid observation, Ms. Lamb."

I turned to Everett. "Did you have something you needed me to examine, my friend?"

"Yes… I arrived here seeing the scene and method of execution with a detached thought. You know how we must process a scene with computer assistance in finding a cloudy idea of where and how a murder like this took place. We set the scene with pointers and guesses. It all takes time and only gives a blurry hunch of what happened after hours of speculation. I-"

"You're a genius, Ev!" I knew exactly what my CSI buddy was getting at. I turned to the body with new perceptions streaking through my head. "You're thinking of height and weight measurements coupled with body position, blood loss, and wound spray determining instant trajectory direction."

"That's the plan, Jed. We've already been on scene almost an hour without determining anything other than the basics."

I knew one thing I needed to appease my little auburn haired Igor. She glanced at me constantly with pathetic gestures of pleading negligible hand movements Erin knew only I would notice. "May I make some measurements and calculations now, Ev? I believe I can get started on an enhancement to do exactly what you have in mind."

"Of course, Jed. Go right ahead. I'll be here to deflect the idiot circus going on. Kelly and I will stand guard while you do anything you need to do, including turning away that dunderhead Haines."

"Thanks. I'll get to it immediately. I set my bag down, retrieved my electronic measuring device with built in video capabilities. While surreptitiously creating all the calculations I would need to make some models at this and a few more future crime scenes to build a prototype, I dipped my little finger in the victim's blood. With my enhanced speed I tasted it faster than the human eye could follow.

A light shined in my face from the church. I glance at it. Blinding instantaneous pain and then nothing. I absorbed the memory of the woman's last moment, reaching out with her final perception, concentrating on the church across the street without looking at it. I felt him. He was still there watching his murder scene, confident no one would be examining buildings for hours. He snuck peeks out of the bell-tower at the Sacred Heart Church across the street. I went about my business, multitasking this killer's intent with my cover situation. I finished. Then a possibility hit me.

"Hey Ev. Who is the victim?" Naturally the politicos didn't mention anything but unnecessary and impossible crap like demands for solving the crime minutes after it happens. I could hear the Mayor still asking what he could say to the media before the woman was even cold on the sidewalk.

"Sheila McRainey. She's US Congressman Del McRainey's wife. I heard the Mayor say Congressman McRainey is on his way to the scene now.

The shooter planned on taking out Congressman McRainey. With silenced rounds, he could wait for McRainey to get there, blow the head off McRainey and easily escape in the confused aftermath. I glanced at Erin, wondering if I could think of a way to disable the shooter for her and Tony to find. I figured the only way to protect McRainey safely would be super-speed over there, find him, do a 'Hulk Smash', and get Erin to discover the incapacitated sniper. One problem – I see the limousine arriving with McRainey. I grinned. I had another idea. Erin would hate it so that was an added plus.

"I'll be right back, Ev. I have to go to my van for a moment. Can you watch my bag?"

"Sure Jed."

I strolled under the front crime scene tape past the small crowd building a moment before the limo screeched to a stop. It drew the attention of everyone while I did my 'Dark Superman' assault on the sniper's position. I stood next to him as he glanced at the staircase access I sped through. When he turned his attention to the scene the sniper saw me. He nearly dropped his rifle with silencer. I slapped him while confiscating the rifle. See, when I slap someone it's usually dumb luck their head doesn't come off. The sniper shot across the room in a heap. He was costumed in priest's garb. I bagged his stuff at Dhampir speed, grabbed him off the floor, and streaked to my Batmobile with all his gear. It took only moments to restrain him completely in the back. I took the precaution of giving him another measured shot to the head of probably concussion strength. I didn't know how much longer I'd be at the murder scene. I took off the Nitrile gloves I had used in my sniper removal exercise.

I arrived at the scene to see a horrific drama of human misery. McRainey stood near his wife's body with fists clenched and lips trembling. I can differentiate between real human emotion and the crocodile tear type. McRainey's grief as he stood blocked away from the body carried with it an emotional upheaval so close to the surface, it radiated from him. I went around to where Everett and Kelly stood away from scene to allow McRainey a moment. He had been afforded the call they don't give to spouses. It may have been a courtesy but I didn't think it was a good idea at all. He knelt shakily with head in hands, his body wracked with silent sobs. I decided to find out who was after him, and deal with them along with the actual shooter in my Batmobile. The police and CSI people moved instinctively around McRainey to block out the media vultures.

"Did you get what you needed, Jed?"

"Yeah, Ev. I will be building a prototype to do what you outlined. I'll need to test it at half a dozen crime scenes. It will be available to you at any time though. I will name it after you and cut you in for royalty action too."

Everett seemed shocked but recovered quickly. "That's very generous of you, kid. I appreciate that very much."

"I'm sure it will put at least three or four field agents on the unemployment line," Lamb said. "Congrats."

"Kelly girl... if you think that 'one percenter' crap you're dishing upsets me, you're hallucinating. I think I'll go over and speak to Erin for a few moments until Mr. McRainey pays his respects."

Everett grabbed my arm. "Don't let Kelly get under your skin, Jed. The work you're doing makes it more and more difficult for us human info gatherers to contaminate a crime scene." He glared over at Lamb who was clearly steaming. "She and her boyfriend broke their engagement because of the New York CSI shakeup."

"Oh... hey Kel, did you ever see that movie 'He's Just Not That Into You'?"

Everett had to intercept Kelly from an assault on an innocent app technician walking away. He had trouble because of stifling his own amusement while doing it. When I reached Erin it was clear she had been watching the drama.

"I'm glad to see I'm not the only one you piss off a step away from insanity."

"In my defense there's nothing I could say or do that wouldn't piss that woman off. This is a bad one, Eerie. I'll have to meet you tomorrow to discuss it."

"Wait a minute." Erin grabbed my arm as I turned away. "Why not tonight?"

"I'm going to dinner at Mom's house. You can come if you'd like but I won't be discussing anything about this scene with you until tomorrow. Dinner's at six. Mom's new boyfriend will be there. Would you like to retrace your timeout from earlier and I'll pick you up at your place around five-thirty?"

"What's with you? You've never held out on me before. I can't have insights with the detectives without any insights."

"I can't speak about this until tomorrow. That's it. Take it or leave it."

"Fine! I'll go with you tonight. I hope you don't think I'll let you alone without an ongoing interrogation throughout the night about this killing."

"Does that mean I'm spending the night? If so, you can interrogate me all… night… long."

"Very funny." Erin blushed. "No, you're not staying the night. Don't go out eating Bambi's Mom tonight either before dinner. You'll embarrass your Mom with those black-eyed pea eyeballs she'll have to explain God knows how."

I planned to feed on something totally different but her point was well taken. I would have to attend to my van visitor very soon so I'd be clear eyed for dinner. "I won't. I'll go snack on Lassie right away so my eyes are back to normal before I take you to Mom's house."

Erin gasped. "Don't you dare feed on a dog!" Her urgent order in fierce whisper was noted by her partner.

"Is Eerie bothering you again, Jed? What's that about a dog?"

"Other than her ordering me around like one… nothing really, Tone. This could be a long time guarding this scene. Will you two have to stay with it all day?"

"No," Tony answered with a head shake, coming over to Erin and me. He lowered his voice. "We're out of here at noon. What did you find over there?"

"Not much other than getting a new idea for an upgrade from Everett. I did make some notes and calculations. They may help shed some light on the murder by tomorrow."

"Congressman McRainey is one of the good guys – pro-police, pro-military, and pro-immigration control, especially from the Middle East. He wants a complete moratorium on immigrants from the sand. I hope you can help the detectives find his wife's killer."

"I'll do what I can with my gizmos. If I turn up anything I'll give the information to my trainer here. Arf!"

"Very funny. Get back to work solving something other than your insecurity complex."

"Arf!" I saw Congressman McRainey leaving the scene so I gave my confederates a wave off and rejoined Everett and the still steaming Kelly.

I rechecked my calculations once more for creating what Everett envisioned. It was an all technical exercise because I knew where the killer was and what would happen to him. What I would be finding out is who hired him and why. McRainey kneeling near his wife's body with head in hands made an impression. I planned to make sure nothing happened to him. I couldn't bring his wife back but I could keep him from joining her, although it seemed as if he didn't share that particular goal of mine.

"What do you think, Jed?"

"I'm no detective, Ev. My prototype would probably confirm mostly what a good field agent or detective would deduce."

"No shit, Sherlock," Kelly piped in.

"Shut up, Kelly," Everett ordered. "I'm beginning to think New York got rid of you for cause rather than displacement due to tech improvements. You've given us good leads before, Jed. It would help to have an outside opinion from someone knowledgeable about murder scenes."

I shrugged as if getting ready to guess. "I can tell the kill wound was from a high powered rifle, probably a .50 caliber sniper rifle like the M82 or M107 Barrett. She was probably shot from the Sacred Heart Church. Did any of the detectives stroll over there to check the buildings?"

Everett looked around at the church and immediate area. I could tell he made the same leaps in logic I did. "I think you're right. The detectives sent uniforms to knock on doors and canvas the area, but did not approach possible shooting origins. That damn church looks like a perfect spot. I'll mention it to the detectives. We haven't found the slug so I didn't want to guess at the caliber. I figured if it had been short range the killer could have used a .45 auto."

"I'll keep you informed about the app, Ev. Bye, Kelly."

Kelly flipped me off without a glance. I left the murder scene to rejoin my sniper buddy. I drove him to an out of the way spot near Pollack Pines where a steep drop near a cutoff road spot would be perfect for a speedy deposit. I could get my exercise for the day while limiting the chances of the authorities or anyone else ever finding his body to slim and none. I heard him groaning a bit in the back so we were ready to begin. I didn't need to do anything nasty to this guy in the way of torture. Once I drank him, I would know everything I wanted to know about his dirty business.

He groaned loudly at me as I went into my van's spacious rear compartment. I smiled at him while removing his gag. "Hi there. I know you simply had a job to do when you killed

Congressman McRainey's wife. Your rather fresh idea to kill her and then the Congressman when he arrived at the scene was ingenious. I felt bad for him seeing his wife like that. Your calculated killing made an impression on me. I'll do the same for you."

I broke each one of his fingers as he screamed... incoherently at the end. I felt marginally better after I completed my sniper hand adjustments. He wouldn't need those digits anyway. "There. I bet that hurt."

"What... do you want? I don't know shit!"

"Sure you do. I'm going to find out what you know in a rather scary way. You've never seen this before except in the movies. I don't want to cause any trauma to your neck so I'll do my liquid extraction from that big vein in your arm. It's a bit slower method but I'm able to hold the mess to a minimum. Drinking the arm allows me to slowly savor the rotten life you've had without my barf reflex kicking in. See... I'm a monster like you. I kill bad guys but only when I have to. What makes me a monster is the way I do it. Sometimes I crush them while they're conscious like the serial killer I took care of a little bit ago."

"Fuck you, poser!" Sniper took the tough guy route in spite of ten broken fingers causing him visible agony. That's okay.

I turned him to the side so I had a clear shot at his arm. I willed my mouth to widen slowly while extending my fangs for him to see the change clearly. I bent to his arm, holding him in an unbreakable grip as he screamed uncontrollably. This wasn't even going to hurt. I don't know what the hell all the screaming was about. Once I slowly entered the pulsing vein in his arm he quieted. They all do. My bite has something of an analgesic to their emotional response to being sucked dry of blood.

This might be the time to reveal another of the quirks I live with. When I drink from humans I absorb everything about them -

their skills, wants, needs, desires, memories, and evil as well as good. Mom told me it's because of my human side's moral character that I can cast out everything undesirable. When I came home with Erin after draining the predator by the stream when we were kids I felt all that he had been. Mom had taken my hand, patted it, smiled, and said, 'cast it out, son. It's not you. It's him'. Since that day I had been able to do exactly that. My sniper buddy was no exception. I kept his skills and memories of what set him on McRainey's trail. I discarded his personal demons, sins, and murderous nature. I have my own.

The sniper, Mitch Bennett, trained in martial arts extensively not that it did him any good against my monster slap. I absorbed many self-defense techniques during my unavoidable confrontations where I had been forced to drain someone. This was my first expert. He studied to be extremely proficient in Jiu-Jitsu, Tae Kwon Do, and the Israeli martial art form called Krav Maga. I now knew how clumsy I was at fighting and why. Goody. I also added valuable firearms and explosives knowledge I could use on a crime scene. I knew where he was staying, had his rented house keys, and knew his belongings there would be valuable in proving his guilt.

The most important knowledge seeped into my head as Mitch's life seeped out of his arm. He hired out his talents on the 'Dark Web', a now famous back alley marketplace on the internet for every sinister transgression known to man. A weapons dealer named Bilal Al-Taei, Bennett suspected in league with Egypt's Muslim Brotherhood, hired Bennett to kill McRainey. The reason Mitch believed the Congressman became a target originated in his leading a growing movement to stop all arms transfers to radical groups anywhere in the Middle East. McRainey publicly built a growing grass roots organization demanding our government stop all transfers of American war gear from past conflicts into the hands of entities like the Muslim Brotherhood. I had to admire Bennett's attention to detail in finding out who and why he was being hired.

"I...I don't want to die." By the time Mitch mumbled that line he was whiter than the proverbial ghost.

I paused to answer. "Ms. McRainey didn't want to die either, Mitch. I'm glad you were so thorough in finding out who hired you. That will save me some time in locating Al-Taei."

"Even... a monster won't be able... to get Al-Taei."

"We'll see, buddy." I resumed feeding. By the time I finished draining Mitch, I glowed – not all sparkly like the 'Twilight' vamps, but I radiated a heated aura which purged what I assumed to be the physical attributes of the liquid red gold.

I took along a plastic bag and gallon container of bleach with a sponge on the trip over the cliff with stripped down Mitch at Dhampir speed. Along the heavily wooded base no one would be stumbling upon my buddy Bennett. I ripped his head off with ragged precision as I wanted my new statement to be seen as the work of the vigilante 'Headhunter'. I chuckled as I bagged Mitch's head after his bleach sponge bath, thinking about Erin's reaction when she heard the news. I selected a sturdy eight foot long thick branch, trimming it of bark with my handy pocket knife, leaving a couple of branch nubs to act as holders as I had done with Gronsky.

After returning to my van, I put on gloves and bent Mitch's sniper rifle into an unusable pretzel for posting with his head. My next stop was his small rented house in West Sacramento which I visited at Dhampir speed with my signal cloaking device to collect all worthwhile accouterments including his electronics gear. I then retreated to my home for some exciting downtime as I assembled a very thorough digital file of Mitch's 'Dark Web' detective work in finding out who had hired him and why. By the time I finished, there was very little doubt Mitch shot Ms. McRainey. I would send the Congressman my findings too after my late night planting session at the Capitol Building. I might not have to go on the hunt for the mysterious Al-Taei.

Erin awaited my arrival at her place in a filmy black dress hugging her in all the places I wanted to hug her, fondle her, and… well… in other words she looked very nice. She smirked at my wide eyed stare of approval, believing I would be an easy mark to pump for whatever info she wanted. Not so, my little Eerie. I had much bigger plans you will only find out about on the news. I admit I might be a little raw about getting dumped again because I could turn her world upside down in an erotic manner. We were much better partners when we were kids.

She poked me in the chest. "You've fed. Your eyes are back to normal, but you're still radiating the cat that ate the canary vibe. You drained something or someone. I want to know right now or I tell your Mom."

Damn it! Erin knows the aura. I thought it had dissipated. I refuse to be blackmailed. "I don't care what you do. One more word out of you and I rescind my invitation to dinner."

Her lips tightened in that petulant look I loved to stroke into a sexual frenzy. "You've been feeding to the point of gluttony. I'm going with you to dinner even if I have to take my own car. You can't fool me, now tell me what you ate."

"I went to the zoo with a recording of Louis Armstrong's 'It's a Wonderful World' and ate the whole cast of 'Madagascar' including the zebra."

Erin couldn't hold it in. Many moments passed as I smiled at her reluctant amusement. "Okay… fine! I'll go with you but I will eventually know what you've done, right?"

"Of course. I also will make good on my promise to update you on the crime scene info tomorrow concerning the McRainey killing. For now, it's just dinner at Mom's so she knows you're okay and not really in exile."

"And so you can have a wingman when you meet Mom's boyfriend. I get it. Afraid you'll eat him in a weak moment?"

"If I had weak moments I would have eaten you. I have no weak moments, Eerie. Sometimes I enjoy your company. This would be one of those times. George Canelo makes my Mom happy it seems. I want her to be happy but having a friend with me might help during the uncomfortable silences if there are any. Usually with you around there aren't any."

Erin brushed her hand over my face. "No need to sweet talk me. I'll go. I need to apologize for acting like a spoiled brat this morning."

"She understood." I gripped her hand gently and kissed the palm. She shuddered, pulling it free while taking a step back.

"Take me to dinner, Fang."

"As you wish, Eerie."

\* \* \*

"Well what do you know, Eerie's back," G'ma boinked Erin for giving attitude this morning. "Hey Ralph, guess who came to dinner."

G'pa came around the corner. He hugged Erin. "I'm glad Jed brought you to dinner, kid. We needed your input this morning. Don't worry about getting upset once in a while. That's what family's for."

"Sorry about that. I was a little cranky this morning. Thanks, Pa." Erin hugged him back. "Mom said to tell you she misses all of you in the neighborhood."

"We had to move on up to the East side, baby girl," G'ma said. "We hit oil with Fang here. You have an open invitation from him to move into a mansion with your folks. He bought you a house already. Play it all the way to the big leagues and stop over thinking it."

"I would, Ma, but my folks won't hear of it. They're pissed at me for letting Jed buy me a house. I told them it was a loan sort of."

"You earned the house," I told her. She did too. Without her day to day insights and help, I don't know if I could have done everything I did. Mom and my Grandparents were exceptional backup, but without Erin in my ear every day as a friend I would have been constantly in trouble. "Maybe soon we can talk your folks into a nice place with all the trimmings. Mom still does whatever chores she wants to do."

Then Mom came in with George. She hugged Erin. "I want you two to meet George Canelo. Sorry, we had to go get a bottle of wine for tonight. George signed a big client so we're celebrating a bit. George... this is my son Jed, and our very good friend Erin Constanza. Erin is a Sacramento police officer"

George stood about six feet tall. He looked lean and in shape - clean shaven with graying brown hair cut short. I also noticed when he looked at my Mom, George loved her. His grip was strong. "I'm very glad to meet both of you. Jill has told me so much about you both I feel as if I've known you two for a long time. You've done very well for yourself, Jed."

"I'm glad you came tonight, Erin. George has a daughter named Marilyn," Mom said. "She's twenty and attending Sac State. She's being stalked by someone. It's been escalating in the last couple weeks. I told George you and Jed do a lot of detective work together because of Jed's CSI app."

"If Marilyn's being stalked on campus, the campus police force employs a sizeable staff," Erin replied. "They have their own department on campus. Has she contacted them?"

51

"Many times," George explained. "So many, they're handling her like a crank complainer. She has a single occupancy bath studio in the American River Courtyard campus living quarters."

"Security cams are all over the campus," Erin said. "If she's being stalked, all it would take is a determined search of the cam footage to find out who trails her from one place to another. Has she explained where she feels most uncomfortable as if being followed?"

"Excuse me." George gestured angrily. "I've been in the middle of this for so long now I assume everyone knows the details. Marilyn knows the stalker. He's in her classes. His name is Seth Dotsenko."

I think I see where this is going. "If I'm hearing you correctly, Dotsenko stalks her openly, either making overt gestures or remarks."

"Exactly." George seemed relieved but I couldn't figure out why. "He threatens her daily. It has become a ritual. She went out with him once. It was a disaster she still refuses to talk about. I want to kill him! No one believes her. She won't change colleges because her friends are all there. Marilyn has told me to stay out of it. My Daughter believes Dotsenko will get tired of the game and move on. I think he'll kill her eventually. His Father is-"

"Nikko Dotsenko," Erin finished for him.

"You...you know him?"

"I know of him. He's an Albanian gangster who entered the country with the other Albanian refugees we took in. Over the last couple decades he's built an empire of drugs, extortion, and racketeering. His latest enterprise involves human trafficking. I can sure understand why Marilyn thinks it best to keep you out of her problem with Seth. I doubt he'll harm her, George. I know that's tough to hear as a father, but if she's strong enough to ride this out, I think the situation will fade away."

I could tell from his facial expression of tired acceptance and frustration that George did not like Erin's common sense option to agree with his daughter.

"Whatever happened to enforcement of the law? Have we simply turned over our country to the gangsters?"

"Erin didn't create the situation, George. Marilyn sounds pretty tough. I'm thinking there might be even more to the story than you know." I could tell he wasn't digging my take on it either. My Mom and Grandparents on the other hand listened intently. "Our leaders allow strands of every vile faction on earth into our country without any safeguards, sponsors, or skills other than creating gang warfare. You have the right idea. Send her to another college. I sponsor promising students all the time. She could attend nearly any college around."

He ran his hands through his hair and into fists at his sides momentarily. "Thanks, Jed... I appreciate the offer. I'll see if I can talk her into getting out of Sac state. Maybe you're right about there being more to her reluctance to leave than I know about. I FaceTime with her every day for a few moments. She always looks off kilter. When we talk her into having dinner with us, she's quiet and withdrawn. Jill said you would probably offer an alternative once you knew her stalker was known."

"Jill knows the only thing we could do for you legally was find out who was stalking her," Erin agreed. "You already know that. Marilyn is refusing to attend a different college so I'm sure there is something we don't know about this situation. She could even take a year off school and test the job market. One true fact shadowing any solution involving a confrontation with Albanian mobsters must be considered: they will kill without hesitation. Getting into a war with them if it can be at all avoided would be suicidal."

George nodded in agreement. He knew raging into this with a Father's righteous anger might be a noble idea, but if it cost his whole family their lives anyway it would be senseless. "I'm glad Jill talked me into sharing this with you. I couldn't see any other way than going behind Marilyn's back and trying to stop Dotsenko… as you say - suicidal. I can't understand why she won't let me send her to a different college. I tried to get her to come with me tonight but she immediately figured rightly I planned to gang up on her."

"Jed and I could speak with her for you if you'd like. We won't be talking her into anything. I can explain more about her options though."

"That would be wonderful," George replied. "Would tomorrow be too soon?"

"Nope," Erin stated. "Jed has some information he wants to share with me tomorrow so we'll be meeting anyway. Write down her address in the Courtyard. I'm familiar with the Sac State campus. I didn't ask you, Jed. Does meeting with Marilyn seem like a good idea to you?"

I glanced at my Mom. She had a pleading look, mostly because in spite of protecting family and Erin at all costs, I was admittedly a monster. I cast out the evil absorbed in draining an evil being, but that fact did not make me an angel. She knew there existed in me a darkness I kept leashed. In doing good as when saving McRainey from the church tower sniper, Mom knew I did such deeds for my own sometimes odd reasons. Gronsky's head on a pike illustrated the quirkiness of my humor. She accepted it as a price paid for my indulgence in a moral sense of right and wrong, but with sometimes perverse results. Erin never accepted the display of my true nature which is why I believed she broke away from me time and again.

"I believe it to be a good idea. Erin's right, George. It would be a necessary first step in gathering some information. As she pointed out, we will be meeting anyway." Naturally, there would be consequences when Erin actually knew the truth about some of my nature she had been avoiding all these years. Maybe my forcing the facts on her would be a good thing.

# Chapter Three

## The Nature of the Beast

"You bastard!" Erin shot out of her front door like a cannonball. I caught her in midair, sweeping her inside out of sight from the neighborhood while stifling her physical assault easily.

I took no offense. I am a bastard. I held her tight. Damn, she felt good with thin black shorts and a red halter top her only clothing. I figured she sat to have a coffee and heard or read the news depicting the new victim of the vigilante headhunter. "Calmness, Eerie. You won't hear the story if I am not allowed to speak."

"Get out of my house!" Erin closed her eyes, clenching fists and tightening her lips in a thin red line of rage as I released her.

See… I don't understand this. I enjoyed the humor of her near insane anger at me for killing a killer but I could never understand why. The only thing I could figure was she felt an entitlement to be in on every decision to kill as If I were her Igor. She knew my passion and love, but wrongly dismissed my dark nature.

"Let's have a coffee, and I'll tell you all about it, Erin. Stop being such a big baby. The sniper deserved his fate."

Erin faced me. She shook her head while folding arms over chest in disgust. "We grew from children to adults together, Jed. Why would you do such a thing? You always confided in me and listened to my counsel. Human beings do not do such things!"

There it is. "I am a Dhampir. You revel in my vampire half when it suits your purpose but you excoriate me for its sometimes dark side."

"You have a will, Jed! You need not give in to these hideous jests of yours."

"Yes, I have a will. I could resist each and every time my inner vampire shadow calls to me. I do not wish to, Erin. I didn't always seek your counsel on the nights I haunted the streets when we were kids. It's time to stop pretending I live my life by your SUCK program guidance. I control nearly all of my impulses. Let's have some coffee. I'll explain why most of what I did had to be done, okay?"

"Okay… but you're beginning to scare me, Jed. I've never been frightened of you. Does your Mom know about these 'Dhampir Gone Wild' events you've had in the past you didn't share with me?"

"She knows. As she explained to me long ago, she can't protect me if she doesn't know the truth. Now share a cup of coffee with me and I'll tell you what happened."

Erin sipped. I mostly talked. After I completed my dissertation on Mitch Bennett, along with the suppositions he made about his employer, Bilal Al-Taei, Erin remained silent for some long moments while absorbing the long ranging effects of my actions. I also explained what I garnered as evidence from his personal stuff they didn't put on the news.

"You've given me a lot to think about. You probably feel as if you've bypassed the system and still dumped useable evidence into police hands, don't you?"

"Tell me where I'm wrong, Eerie. Everything gathered and planted with Bennett's head remains anonymous. It also remains useable by the police. In the case of Al-Taei. Sure, I added my own brand of sick humor to it, admittedly because I knew it would probably make you crazy."

I stroked her arm. "You make me crazy. I want you so bad sometimes my fangs want to jump right out of my mouth. Admit it since we're being honest. You've suspected I wasn't following every guideline you gave me."

"I didn't know how far you'd go. You did that gang guy who moved into our neighborhood when we were twelve, didn't you?"

"Among others I know you suspected. Every corpse found drained of blood must have beamed my name into your head, Eerie. If you had asked, I would have told you the truth. You didn't want the truth. You can't handle the truth!"

Erin couldn't hold in her amusement at my Jack Nicholson imitation of his lines in 'A Few Good Men'. "Enough! So I suspected and didn't want to know. Does that mean you've escalated to these Headhunter displays because you needed me to admit I know you're a monster?"

That didn't sound as good as I thought it would. "Maybe. When we're together body and soul we make fire. Then you let the hidden thoughts of what must be true about me break us up. It's all because you can't live with the truth. I'm not certain you can have me for a friend knowing the truth. I'm tired of ducking the question myself. The cards are on the table. You know what I've done. What's it going to be, Eerie? I'm the judge, jury, and executioner for many bad men who cross my path. When I have to survive for very long without human blood you know I'll even eat Bambi's Mom. I need blood. Let's get that out in the open as an immutable fact. Talking about will power and fortitude may make you feel like you're my muse but it doesn't do shit for the craving I have."

Erin reached across the table to grasp my hand. "I know, Jed. You're right. I've been pretending. I assumed you used the blood bank to overcome the craving. You joke about the blood bank making you like a Hollywood movie vampire so you don't have to feed. I went along with it."

No use stopping the 'Sin City' train of admissions now. "I'm a predator. Drinking blood out of a bag may seem like a harmless and wonderful way to avoid my darker side, but it doesn't curb the murderous impulses to hunt. I can feed and heal. I don't always kill unless what I find on a late night hunt provokes the predator inside. What I had been missing hit me the day by the stream when we were kids. There was no turning back from it then. Mom awaited me after one early morning return. Being a kid, and not very proficient at cleaning my mess, I made too many clothing items disappear. She could tell I couldn't erase what I was. I made a pact with her I've never broken. Mom knows I don't kill for the sake of killing. She also knows I only kill other predators... bad ones."

"Where do we go from here?"

"I love you, Erin. I don't care where we go from here if I can be with you in any way I can. We can do a lot of good together. We've proven that. I can understand if you don't want to be more than best friends. Don't throw what we have away. Believe this. No innocents were hurt at any time."

Erin kept hold of my hand. That was a good sign. "I guess I can't forbid you to not do your extracurricular activities, including last night's horror, huh?"

"You can forbid anything you like. I probably won't listen though. Your input would never be ignored out of hand and would always be considered."

"So from now on if I suspect you'll be on a night time purge I can ask if you're going to eat someone and you'll tell me the truth?"

"Yep."

"Have you told your Mom about last night?"

"Yep. She said your head would explode when you heard about the Headhunter's second mission. Mom was pretty close. I couldn't believe you actually flew out of the house in assault mode, Eerie. You were so mad you forgot what I am completely."

Erin shrugged after batting at my hand instead of continuing her hold on it. "Yeah, I did. It is a bit disconcerting knowing what you could do to me if you wanted. Have I ever provoked you to the point you thought about teaching me a lesson?"

I hesitated a split second too long in my answer. She gasped. "You have thought about it, you blood sucking fiend!"

"Fiend... really?! My thoughts in that area were very tame. Besides, if I wanted to get nasty, I could simply compel you to do anything I wanted to do."

"Bullshit, Jed! What? Now all of a sudden you're like one of those TV 'True Blood' vamps running around in the script 'glamouring' humans? I would have seen it before if you could do that."

No, you wouldn't have seen it because I didn't want you to see it, Eerie. "Heh... heh."

"Prove it, you poser! You're just trying to get a rise out of me now. We have to go see George's daughter. Finish your-"

I had her the moment she looked into my eyes without blinking or turning her head for a couple of seconds while she spoke. I admit it. I've been playing around with my victims for years. I'm pretty good at it too. The less offensive bad guys I caught at night burglarizing homes in our area, and near my new place when I got older, I 'perfect stormed' them which was my term for what I do. I smiled at my little Eerie, her eyes big as saucers. I held her without movement or speaking. I compelled her to remain in place while I cleaned off the table and put our coffee cups in the sink. When I returned to her, I knelt down beside her chair. Tracing one fingertip over her bare leg from ankle to upper thigh, I spoke to her in scholarly fashion.

"And so you see... my dear Eerie... I do indeed have the power to compel even a strong willed woman such as yourself. I use my rather awesome intellect to do good not evil. I refrain from childish displays such as this to prove a point."

I stared into her eyes once again, smiling. "Shall I release you now to sin no more, my dear Eerie? Yes... I see it is the right moment for release. Remember though, you asked for it. Don't do anything silly like attack me, okay?"

I released her. She launched out of her chair like a moon shot. I perceived Erin had turned every cell in her brain to the task of movement without success. Naturally, when I released her, I also needed to soften her landing. Erin trembled in my arms, gasping for breath, her face turning red with the effort to regain control.

"Oh... my... God... Jed! That was amazing. Tell me the truth! You've never compelled anyone on a lark or to get your own way even when we were kids?"

"Never. I'm not that kind of monster." I stroked the side of her cheek. "Before you ask, yes, I could compel you to be my sex slave for the day, and then mind wipe the memory from you of doing it when I was finished with you."

"Good Lord... you've been practicing on people, haven't you?"

"Yep. Most of the bad ones I play with for a time to hone my skills. The first time I did it was on our down the street neighbor, old man Jenkins. I suspected him of being a monster. I was right. One night when I stalked the pervert, he attacked a young woman outside a bar I followed him to. I clipped Jenkins in the head at Dhampir speed. She saw Jenkins hit the wall next to her out cold and ran for her car. I carted my prey into the darkness. We had watched an old Dracula movie where the actor had compelled his victim so I tried it on Jenkins. I gave him a full range hit and turned him into a vegetable. It freaked me out a little. I fed on him for a bit, healed him, and left Jenkins to be found."

"So that's what happened to that bastard! He tried to get me into his house one Halloween when my Mom had let me trick or treat up the street by myself for a couple houses. I kicked him in the shin and ran back to the house where Mom was chatting with my Aunt Cheryl. She didn't believe me. I had made up so many stories Mom didn't know what to believe by that time. I never went near him again. I wondered where he went."

"They had to put him in a hospice place or something. I watched the cops take him away. He could walk, but he just babbled, making weird noises and muttering incoherently. Anyhow, I toned down my act while practicing over the years."

"Can you compel bad people to not be bad?"

"I tried. I can't change them."

"How do you know?"

I paused, wondering whether I should be going this far with my Erin reeducation seminar.

"Don't hold out on me now, Fang!"

"I drank from them, then compelled them to never do evil again. You know I can sense everything about the person when I drink from them. Well, when I tasted them again, their inherent evil nature was still intact. I imagine my compelling them could have held them in check for a time, but eventually they would have returned to their true nature. Just as I can't alter my nature, I can't alter anyone else's either."

"This is incredible. I'll go get dressed. You stay here," Erin ordered.

"Are you going to shower first?"

Erin stopped, popping an arm in the air while she sniffed for any telltale odor. "Why, do I stink?"

"No. I figured if you were going to take a shower, I could show you a few more of my incredible powers. They even work underwater."

Erin blushed. "You stay right here, Fang. I'll be down in a few moments."

I confessed to having dark moments so I added another. With Dhampir speed I may have enjoyed Erin's change into other clothing without her knowing it. Unfortunately, Erin knew me a little too well. She came down fully clothed and slapped me in the face. She knew when I didn't stop her that she had guessed right.

"Shame on you, Fang. Don't bother with the 'it's in my nature card'."

Erin dressed in a summer dress with shoulder straps begging to be pulled down over her shoulders to reveal the braless look she chose to drive me insane with. She moved around the table to sit and drink her cooling coffee. I struggled mightily and won yet again. I don't think non-vampire humans would ever understand. When a being can do things I can do, it borders on the insane at all times. I resist everything. The predator inside me sees a nasty look, feels arrogant displeasure at my presence, and knows when he is being blunted. The fact I restrain it all within as I enjoy Erin's unknowing challenge to my predator's nature builds strength. I use and funnel it into my daily life.

"As you wish, Eerie," I responded meekly. "Don't forget the truth you hold now when we are together though. I believe we have changed the paradigm of our relationship. When you forbid me or try to dominate me, always remember the truth, and never discount fear."

"Is that a threat?"

"No. It is a promise of life I give to you every day we are together. I could never hurt you in any way, but the reason is because of restraint. If you keep that in mind, you can interact with me more as an adult, especially when you do stupid things like you did with Gronsky. We both know I don't exist as a thread for you into the detective unit or your personal bodyguard. I'm a monster. That I love you makes an infinite number of threads in life possible. I will help you from now on under my own terms."

Erin glowered at me with her fists on the table. "I don't think I like the sound of that."

I popped to my feet to face her with fists on the table. "Too bad, Eerie. Take it or leave it, but I add one other item to the mix. If you bail, I will no longer protect you. When you do something else stupid, I will leave you to pay the consequences. After you pay for your stupidity with your life, I will kill until the taste of you no longer exists in my memory."

I had her then. I did an academy award winning performance. I saw fear and projection of thought in her mesmerizing azure eyes. Yes! Sure… I'm a liar. I would kill anything and everything that ever threatened or harmed my Erin in any way, shape, or form. This meeting of the minds had to do with her not taking that fact for granted. Then, my world came crashing down. Damn it!

Erin grinned, reaching across the table to stroke my cheek. "I own you, my monster minion. You're mine and you know it. I may not be able to make you do everything I order you to do, but I still own you."

"I'm beginning to lose impulse control. If you don't want to find yourself skipping down the street naked, singing 'If I only had a Brain' we'd better go see Marilyn."

　　　* * *

We introduced ourselves at the American River Courtyard housing complex as a courtesy. Marilyn Canelo occupied a one bath studio apartment. As we neared her quarters we noticed two men following us. I began to suspect we should have visited without the courtesy call. Our shadows, casually dressed in dark suits, shirts, and ties were both over six feet tall with stylishly over the collar length hair. It didn't seem like an interested security detachment. When we approached the entrance, they speeded to block the entrance with smiling faces.

"Hey." Erin showed them her SPD identification. "What's this, an entourage? We're here to see Marilyn Canelo at the behest of her Father. I'm police officer Erin Constanza. This is SPD consultant, Jed Blake. Why don't you two move aside so we can talk with Marilyn."

"Marilyn not seeing visitors today," the huskier man with brown hair said with an accent. "She is fiancée of Seth Dotsenko. She has been having trouble with unwanted visitors. We are her security detail. Please go away."

"Not until we talk with Marilyn. Once we find out everything is okay, we'll be on our way, but not until then. I'm not campus security. I'm an SPD officer. If you keep obstructing our visit, I'll have campus police remove both of you."

I could tell they didn't like that development, but without any real alternatives, they stepped aside. Erin rang Marilyn's doorbell. Marilyn opened the door with some surprise, glancing at her supposed security detail with some fear showing on her features. This was getting more interesting by the minute.

"Ah… my Dad called and told me two people were coming to see me. You must be Erin and your friend is Jill's son, Jed. My Dad really likes her. I see you've met the Dotsenko men."

"She is fine," our talking shadow told us while reaching for Erin's arm. "Tell Dad she-"

I blocked his hand. "No touching."

He tried a couple more thrusts past me with the same result before his friend moved next to him. Erin put her hands on hips.

"I will arrest you two bozos if you don't back the hell away."

The one I was playing patty-cake with jabbed a finger in my chest. "I don't like you."

"I'm very hurt. Erin can tell you. I'm very loveable." I used my most award winning smile on him but he didn't seem interested in making friends.

"Maybe we talk after. You big guy. I like big guys."

"I don't date strangers."

"Not date, smart-ass!" His friend was yanking on his shoulder. "I see you outside. Maybe you tell cop friend to go get coffee while we talk."

"Forget him, Jed." Erin tried to tug on me but I was getting romantic feelings. "Marilyn. We need to talk. Invite us in."

"Sure… come in. Sorry. I haven't been able to invite anyone over for some time, not even my girlfriends." Marilyn moved aside for us to enter. She wore jeans and a dark green, Sacramento State Hornets sweatshirt. Her brown hair, left wavy and free, framed her angular face attractively.

I gave my new buddy a finger wave. He tried to grab me but I blocked his hand easily, which did nothing for his disposition. "No touching I said."

Inside Marilyn's one room studio she gestured for us to sit while closing the door. It was a very small place. "Please sit down. Can I get you a coffee?"

"No, but thanks," Erin said without even looking at me as she sat down at the small kitchen table.

"I'd like a cup if you have a pot made." I endured the usual Erin sour look whenever I thwart her will.

"I just made one." She handed me a cup and sat with us. "It's so nice to have someone here visiting. I go to classes with an escort and then I get walked back here. I guess my Dad explained the situation."

"He's worried you'll be hurt," Erin said.

Marilyn shook her head. "Seth would never hurt me. He's obsessed with me. The campus police said I could get a restraining order against him and his goons. I…I figured he'd get tired of this game and leave me alone. I don't want my Dad involved. Seth's Dad is Nikko Dotsenko. He's bad news. I've checked him out."

"Your Dad said you dated Seth once," Erin said. "I don't understand how you could go from a simple date to having round the clock gangsters escorting you around."

Marilyn blushed. "I slept with him at his place. I met him at the 'Dive Bar' over on K Street. You know… the one with mermaid costumed women swimming in tanks."

"I've heard of it, but never been inside," Erin replied.

"I was with friends. One moment he's buying me a drink and the next I'm in his bed at this lavish place on West River Drive, the Regatta Apartments. I know he slipped me something, because my friends told me I simply got up and left with Seth, draped all over him. Luckily, I'm on birth control. I didn't tell my Dad because he would have done something crazy and gotten killed."

"Why didn't you go to the police? The morning after they could have done a rape kit and tested your blood and urine for traces of what he gave you," Erin said.

"That would have been exactly what I would have done except he kept me at his apartment under guard for three days saying it was for my own protection. He convinced me if I went to the police, his Father would have me killed. I believed him. Seth tried everything of a romantic nature to win me over during my apartment incarceration. He didn't rape me again. I refused to drink out of anything not sealed. After three days, Seth took me to my place here, saying he was my fiancé from then on, and his men would be looking after me. I figured it would be only until there was no way the police would ever believe my story. On the contrary, Seth comes over every night even though I won't let him inside my door. You two are the first ones allowed to see me. I have to tell Seth whenever I meet with my Dad, and he made it very clear what would happen if I told him what was going on."

"We can help you," Erin stated.

"How? I can't have the police involved or tell my Dad what happened. I'll have to continue this farce until I graduate or Seth loses interest. I'm betting he drops this in another month… tops. I appreciate being able to share this with someone but you have to promise me not to tell my Dad. I know you'd never endanger us on purpose, Erin. You're a police officer, so anything you say or do to help me could get my family killed. Please... accept my thanks for listening and let this go. Everyone knows what happens when you testify against a gangster. They own the law. Everything is in their favor. They intimidate witnesses and even jury members. They kill and are never caught. Unless you have a plan to catch them cheating on their taxes, I have to wait this out."

"We can't surrender the state to gangsters, Marilyn. We'll think of something. Won't we, Jed?" I received the knitted brow 'don't you dare undercut me' glare.

"I actually think Marilyn has the right idea. Seth won't keep this gangster house arrest thing going indefinitely. Some other woman will turn his head. Once he knows he's safe from legal threats with the law, he'll walk away. I respect what you're doing, Marilyn. You're a survivor." I handed her my card. "That's my personal number. If this gets too much or you feel you're in danger, call me. Thanks for the coffee. We'll get out of here before we cause you more problems. Call if things change, okay?"

Marilyn hugged me. "Thanks for your understanding. I just want to do my schooling and hopefully get free of this mess without anyone getting hurt. I always thought these things happen to other people. I know now there are predators out there no one can protect you from. I will call if it gets to be too much, Jed."

"You do realize this will happen to other women at his whim, don't you?"

Marilyn nodded with grim determination. "Yeah, I do, Erin. I also know this isn't a TV movie. Getting my family killed won't help those women either."

"Come on, Erin," I urged. "Those guys will have called Dotsenko to let him know what's happening. We need to get out of here before we cause her more problems."

"Okay-"

Someone pounded on the door and Marilyn gasped. "Oh shit!"

Erin grinned at me. "Well, Jedidiah... Mr. Fixit... get us the hell out of here without causing any more problems for Marilyn."

"There's no need to get snarky, Erin." I answered the door with a smile.

I received an immediate punch in the face for my trouble. I mean my face was the target. The fist however only landed inside my fist. I squeezed and broke all the bones inside it. Then I threw the punch thrower off to the side. It was my beany baby buddy who planned on giving me a good talking to. His screams of agony while rolling on the walkway caused his buddy to reach for an illegal weapon on campus. I pulverized his wrist, taking the weapon away from him in a split second's snatch. The nicely dressed gentleman behind the gangster duo cringed away from the screaming men. I figured him to be Seth. He was lean, tall, boyishly handsome, with long dark shoulder length hair. I could see why Marilyn had accepted a drink from this player.

"Hello there. You must be Seth Dotsenko, son of Nikko Dotsenko. I'm Jedidiah Israel Blake. My Mom is very taken with Marilyn Canelo's Dad, George. That means we may be kind of family in the near future. It would be very bad for you to cause her any more hardship, Seth. I'm afraid after my friend Officer Erin Constanza arrests these two for carrying weapons on campus illegally, you and your boys will not be welcome here any longer. Am I right, Officer Constanza?"

"Yes, Mr. Blake, I can guarantee you that. I've already called the campus police. They will be here shortly."

"It would be to your advantage to stay out of this."

My 'good talking to' buddy tried to reach with his undamaged hand for his weapon. Erin kicked him in the face and disarmed him.

"Officer Constanza and I were staying out of it. You ordered your minion to rearrange my face. Now, I'm involved too. Marilyn already agreed not to do anything to get your raping ass into trouble. You're safe, so why don't you go away and hump someone else's leg?"

Seth started to reach for me, glanced down at his minions, and decided he liked the way his hand and wrist bones were at the moment. He pointed at me from a safe distance. At least he thought it was safe. "Mar is mine, Blake! She'll be mine until I no longer want her. No one takes what's mine, asshole! If you keep poking your face into my business I'm going to become your worst nightmare!"

Erin laughed at that remark. "You're funny, Seth. You think you know what a nightmare is, huh? Here come the campus police. It would be best if you start creating a story of why you have two armed hoodlums shadowing Marilyn because I guarantee they're going to be asking you."

"It would be best if you tell them this is a misunderstanding, Missy."

Uh oh. I stepped away. Erin ran into Seth's airspace in a split second, grabbing him by the chin.

"Did you just threaten me?"

Silence. Even Seth knows you can't publicly threaten a LEO. Erin gave him a shove back. "Yeah, that's what I thought, poser. I'm not Marilyn. I charge. I arrest. I testify. Call your lawyer because you will need him to get clear of this mess."

Three campus police officers arrived. Erin showed them her ID and explained what happened, showing them the weapons we'd confiscated. Seth's men did not have any permit for the weapons they carried at all. They were arrested on the spot, although they would have to be transferred to the emergency room due to my adjustments. Things became interesting when Erin requested the officers find out if Seth was armed. He was and also without a permit. None of them were law enforcement officers so it wouldn't matter anyway. Seth was not happy. This was going to get ugly because Seth and his men were going to jail. I added an assault charge with Erin's backing my statement of being attacked and defending myself.

We didn't bring Marilyn into the conversation, but she volunteered the information that Seth's man had tried to sucker punch me as I answered the door. She also confirmed the men were watching her day and night. When the campus police found out they were arresting Nikko Dotsenko's kid, they were less than ecstatic. Being armed and coming onto campus property was a no brainer though.

Officer Mendez, a thin dark haired woman with a kind face, perceived what was happening. I could tell she didn't want to get involved in gangster problems. She also realized allowing the three gangsters to walk away in front of an SPD officer was never going to happen. She called for backup because of the injured men needing more than simple holding or transport. Erin supplied her with all venues to reach her, promising to fill out any complaint forms necessary to get the arrests rolling along. The police took Seth and his boys away, leaving us with a distraught but resilient Marilyn.

"That went well. I know you had to defend yourself. How did you do what you did, Jed? I saw it, but I can't quite believe what I saw."

"Jed's speedy and strong as a bull," Erin filled in for me as she often did. "I'm sorry we couldn't let things proceed the way you wanted them to. You'll still have the opportunity to keep what you say at a minimum. Jed and I will do whatever it takes to put the guys behind bars. Seth and his men will be banned from campus. I can guarantee you that. I'm not sure what difference it will make in everyday campus life. I also don't know if Seth will simply put two other guys on you without weapons. They're used to getting what they want so I don't see this going away, just as you perceived. Keep Jed's card with you. Call if you need us."

"I hope you're still alive to call," Marilyn replied.

"I'll be okay," I told her... the Dotsenko mob maybe not so much. It was too bad we couldn't let her plan have time to work. Nothing much could be done right now unless I wanted to get proactive with the situation. I could start with Nikko, and work my way down the ladder. I'll ask Erin when we get past the paperwork.

* * *

Erin and I drove toward my Mom's house. We'd need to make a report to them. They would be in danger to some degree. I had safe-rooms both upstairs and downstairs in Mom's mansion. I also built the security system myself. All the window glass was protected with security shutters. I paid a lot of money so in case the villagers arrived with pitchforks and torches I'd have time to get my family out of the mansion. I always figured they would come for me in Pollack Pines if it ever happened. I'm very dangerous in the woods so if I am ever deemed a threat to humanity they better use a Reaper Drone missile strike.

"You're quiet after all the 'Erin… let's just allow time to work this out crap', Fangster."

I knew this was coming. "Marilyn gave us solid reasoning. If Dumbo hadn't taken a shot at me, she would be working this out on her own which may have been the best way. Obviously, the boys called Seth and gansta' arrived to order a beat down. What bothers me about his reasoning is he knew I had an SPD officer with me. I figured you would be more concerned with that fact than you are."

Erin shrugged. "I gave it some thought. You're thinking he owns someone high in the SPD ranks. I'm not buying it. Seth throwing a valuable asset like that on the table over a scene he could have avoided by simply ignoring us makes no sense at all. I think he's so obsessed over Marilyn, he treated the situation like the spoiled prick he is. Seth figured his guy would cold cock you and I'd let it ride rather than cause a big scene."

"If he's that dumb, what do you think his next move would be? If you believe what you said, he's going to take this real personal. I'm not familiar with Nikko the mobster. How bad is he? Would he even get involved in a goofy extortion plan like Seth has been playing?"

Erin put a hand on my arm as I drove which she never does. She'll slap the back of my head but she's not much on gentle attention grabbers. "I'm wondering if maybe we need a monster, Jed. Nikko is Columbian Drug Lord bad. You've been doing it for years. Since our dynamic has changed, how do you feel about a preemptive strike?"

War with the mob in public would be dangerous and stupid. Their hierarchy dying one at a time in the dark of night makes a lot of sense. Since I'd already considered it all I had to do now was thoughtfully agree with my Igor. It seems I received my answer without having to ask. I wonder if this preemptive strike venture should be handled now or after a few days keeping track of Marilyn and our own families.

"Lay it on me. When would this preemptive strike occur in your mind, Eerie?"

"We're too close to this confrontation right now. If we're in the process of pursuing Marilyn's problem on a legal front, suspicion when Nikko and Seth die would be cast on rival gangs. I think we need to wait for a time. Do you think it would be safe to wait a couple of weeks?"

This new blood thirsty Erin needed contemplation. "I think that would be wise. What have you done with 'by the book Erin' who would never think of acting outside the law, and especially not using a Fang to do the dirty work?"

Erin stayed quiet for a moment gathering thoughts for a cogent answer. She finally lifted a hand in a 'What Me Worry' gesture. "Gronsky nearly turning me into a dismembered corpse jolted my complacent know-it-all attitude. Visiting Marilyn with you and finding out how easily an innocent citizen can be legitimately cowered into a caged prisoner blew my last conception of justice. She's getting hosed. Maybe the city needs a 'Headhunter' vigilante."

"Outstanding. You could be my sidekick 'Gives Head'."

That remark earned a head slap with attitude. "Very funny. After seeing the situation forced on Marilyn by the Dotsenkos, reading about the police finding their heads on poles at the Capitol Building doesn't seem as horrifying as it once did."

"Twice is all I can pull off at the Cap. I can pick other head destinations though so I don't mess around with my cool vigilante tag name."

"I must admit you made a hell of a splash with the sniper's head and evidence," Erin said. "Having a high profile case like the McRainey killing snatched away by a vigilante supplying proof, next target saved, and probable suspect that hired the killing done, does not make friends in the police department."

"Two things on that score, Eerie. The Headhunter cares not for friends in the department. Secondly, he was going to kill Congressman McRainey on the spot. I moved without you or the cops because I knew I could take him out before he hurt anyone without being caught. You can bet Mitch Bennett would have shot his way out or tried to, thereby killing or maiming any number of cops."

"I know you saved a lot of lives, including McRainey's, Jed. I should never have jumped all over you about it. The heads on poles I considered a bit over the edge, Fangster."

"Heads on poles makes an unforgettable statement," I replied. I didn't add the real reason was to make her head explode. That would have been a bit over the edge. "Let's put that behind us. We're on the same page now about what I am and what I'm not. You want in then fine… you're in. I'll consider anything but the detective business. Boring. I don't want to be Sam Spade. I want to keep being the invisible force behind great technological advancements."

"Except when you're ripping heads off."

"That's very small of you to point that out, Erin. Back to the point, let's stay on guard. This won't be a game. The main drawback to not doing something immediately is it gives them time to set something in place to kill or maim family. That is how they keep people in line. It's not a bluff. Nikko-"

My phone rang. The Batmobile Bluetooth put my Mom's voice on. "Did something happen today, Jed? There are three black vans parked in front of the house, no license plates. The glass is so tinted I can't see a damn thing. Are the Men in Black finally catching up to you?"

"Ah... no Mom, but the gangsters terrorizing George's daughter may be over to make a statement. Stay inside with the security shutters down. Erin and I are only a few minutes away."

"Fang!" G'ma grabbed the phone. "Let me get my shotgun. I'll fire a couple shots and play the terrified old lady card."

"Please don't, G'ma." Erin was holding her mouth with both hands, comically trying not to descend into uncontrollable laughter at G'ma's offer. "If they try to break in let 'em have it."

"Okay... but I have plenty of ammo if you change your mind."

"Thanks. I'll let you know." I disconnected. "Well... this is another fine mess you've gotten me into, Eerie."

"Me? You're the one beating innocent bystanders. How do you want to handle this?"

"Couldn't we simply call the police? They respond to strange people and vehicles casing a neighborhood house, don't they?"

"You're right." Erin plucked her iPhone from her purse. She reported the incident, explaining who she was and how she knew the vehicles were unknown to the resident. "They're sending a couple cars over to check it out. Are you going to park down the street a bit and go check out the vans in vamp mode?"

I grinned.

"Don't grin, Jed. I hate it when you grin. I know you're contemplating something entirely illogical. Resist temptation. Go have a quick look and come back."

I don't think so. I parked the van nearly a half block away from the entrance to my Mom's estate. I reached into the glove compartment where I had a pair of gloves stashed, the bulky kind with hardened knuckles. "I'm going to create an enigma."

"You're scaring me, Jed. Think this through. Your Mom can handle anything on this earth, visitor from another dimension where they manufacture your kind."

"My kind? What the hell does that mean?" We're hitting undiscovered territory here. Erin never shared anything concerning her thoughts on how I came to be. "Never mind. Hold that thought while I go create my enigma."

I didn't give Erin time to reply. I flashed down the street at Dhampir speed. With my usual precision I never get credit for I busted all the windows out of every van on one side. After rounding the lead van, I busted all the windows out on the opposite side. Each one had surprised gangsters cringing in it. I returned to find Erin, laughing her ass off while looking through a pair of range finders I keep in the glove compartment. Maybe Erin really did have a revelation after the Gronsky scare, coupled with my 'Headhunter' antics.

"That will definitely be an enigma. Oh my God, Jed, that was funny as hell. How'd the guys look inside the vans?"

"Like they were being shot at by automatic weapons fire." I started my van and did a turn to go the other way. "We'll drive around until the police arrive. Once they laugh at the startled criminal minions, we'll drive into the driveway past the scene, stroll over to identify ourselves, and see how things are going."

"This should be fun. I didn't mean anything when I said 'your kind'. You didn't really think I simply accepted the fact I grew up with a Dhampir without me wondering how the hell you could exist, did you?"

"Actually, that's exactly how I figured you coped with being my friend over the years. If you start thinking origins I can understand the 'visitor from another dimension' remark. Why haven't you ever mentioned the subject before?"

"I admit to not really wanting to know the answer. I speculated your Father may have been exposed to a mutated virus like they explain away zombies with."

"There are no such things as zombies." Wait for it... wait for it.

"There are no such things as Vampires and Dhampirs."

"Exactly. I am a figment of your imagination, Eerie. I like your other dimension theory. My theory was Dad survived through all the centuries from a prior age when vampires existed. Someone came along, bled on him, and he reanimated into the present day like in the Dracula movies. He then frolicked all over creating Dhampirs one at a time as he seduced young coeds like my Mom."

"Not a bad theory, but if he could procreate all over the country why wouldn't we have heard Dhampir stories? You don't really think you have half siblings throughout the nation, do you? What does your Mom think? Did you ever ask her?"

"I asked. She doesn't like talking about that night. Her story doesn't change by even a word, which made me suspect Mom was always holding back something. The story is stark with very little detail. I figured maybe the experience was so bad she created a version she could live with and stay sane."

"Now you've done it." Erin sat straight with arms folded.

"Done what?"

"I've got to find out the story from your Mom. We'll double team her while she's weak from this Dotsenko mess. We need to know everything. Maybe we could get your grandparents involved. I always thought your Mom's story was written in stone. I didn't know you suspected she knew more than she woke one morning, after a dark stranger one night stand, pregnant with you."

"I'm not gang tackling my Mom. I will ask her again with serious intent. I haven't asked her anything more in years. I asked her if she thought my Father was dead or alive. She changed the subject, telling me I should concentrate on our lives and forget the past. I took that to mean she was done talking about that night. Come to think of it… you changed the subject from my enigma tornado. You thought it was funny. Are you being seduced to the dark side, Eerie?"

"I'll let you know after I find out what happens with this surprise Dhampir assault on innocent criminals and what really happened the night you were conceived. This should be a fun night."

# Chapter Four

# Origins

I turned onto my Mom's street once again. There were two Placerville police squad cars on scene. They were questioning a bunch of suited thugs. More squad cars arrived as we entered Mom's driveway and parked the van. It became obvious the cops had called for backup because they saw these guys were loaded for bear. When they spotted their fellow officers arriving on scene the four officers in attendance immediately drew down on the gangsters. We stayed in the van until the gangsters were ordered to their knees, hands behind heads. Interesting. This ploy of mine may garner a few entertaining results. The criminal minions were not happy. Erin and I stepped from the van slowly without slamming the doors, our hands in plain sight. Erin had her badge ID in hand too. We stood still until one of the officers motioned us to approach.

"Officer Constanza," the black police officer with Robbins on his nametag said after peering at Erin's ID in a glance while keeping hand on weapon and watching his partner restraining five of the men from the middle van. "Do you know something about this? There's a dozen armed guys here with nothing to say except they were attacked by a mysterious force."

"It all depends on who those guys are. This is Jedidiah Blake, a CSI consultant with the SPD. This is his parents' and grandparents' home. They called us, saying three strange vans were parked in front of the house with windows tinted too dark to be legal or to see through. We came as soon as we could. We were investigating another complaint a friend of Mr. Blake's Mom asked us to look into. His daughter, Marilyn Canelo, is being stalked by men tied to Seth Dotsenko. I'm sure you recognize the name. His Father is Nikko Dotsenko."

"I know the name. I take it you suspect these guys work for Dotsenko. They won't say anything about who they are or why they're hanging out at this residence. All they will say is some mysterious entity attacked their vehicles, busting the windows out. My partner and I saw guns in evidence when we arrived. I called for backup. We kept them talking until I had more guns than they did before taking them down."

"Smart move," Erin said. "Can we stick around until you ID them? If they're part of the Dotsenko mob, Mr. Blake and I may have a problem."

"Are you armed?"

"Yes."

"I'd appreciate it if you stand in with us while we complete the process."

"Of course. Where would you want me and do you want me to draw my piece?"

Robbins pointed to another woman officer with her weapon out, keeping five of the van occupants under guard while her partner restrained the men. "Stand with Terra and draw your piece once she sees you. Thanks for the help."

"You bet." Erin walked toward the other woman officer.

"Terra!" Robbins called out. "That's Officer Constanza, SPD. She'll help."

"Thanks, Mike!" Terra greeted Erin with relief plain on her face.

"Are you armed, Mr. Blake?" Robbins glanced away from his partner's restraining task.

"No Sir. I only consult with SPD." I had another thought though. "I've had some experience with interrogation techniques. Would you mind if I gave it a try? I noticed there were five men in the back van, five in the one you're taking care of, and only two in the front one. I think it possible the two in the front van might be the leaders."

"That's how we figured it. I have no objection to you taking a shot at it." Robbins' partner finished restraining the men they were handling. "Watch them for a moment, Pete."

Robbins walked me over to where a single officer watched the two men kneeling with their hands locked behind their heads. Robbins quickly used plastic restraints on the two remaining men. I watched them carefully. One kept making noise claiming they were victims. The other guy wore a sullen, impatient look, his mouth tightened in a thin muzzle against saying anything that would prolong the ordeal.

I planned to change my interactions as Erin seemed comfortable in doing. I've lived within Star Trek's Prime directive of non-interaction with other species long enough. Erin was probably right about my origin not being of this earth for all I knew. This could be fun acting the part of a visitor from another world. This would be a perfect trial for a public dose of Dhampir power without breaking anything. I helped my target to his feet. He stared at me with the intention of belligerently putting me in my place. A few seconds later I owned him. I turned to Robbins.

"Have you read him his rights yet, Officer Robbins?"

"No time. I will now if he'll acknowledge the Miranda reading. Should I record it?"

"Yes. He'll acknowledge everything. I could tell this guy wants to help in any way he can." I turned to my new gangster zombie. "What's your name, my friend?"

"Zack Algonac."

"Cooperate with Officer Robbins, please."

"I will."

Robbins sounded skeptical but read the Miranda warning to Zack. He acknowledged understanding what he had been read. The whiner still kneeling stared at Zack in disbelief.

I put my hand on Zack's shoulder. "Tell Officer Robbins who sent you here and what exactly your crew had in mind to do here."

"We work for Nikko Dotsenko. His son called us with a problem. Nikko told us to handle the problem. We were to intimidate and wait for Seth's call."

"Shut the fuck up, Zack! Are you crazy!?"

Zack glanced down at his companion, his brows knitted in confusion. "I have to tell them what we're doing here, Derek."

"How far are you to go with this intimidation, Zack?"

"As far as Seth wanted us to, including burning the place to the ground."

"Nikko's going to kill you, dummy!" Derek edged away from Zack as if he were in danger of being shot for being too close.

"Come along with me and Officer Robbins." I led him toward the squad cars with Robbins following. When we were out of Derek's earshot I stopped him with Robbins still indicating he was recording. "Do you have a phone on you that Seth was supposed to call with orders?"

Zack dipped his head toward the inside suitcoat pocket over his left side. I removed one of those throw away phones you buy when you're broke, or selling drugs, or being ordered to kill people. "When were you guys to leave if he didn't call?"

"What time is it now?"

"3:10," Robbins told him.

"We were to leave in another twenty minutes no matter what."

"How did you guys figure to get away in broad daylight after destroying and killing?" This intimidation plan of theirs bordered on insanity so far. Placerville's a small city on the way to Lake Tahoe, but it's not a lawless wild-west show or mob owned mecca of criminal activity. They have a good police force as evidenced by Officer Robbins.

"Nikko owns the police chief. It shouldn't have been possible for the people to call for police help without a delay in place to allow us a warning. In the event we did destroy the property, we were to get twenty minutes to disappear, but it would have been done after dark."

"Damn it! He's right. We did get called back, but I overrode the recall because I explained a Sacramento Police Officer called it in." Robbins walked off for a moment as if lost. He turned suddenly after a few steps. "What the hell do I do with this, Blake?"

"I would suggest waiting to see if Seth calls. If he does, Zack will answer with it on speaker. You can record it. We have your permission to record any call that comes in, right?"

"Of course, Mr. Blake," Zack answered.

Robbins pulled me over to the side with me allowing him to. "Jed, is it?"

"Yep. Just Jed."

Robbins shook my hand. "Mike to you. How are you doing this, Jed? I have no complaints, but why is this Zack guy acting like your hand puppet?"

I shrugged off the question. "It's something I've had for as long as I can remember. People trust me and want to do the right thing when I speak to them. Until now, it was a party trick to do on Halloween or New Years. This is the first time doing it has meant anything." Most of that was true... well... half true.

"That's a gift!" Mike was swallowing the bait and hook. He couldn't explain it other than I was doing Star Wars Jedi mind tricks on crooks. "What should happen if this Seth Dotsenko calls with orders to torch the house?"

I couldn't think of anything uncomplicated for Mike to do. I planned on killing the Dotsenko Father and Son duo. Then, I might settle with the Placerville Police Chief too. "That's a tough one, Mike. Officer Constanza and I would leave the facts in your hands to deal with. I give you my word we'll stay out of it. I have no idea what it would take to bring down an active city Police Chief."

"Thanks for your understanding. I give you my word no cop will turn a blind eye to helping your folks in the house."

Then Zack's phone rang. I took it over to Zack with Mike Robbins again recording. "You know what to say, Zack. Answer normally."

I flipped open the phone and put it on speaker. I nodded at Zack. "Algonac here."

"Listen carefully, Zack!" Seth sounded to me like his head was about to explode. "Call my lawyer! They're trying to hold me overnight for a hearing in front of a judge. Burn that damn house to the ground with everyone in it. Is that big Blake guy there?"

"Yes… he's here."

"Good! Did he have a little auburn haired bitch with him?"

"Yes."

"Kill them all. I'll put a call into Lemanski before they take my phone away from me. He'll give you the time needed to leave the area. Get it done! Hear me?"

"Yes Sir," Zack replied. I closed the phone.

Robbins looked like someone shot his dog. "Lemanski is the police chief in case you didn't know."

"I know." I saw what they call the meat wagon arrive on scene. I wondered how many of these guys would be back on the street inside of a few hours. "May I suggest keeping Zack in protective custody? I don't know how your DA is here, but he'd be very valuable. I believe Zack has had a life changing moment and he will help you build a case willingly if you can keep him alive."

"Can you really say he'll help us now without you around?"

"I think so." I know so. "Let's walk over and ask him."

"Zack. Officer Robbins wants to put you into protective custody so you can explain your work with the Dotsenko mob. Would that be okay with you?" I had repaired a couple of wires inside Zack's head. If the mob didn't kill him, he'd be very helpful.

"I would be glad to help, Mr. Blake."

"You stay with me then, Zack," Mike told him. "I'll get the other prisoners loaded. Thanks again for this and keeping a lid on it until I can figure a course to follow."

"You bet, Mike. Good luck." I walked over to Erin where she was being relieved of guard duty. She joined me at my gesture away from the police activity. I explained my breaking the self-imposed Star Trek Prime Directive simile which she enjoyed.

"So this Zack took the call from Seth with Robbins recording but Dotsenko owns the police chief. We're backing away to allow Robbins the opportunity to handle it in house. I go along with you so far but you haven't addressed the danger factor. Nikko or Seth can order hits from inside any place they're at, including jail."

"Yes, unless they're not breathing. I hope you haven't jumped ship already on the cruise of the Dhampir Rising."

Erin stared at me for a second trying to read whether I was serious or not. "Look, Jed, when I talked about an active proactive part, I didn't think you would take it seriously enough to take on the mob. How do you know someone's not waiting in the wings to come after you in ways you've never dreamed of?"

"That's why we have the 'Headhunter'. I don't plan on doing Nikko and Seth so I can plant a flag in their asses, declaring them as a 'beware of the Blake' warning. I'm not waiting for the mob as you call them to make our lives a living hell. I will hunt down and kill every single one of them until there is no threat. I'm not playing games as Marilyn decided to do. She's helpless to do anything else. She created a way to deal with the circumstances. That's what I'll do too. In doing so, I'll solve her Dotsenko problem while I'm at it. It's a win/win situation."

"What the heck has happened to you, Jed? You're talking about mass murder. You respected what Marilyn was doing. What's with this new mob extermination plan?"

"When they arrived in black unmarked vans specifically to await orders from a lunatic as to whether or not to exterminate my family. Now's the time to walk away if what I've said bothers you, Erin."

Erin took my arm, walking me toward Mom's house. "I need time to absorb this, Jed. We're on the voyage of discovery between us with me hearing about things you've done without me knowing or suspecting them. Can I ask your Mom about your origin or not? Maybe with all that's happened she'll be more forthcoming with what happened the night of your conception."

"Yeah, or she could tell us to mind our own business and throw us out." I admit to always being a bit in awe of my Mom. She's like a good looking Star Wars female Yoda, who knows everything, smiles at you when you say something stupid, and changes your mind without saying anything. She's scary good.

"Your Mom won't do any such thing. She may refuse but she won't get mad that we asked. C'mon, Fang. Admit it. You want to know all the details from that night."

"Fine. Ask if you want. I don't know how much or little I'll join in on the interrogation though. Some things are best not known."

My Mom with the Grandparents staring over her shoulder awaited us at the entrance. "They arrested them all. That's a good sign isn't it, Jed?"

"In some ways it is," I replied, hugging G'ma and shaking hands with G'Pa. I saw George waiting in the wings. I thought so much for interrogating my Mom. Boy, was I wrong.

"Come in, Jed. George had a lot of questions about us. I told him everything. I'm in love with him, and he's in love with me. I don't want to pretend anymore or hide anything from him. He thinks I'm nuts. Although he hasn't said anything since I explained what you are, I can tell he thinks I'm missing a couple of pancakes from my short stack with syrup."

Am I hearing this right? "So… you want me to prove I'm a Dhampir for George? Have you thought this through, Mom? There are a lot of complications in Marilyn's circumstances. Some will have to be handled violently right away."

Mom nodded her head with attitude as she closed the door behind Erin and me. "I want him to know. If he has any reservations afterwards about either of us I want him to leave and never come back. Show him, Jed."

"Okay, Mom." I would do anything for her, including risking my own existence with a stranger. I walked over to George with my hand out. He shook it. "I had an extensive talk with your Daughter Marilyn. Mom told me you don't believe I'm what she says I am. She loves you and understands my secret will have to be known by you. Mom's never asked me for anything. She wants you to know so you can make a decision whether to continue seeing her. I hope you will. May I show you?"

"Look, Jed, I understand you may think you're some superhuman freak and have been since birth. Really, I think you must know Vampires and Dhampirs don't exist, right."

"Hold that thought." I turned into full on Dhampir mode, black iris eyes, dark lined facial features, and fangs I grew out slowly to full length with him watching in horror.

Erin came over and gripped his hand. "Jed is a Dhampir, George. I've known since we were kids. He's not a monster, but he takes some getting used to. Are you okay?"

I stayed still and let Erin speak. George didn't look so good. "Maybe you should sit down, George."

G'pa put a chair next to George and he sat down heavily. Mom brought him a double shot of amber fluid which he threw down in one gulp. His eyes cleared a bit after that. It was a few more moments before he could speak. "I...I don't know what to say."

"Fang's a good boy," G'ma said, taking my hand as George again looked in my direction. "He sometimes hurts bad people, but he's very conscientious about it."

"Jed had to hurt a few of them around Marilyn today, including Seth Dotsenko," Erin told him as I willed myself into normal form. She then went over the entire series of events and possible consequences when we were all seated at the kitchen table.

"Dotsenko owns the police chief here in Placerville. That can't be good," George said. "I'm really sorry to have involved all of you in this. I had no idea it was this bad. Do they really have that Seth guy now with what he said on the recording?"

"It depends on the judge," Erin explained. "California has recording laws prohibiting people from recording others taking part in a conversation without their permission. I'm not certain Officer Robbins could use the actual recording, but he can use it to prove he heard the conversation. Then it would be established that he was there on scene."

"They're not going to stop trying to kill you," George replied. "If anything, the Dotsenkos will hold off their intimidation tactics until a trial date nears. Their underlings could finish what was started today."

"Let Erin and I handle the threats," I told him. "Marilyn is doing well under the circumstances. The police have a handle on the situation right now. Robbins will find out what is possible and what isn't in regard to the police chief."

"I don't understand what you and Erin can do to prevent these psychos from carrying out whatever they plan in secret. They own police chiefs, incorrigible crews of men to do their bidding, and enough money to fund the best lawyers in the country to defend them. They can intimidate witnesses as well as victims. For all we know they own a bunch of judges too. How can... wait a minute. Are you planning to kill the Dotsenkos, Jed?"

"I'm not going to reason with them. Officer Robbins will send squad cars periodically to check Mom's house, but even that may end after an initial time. If he can't find an internal affairs officer or a district attorney capable of neutralizing the police chief we'll have to create a way to deal with Nikko and Seth."

"Meaning what exactly?"

"Whatever Jed has to do to protect us," G'pa stated. "C'mon, George. Have you been listening at all? Dotsenko's had your daughter held prisoner since he raped her. He gave a kill order on the phone for all of us. The police can't protect anyone 24/7."

"Sorry." George hugged my Mom standing next to him. "I don't want you to think I'm not incredibly grateful for what all of you have risked for me and Marilyn. This news about what actually happened, and what Seth has been doing, makes me want to get my gun to hunt the bastards down."

"Honey," Mom said. "Let Jed and Erin handle this. We'll stay on guard. My Dad is a Marine. There's no such thing as an ex-Marine. He has guns and he knows how to use them. We have a first class security system. We don't want you in prison. Jed can do other things besides grow fangs. Show him, Jed."

I moved in Dhampir speed to a spot next to him. George's naked eyes would see me as a shadowy blur appearing next to him as if by magic. I then lifted him in his chair to the ceiling, holding him there as he gasped deep intakes of air. After I put him down slowly to the floor, he jumped from the chair, facing me with his chest heaving.

"Good Lord! Can you turn into a bat and fly around the room too?"

"He can compel people like the vampires in the movies," Erin answered. "Want a demonstration?"

"No... I'm good. I admit this will take some time to process, but you're certainly capable of facing anything short of getting blown up. Do you heal like the vamps on TV?"

Good question. "Yeah, I do. I haven't been shot or anything like that though. Cuts and scrapes have healed instantly. I fractured an ankle and it healed instantly when I was younger. I admit I tried turning into a bat after seeing some old Dracula movies."

That elicited some laughs. Erin did as she told me she would do.

"Jill. Tell us what really happened the night Jed was conceived. I know you'd rather leave it in the past, but it's too important."

Mom looked at me. I smiled. "C'mon, Mom. Do you think I can't handle anything in the way of a story about my Dad? You've found someone you really care about. He knows about me. Soon, he'll be wondering about my Dad too. I can tell from their faces, G'ma and Pa are just as interested. I'll bet G'ma has asked you a thousand times about that night."

"Damn right I did. Fang deserves to know, Jill. We want to hear what the hell happened the night you were raped by the Count."

With an attentive audience, silent and enthused, Mom took a deep breath. "Okay, but the story's not a pretty one. I was a stupid kid at a party just like I told you many times. My friends I came with split to different places all over the frat house. It wasn't 'Animal House' crazy in there, but it was dark, noisy, and all the usual mind altering substances were in attendance. A tall dark brooding guy with a smile much like Jed's chatted with me for a moment. I thought he was into Goth stuff, dressed all in black. I remember him saying something in the noisy room that pierced the scene and jammed me right between the eyes."

"He told me he was a vampire, hundreds of years old. I listened like any other coed dimwit would to a juicy make believe story told so convincingly. He told me his name was Aaron and he had been a vampire since Italy in 1558. He was buried alive after being turned by a French vampire during the Italian wars of 1551 – 1559 at the Battle of Gravelines near Calais. Aaron claimed to have been discovered accidentally only a month before, feeding on his finders, a pair of young archeologists exploring the battlefields of the Italian Wars. As Jed can attest, he acquires all the skills, knowledge, and moral trappings when feeding on another human."

"Aaron traveled to America, using the young archeologist's passport because of his close resemblance to the young victim. He haunted the Sacramento State campus, feeding, stealing, pretending, and compelling any help he needed. His disadvantage of course was daylight. Although he did not burst into flame or anything when exposed to the sun, daylight hours made him extremely lethargic as if drugged. Aaron explained he needed someone to become his mate, a partner who could care for him during daylight while guiding his endeavors, much as Erin has done for Jed."

"I thought he was a joke. I made light of everything he said, trying to edge away from him. His story had fascinated me as any good vampire tale would. Aaron's request for a mate to be his human caretaker kicked in my predator alert. It was too late. He grabbed my chin. I looked into eyes black, without reflection. They devoured me. The next thing I knew was driving away in his new two seater sports car. He drove me to a cabin north of White Hall in El Dorado County on Ice House Road. I could do nothing. I knew what was happening. I willed myself to stop all resistance, allowing him to invade my mind completely as he made love to me."

Mom put her hands over her face. Tears streamed down her cheeks. "God help me. I felt completely in thrall to a monster, but acted as Aaron hoped, convincing him I loved the incredible thrill of being his mate and partner. He fed on me, tasting everything about me, violating me to the depths of my soul. When morning came, the daylight brought lethargy just as he had explained. I had been so willing and enthusiastic Aaron left me unbound. While he paced around the cabin as if in a trance, I found a weapon – an oaken dowel pin in the kitchen drawer. At midday, Aaron reclined on the bed, beckoning me to him. I came willingly, cuddling next to him. The moment he closed his eyes, I staked him with all the vicious force and fear electrifying my entire body. In one nightmarish split second, Aaron's eyes popped open in sad surprise. He crumbled into dust like a vamp staked in a 'Buffy the Vampire' episode."

Silence so tense as to be palpable followed Mom's ending of Aaron the vampire: my Father. She stood and went over to where the whiskey bottle was that she had poured George's drink from. Mom poured her own double, taking a large gulp, and then refilling it before returning to the table.

"You staked Dracula!" G'ma pumped a fist. "Damn, girl, why the hell did you wait so long to tell us the story?

"He wasn't Dracula, Mom. Aaron was Jed's Father. I didn't see any reason to expand on the story I told. It was the truth. I was in denial until Jed was born. In knowing what Jed was I came to grips with the truth of what had happened. I'm sorry I didn't tell you before, Jed."

"I wondered if there were more like me out there and if my Father was creating a horde of Dhampirs. You answered that concern. What did you do after you staked him?" My Mom, the Vampire Killer.

95

"I wiped down his sports car. After I swept Aaron into a garbage bag I used a couple of cloths to drive the car down to the Sacramento campus. I parked it off campus before depositing the plastic bag in a waste bin. I'm sorry, Jed. I don't know how else to tell this in a less than gruesome manner."

I already knew my Dad was a monster. I'm trying to be a good monster, but I know I still take after him in some ways. I don't kill indiscriminately. Maybe Aaron didn't either. "It's okay, Mom. He was going to make you into his sock puppet. Did he speak about creating other vamps the way they do in the movies?"

"No. He didn't say one way or another. Someone made him though in the Middle Ages so there must have been a way. Aaron only spoke of feeding on people. He compelled them, fed, and left them alive. He mentioned he did not want to run afoul of the law which made sense. Unlike the movies, leaving trails of dead bodies everywhere would have been disaster for him. You all know now everything I know."

George sat next to her, gripping Mom's hand. "You've had obstacles to overcome in your life that would have driven anyone else insane. I'm glad we've found each other, Jill."

Mom grinned. "Hold that thought. I haven't introduced the werewolf family tree yet."

George tried to hide the startled look but couldn't. He realized Mom got him when the rest of us started laughing. "Okay... you got me on that one. I hope we can all get past this rough sharing of the past as it clashes with the present and future. I'm going to see Marilyn tonight. I'll phone with details on how it looks over there."

"We'll take my van, George. I'll drive. How about it, Erin?"

96

"I'll go. I have early shift tomorrow, so you'll have to drop me at my house right after, Jed."

"Okay. C'mon, George." He followed me to the door after kissing Mom goodnight. "I'll stop by tomorrow, Mom. Stay in the safe rooms tonight. Erin and I will check on her Mom before I drop her off and come home."

"Watch your back, Fang," G'ma ordered.

In the van Erin sat behind George. "No one should have been able to post men outside Marilyn's place yet. Will she take your call, George?"

"I'll give it a try." George took out his iPhone and tried a call session with Marilyn. I waited to see if he got through to her. He did.

"Dad?"

"Yeah, honey. Jed and Erin are driving me over to see you. Has Seth tried to post different guys at your door yet?"

"I don't think so. I stayed inside studying all today. I'll take a look outside."

"Don't Erin." I called over to her. "We'll check around when we get there. Let's not take any chances."

"Jed's right. We'll see you in a half hour."

"Okay. It will be good to see you, Dad."

"Be there in a few, kid."

\* \* \*

I parked in the designated area for the American River Courtyard housing. "You two stay here while I-"

97

Bullets hit my front windshield as two men walked toward the front firing what looked like silenced machine pistols of some kind. My vehicle glass held as George ducked down. Two more shooters approached the van from our sides, firing as they came.

"Keep George safe, Erin. I'll be back."

I opened the driver's side door a crack so I could streak out the opening, locking the door behind me. The shooters never had a chance. I ran over the driver's side shooter in locomotive fashion, smashing his weapon into his head. The shooters in the front went down under my assault from the side using the infamous clothesline right arm held still stiff. I snapped the first one's neck, caught the second one high. He pitched to his side. I followed with an elbow that caved in the side of his head. The passenger side shooter, noticing he was firing alone, held fire long enough for me to smash him to the pavement with a blow to the temple.

It was time then to find out quickly who sent the assassins. I fed on him, my fangs slashing into his neck, feeling both the exhilaration of the blood coupled with the panorama of resulting visions. I healed his neck wound and finished him off with another elbow. Seconds later, I unlocked the van, and drove away with George and Erin silently awaiting my direction. I waited until we cleared the campus. I parked on a darkened street nearby.

"I'm afraid it's time to bring Marilyn in from the cold. I'll go bring her out here. It would probably be a good idea if you got ready to drive away, Erin. Leave the passenger door unlocked. I'll take her directly into the back. You drive toward my Mom's house. George and Marilyn will have to be house guests for the time being. Those guys were sent directly from Nikko. He has her phone tapped. They knew we were coming. As you could see, they were here to kill us. There are two others dressed as campus security cops near her place. I'll be back with Marilyn as soon as I can."

"Okay, Jed," Erin said, exiting the passenger compartment. "What about the killers?"

"All dead. We'll let the cops draw their own conclusions when they discover four dead men with silenced machine pistols. I'll write their names down for you later. Hang tight, George. I'll be back with Marilyn, safe and sound."

George began to speak, but then simply nodded in acknowledgement. Erin hugged me momentarily before taking my place behind the steering wheel. I spent a few seconds going into predator mode. I knew what the fake security guards looked like. I also knew from what vantage point outside the American River Courtyard building they were watching Marilyn's place from. I moved in full Dhampir mode from shadow to shadow until I was in position to see my prey. I grinned. They thought we were already dead I'd bet. I took my visual scrambler out and turned it on. I raced at the one nearest me nearly decapitating him with a side hand chop to the throat. He swung around as his companion reached for him, not having noticed what took his friend down. I twisted his head all the way around on his neck. After depositing the two corpses in the building shadows, I proceeded to Marilyn's.

She answered my first ring. "Hi, Marilyn. I don't have a lot of time to explain but can you pack your college materials and some clothes for a few days. We have to keep you and your Dad in a safe place until my friend Erin and I can clear some obstacles away so you can return."

"Uh... sure... I'll only be a few minutes."

True to her word, Marilyn rejoined me at the door with a small suitcase. I took it from her. We left the building. I took her by a side route toward where Erin and George waited. To her credit, she didn't question my choice of exit from the campus or why we weren't parked in her parking lot. I could have scooped her in one arm to the Batmobile in seconds but I thought it best to keep George as the only new confidant of my secret identity. The incoming sirens were blaring by the time I reached the van. I helped Marilyn into the back and Erin drove directly away from the campus until she could get turned onto a street leading to the freeway. George and Marilyn had an emotional reunion. I didn't phone my Mom because I was unsure how many phones were tapped.

At Mom's house, a squad car was parked near the driveway. The police officer waved as we drove in the driveway. Erin parked near the house entrance.

"Stay inside while I check out our police guard." I didn't wait for an acknowledgement. I walked toward the squad car.

The two police officers inside the squad car met me near their hood. "Hi. Is everything okay, officers?"

The taller dark haired officer nodded. "Everything's okay. Mike told us to watch out for your Mom's place tonight. He described your vehicle and you. You're Jed Blake, right?"

"Yes Sir." I shook hands with the officers.

"Mike explained how you helped us out today. He says we have an internal affairs problem that is endangering your Mom and Grandparents. We're here to make sure no one approaches her place but you."

"Thank you. I'm hoping everything will be fixed in a few days. I really appreciate your help. I'll check on my Mom. She's going to have a couple of house guests until conditions improve."

"My partner and I heard rumors it's the Dotsenko mob behind the small army that was arrested here earlier. Do you know if that's true? Mike couldn't tell us anything for fear word would reach the wrong ears."

"I believe the rumor you heard to be true. Thanks again for the added protection."

"We'd do anything for Mike. He gave us your number. If things change we'll call you. Here's my card if anything changes in your situation."

I took his card. "I'll call if anything changes. We have George Canelo and his daughter Marilyn with us. She's the target. My security system is state of the art and there are two safe rooms inside. Sacramento Police Officer Erin Constanza is with me at this time too. We'll be leaving soon to check on her loved ones next. Thanks again."

"You bet, Jed."

I rejoined my charges in the van, explained Mike Robbins had a squad car watching the house until a decision was made concerning 'internal affairs' as the officers outside called the problem. "Let's go inside. At least Marilyn is no longer within the Dotsenko mob's reach at the moment. We'll fill in my Mom on details. Then Erin and I will check her folks' house after."

"Will I really be safe staying here?"

"You'll be as safe in my Mom's house as anywhere in the state, Marilyn. Give Erin and me some time. We'll solve the rest of this problem somehow. For better or worse we have a part to play in this."

I began to get nostalgic for my life from a couple weeks ago. It appeared Erin's backfired ploy to get a detective's shield by capturing Anton Gronsky upset the linear discordance factor or some other weirdo building block of reality. Not long ago, I created apps for computers and mobile devices, along with once in a while taking out a bad guy or tasting blood at a crime scene to help Erin. All of a sudden, I've dive bombed into the vigilante 'Headhunter' while trying to be monster cute. Then I decide on being some kind of super bodyguard in an attempt at trying to be a good son. I now have probable enemies in a gangland mob, an Egyptian arms' dealer named Bilal Al-Taei, and even a CSI assistant I somehow pissed off by inventing something to make her do better at her job. I was indeed on a roll.

When inside, I pulled my Mom aside to update her on the happenings. "Keep your iPhone by you at all times. FaceTime me at any time."

"You've really stepped in it this time, Jed," Mom replied in a hushed voice. She rightly assumed we didn't dump my story on Marilyn yet. "I admit to having some responsibility in this, son. Do you have a plan?"

"Other than killing the Dotsenkos... ah... no. I'm open to suggestions."

Mom smiled at me. "It's getting easier to see the killing as a solution, huh? I didn't mean my seeing George on a serious basis to ever cause an upheaval with gangsters and police."

She always could read me which made keeping her informed all the way the only real choice I ever counted on. "Don't worry about it, Mom. We have to make things safe for the people close to us. A couple less Dotsenkos seems like a good trade to me. You and George will have to feel out Marilyn as to whether she can handle being in on the family secret. Erin and I will be over at her Mom's house to make sure her folks are safe. Keep your heads down until I can adjust a few things."

"Do you know where to find them from the feedings, Jed?"

"Yes. Father and Son will be at Arthur Henry's Supper Club on Broadway in Sacramento, establishing alibis while their minions are out working the streets."

"Have you ever taken someone in a public place like that?"

"I normally stalk the one I'm after until they aren't in public. The Dotsenkos arrived at the supper club by limo. That's all the guy I bled knew. There won't be many limousines parked in the area. Erin and I will reconnoiter the streets near Arthur Henry's. If I can find the limo in service to the Dots, I'll bet I can compel the driver to bring them to a place where I can make the Dots safe for civilized society."

"How do you... oh... I guess it is the only way," Mom said, hugging me. "I'm sorry I waited so long to tell you what happened to your Father. I know you could have handled it. Could you simply go in the restaurant and compel the Dotsenkos?"

"If I wanted to be the last person seen with them I could." I grinned as my Mom rolled her eyes. "You're thinking I'm getting a little too good at this killing business, huh?"

Mom slapped my shoulder. "Get out of my head, Fang. What about the other deal with the sniper? Do you have to handle that right away?"

"No. I left enough evidence for the police to put Bilal Al-Taei at the top of their suspect list. If I see McRainey is still in danger I'll look into the situation again."

"You'd better get going. I'll handle our guests and your Grandparents. How's Erin doing with working outside the law?"

"So far, so good since I compelled her."

Another smack... this one at the back of my head. "You did no such thing. Get out of here. You'll call me one way or the other, won't you?"

"Of course, Mom," I answered, grabbing Erin's arm as I walked toward the door. "C'mon, Eerie. We have work to do. I want to make sure your folks are safe before we hit the outlaw trail."

"Don't call it that," Erin ordered, waving back at the Canelos and my Grandparents on the way to the door. "We're forced to work around some of the tenets of law."

103

"Way to relabel the outlaw trail, Eerie. We've been 'working around the law' since we were kids. I always thought once the apps I created took off I would be able to resist my baser tendencies. Unfortunately, having a fortune has made it easier to work in the dark."

Erin stayed silent until we closed the doors of my van. "You're getting off on the blood now, aren't you? I mean I know you feel exhilarated after feeding, especially on humans, but the temptation has been increasing, hasn't it?"

I drove away from Mom's house with a shrug. "I'm more comfortable doing it, but there are plenty of bad guys. The blood bank is a great front for me to pretend I'm a good monster. The truth is drinking blood out of the bag sucks... pun intended. Why resist when I can drink at the trough of evil doers everywhere."

"Gee, now you're a poet, huh? I wish I could say you'll run out of bad guys but I can't. What about women?"

"If I find them doing bad things I handle them the same way. Drinking their blood gives me a lot of insights you wouldn't be comfortable with me knowing, Eerie."

"Like what... no! Never mind. You're right. I don't want to know. Some of those guys you killed tonight were Russian or Ukrainian. Can you speak the languages of the people you drink from?"

I nodded. "I can and I do. I keep that to myself though. I'm certain I could claim to be incredible with languages, but it would be odd if I suddenly revealed I knew a multitude of languages."

I then told Erin my plan for the limo and the Dotsenkos. "I'm sure the limo driver has a spot he parks in while he has to wait for his patrons. We'll park near him. I'll go have a word with him and a bite. He'll get the call to pick the Dots up. He'll get them inside and drive them to us. I'll be inside with them in a heartbeat. Then the fun begins."

"What fun? C'mon, Jed, you're beginning to worry me again. What fun are you talking about?"

"I told you when I feed I know my prey inside and out. That includes bank accounts, offshore accounts, and safety deposit boxes. Over the years I've accumulated a lot of wealth on my own. When I was starting out, we needed money to help us with my college bills. I would confiscate it from my prey. Now, I just give it away mostly – anonymously to the Salvation Army or to the various veterans' groups."

"So in other words you're going to play Robin Hood with the Dotsenkos' ill-gotten gains? That does have a rather attractive side to it. Do you want to look into who they'll be leaving behind?"

"Nope."

"That's cold, Fangster."

"I'm a Fang, not a priest. We're going into Arthur Henry's to stir the Dots a bit, or at least I am. If you'd like to go with me, you're welcome to come along. I've been there before. It's a nice place. We can have a coffee while we're bearding the Dot's in their lair."

"You are seriously nuts. What's gotten into you?"

"Some of it's always been there. As I explained, you don't know everything about me. What's the use of being nearly superhuman and acting like Casper Milquetoast? I'll set the driver on his path of helping us. Then we'll go have a coffee with the Dots. There's the restaurant ahead on that funky looking outcropping of Broadway and 34th Street. Did you call your Mom?"

"Mom promised to be on guard and will call at the first sight of any strangers or strange vehicles. She will lock down for the night. Mom, of course, wants a complete explanation when I see her. At least we don't have to drive by the house tonight. I've driven by Arthur Henry's before on an officer needs help call. This Oak Park area is part of the good, bad, and ugly. What's so special about this place?"

"It's a nice place and has a great bar with one of the few half naked lady portraits over the bar I've ever seen – very tastefully done I might add."

"You mean it's not done in glow in the dark felt?"

"This is why I never take you anywhere nice, Eerie. You're too caustic."

Erin chuckled and then pointed. "There on the 34th Street side. Nice limo. The Dots know how to travel."

I parked the van near the next corner of 3rd Avenue and 34th Street. "I'll be right back to get you once I introduce myself to the driver."

"Don't forget your eyes, Jed. If you feed on the guy, you'll have to wear your sunglasses in the bar. That's going to attract attention."

Damn it! I forgot about my eyes. "Thanks, Eerie. I'll wear the sunglasses. It will make me stand out more for the Dots to notice."

"Because being six and a half feet tall with a physique like a heavyweight boxer doesn't make you stand out?"

"Don't be snide. See you in a few."

# Chapter Five

## Connecting the Dots

I moved fast along the shadowed tree lined 34th Street. The driver smoked a cigarette with his window open, blowing clouds of putrid stink into the outside air. Ever notice how smokers can't stand to be in their own stench. I have no problem with them doing all the crappy things to their bodies they want. I probably wouldn't care about sharing air with them if my damn olfactory sense wasn't off the charts. I'm like a bloodhound on speed. I guess it's no worse than the body odor, aftershave lotions, perfumes, and bad breath I've had to consciously blunt or go stark raving mad. I yanked him out of the driver's seat and into the shadows of the building near the limo. I drank from him in rapid, violent manner before healing my bite. He didn't get much more than a gasp out of his mouth when he dropped his cigarette before I owned him. If you're wondering how I knew for sure the limo belonged to the Dots... I didn't. No harm, no foul, and he was the driver for the Dots. I explained in detail what I needed him to do and cured his smoking habit. His name was Marko Blevins.

"Do you understand, Marko?" I held his bulky frame in the air easily.

"Yes Sir. I wait for Nikko's call, pick him and his son up - then drive them over to you in the black van down the street."

"Very good. I will see you soon. Thanks, Marko."

"I will not fail, Sir."

At the van, I grinned in at Erin. "My main man Marko is all mine. Let's go have a coffee with the Dots. What do you think they'll do when they see us?"

"Shoot us in the head I would imagine." Erin left the passenger seat, closing her door, and walking in the sensuous manner I find unnervingly erotic even when she has jeans on. Tonight she wore a tight fitting gray skirt with off the shoulder red blouse. Erin brought along a light tan leather coat too because the chill was in the air. She took my arm. "In for a penny, in for a pound. Lead the way my dear Fangster."

I took out my excitingly fashionable Ray-Bans to shut out the black marbled eyeball look I had after feeding. Oh man, I felt good. Nothing like a little fresh human blood to stir my monstrous impulses to the max. I don't know what I was hoping for. I enjoyed Erin's arm threaded inside the crook of mine. I loved her scent of a woman. We walked into Arthur Henry's Supper Club to a greeter not impressed with us at all.

"Do you have a reservation?" He was instantly nice as you please when I gave him a hundred dollar introduction note. "Indeed you do, Sir. Where would you like to be seated?"

I glanced at his nametag and gave him another hundred dollar bill. "My friend and I would like to go into the bar for now, Enrique. May we ask for you if we decide to get a table?"

"Of course, Sir. I will be here until closing."

"Are you familiar with Nikko Dotsenko?"

"Why yes... he's a regular. Mr. Dotsenko and his son are in the bar now with a couple of their security people."

"Thank you, Enrique. I hope to see you later."

"My pleasure, Sir."

Erin giggled annoyingly while we were walking toward the bar. "I bet you didn't figure on him bringing bodyguards, did you?"

In the end, what difference does it make? I needed to get Erin on course. "Listen Eerie, we're making sure my folks, your folks, and the Canelos walk away unscathed from this interaction with the Dots. We can't do that by leaving Nikko alive to whack us by remote from inside prison if we ever do get him convicted. That would be if he didn't bother waiting for the verdict. If we have him arrested now and charged, what will keep him from constantly endangering our people? He'll be out on bail in an hour with his lawyer... probably suing us."

"I know, Jed. Calm down. Do you have a plan for the Dots' henchmen?"

"Let them make the first move. I have a very good idea what Nikko will want those guys to do to us. We'll use that for a redirect." I grinned as I scanned the room.

I saw Nikko and Seth right away at a table against the wall. Nikko's hired thugs looked up to the mark... but not my mark. When Seth glanced in our direction, I waved with a bit of playacting animation. That triggered an intense, rapid fire conversation with his Dad, who gave me his best snarly Godfather face stare down. When he couldn't win, he spoke to his two goons who simply nodded their understanding. They sauntered toward us. Erin elbowed me.

"You certainly got their attention. Is this according to your plan?"

"Yep. Nikko did one of two things. He either ordered them to muscle us to his table or outside. He knows you're a cop. No way does he order his men to shoot us down in the dark. Be ready if they're supposed to take us back to the table. The threat-a-thon will be in full swing then. Nikko will make it clear we'll be killed along with everyone we love if we don't stay out of his business."

"Since he plans to kill us and our loved ones anyway, what's in it for us?"

"Exactly. Elementary, my dear Eerie. The goons are smiling. That means we're getting murdered in the back room of some warehouse, right after the big scene where Nikko plays his dream role of Godfather sending us to our death. This conversation should be so neat!"

"You're nuts, Fangster." Erin allowed the smaller of the two behemoths to clutch her arm. "Hey, big boy, want a date?"

The other henchman noted my size. He reached into his jacket instead of grabbing me. "Our boss would like a word with the two of you. Come along quietly and no one gets hurt. Make a scene and Nikko says we're to take you outside."

"And if we don't want to go outside?" There was no mistaking these two guys. They were killers. "Did Nikko tell you my friend is a Sacramento police officer?"

The other guy hanging onto Erin laughed. "We don't talk. Vick and I get orders. We carry them out. If that means blowing your brains out right here in the bar, then that's what we'll do. Do yourselves a favor and come along to the table. Maybe Nikko's in a good mood tonight."

I grinned and nodded at Erin. "We better do what he says, Erin. I want to do exactly what my Mommy would want me to do in a situation like this."

"At least you guessed right. Man… being a cop used to mean something! Now any bubbas with an ax to grind, order their minions to drag us around like someone's huckleberry."

"Good one, Erin." I turned to my conversationalist. "Erin's right. I'm your huckleberry. Take us to your leader."

"I don't like you, pussy. You think you're big and bad. Harv and I eat rubes like you for breakfast. The only reason we haven't clamped onto you and the girly big mouth for a quick smack-down in the parking lot is Nikko believes he may be able to reason with you idiots."

"That's very hurtful. I like you. I bet we have a lot in common. Do you play chess? We could have a game over coffee sometime when your minion duties are done for the day."

I thought he was going to draw down on me, but he regained control of his emotions at the last second before his head exploded.

"Walk ahead of me to the table. Don't say any more or I put a bullet in your fuckin' head right here in the bar, wise-guy. The girly cop doesn't mean shit to us. Reach for your piece, girly, and we cap both you and your dimwitted partner. Move, dummy!"

"Okay... okay... I didn't mean to start anything with you two. We'll be glad to walk over and say hello to the big man."

Nikko grinned at us while Seth simply stared down at the table. I could tell he wasn't excited about seeing me. His Daddy probably didn't believe a word he said concerning my thug adjustments outside Marilyn's place. Seth sensed something out of order in me dangerous to his wellbeing. He wanted a report of me dead. He didn't want to see me in person, even in a public place. Seth knew deep down inside his life was in danger around me. Oh, how right you are, Seth. I've come out of the 'monster' closet now. You and Daddy Nikko will do your part to make things safe in Dhampir land. I've only discovered how much fun killing bad guys is, and especially ones trying to kill my loved ones.

"Hello Nikko and son," I greeted them happily. "Wow, it didn't take you long to get them to release you, Seth. I noticed you're really surprised to see my friend Erin and me. We're not so surprised to see you and your little friends. We figured when you heard we weren't dead, you'd wonder how that could have happened. Erin and I decided to come over and explain it to you."

111

"How did you know we were here," Nikko asked with a no nonsense frown of impatience as things were not proceeding as he had pictured they would.

"I'm glad you asked. Erin and I thought about where we'd be if in pursuit of a nice place where we could be seen by a lot of people while ordering and awaiting the murders of innocent people. We decided a nice supper club like this would be perfect. You're regulars here, so everyone working tonight would be able to say, 'oh sure, I saw Nikko and Seth'. Very perceptive of us don't you think?"

Vick started to reach for me, trying to act like a good little minion upset over disrespect toward his boss. I backed away while holding up a hand of warning. "Now Vick, don't get over zealous with the hands. I'm sure your boss would like to have a friendly conversation, right Nikko?"

"Vick gets impatient with smartass know-it-alls like you. I called you over because I don't want you or your cop friend here. Vick and Harv will escort you both to your vehicle. Whether either of you gets there in one piece will be up to you. If I were you I'd go quietly. Now get lost, asshole!"

"Sure, Nikko, Erin and I will get a breath of fresh air but we'll be back. We'd be glad to have some company while we take a short walk, right Erin?"

"Oh yes, Jed. It was lovely outside, but I would still like that coffee you promised me."

"Of course."

Vick gestured toward the exit. "Let's go. Maybe we'll let you go home to get your coffee. Big mouth might need to drink his through a straw though."

"You're quite the comedian, Vick," I told him. "You'll need that sense of humor. How about you, Harv? Are you a comedian too?"

Harv smiled at me in what he thought was a frightening way. "Not me, pal. I'm always dead serious. I have it in mind to gut you like a trout if you keep talking."

"That's not very nice. We're very offended at your tone. Aren't we, Erin?"

"Yes. I thought you were going to be nice, Harv," Erin admonished while Harv guided her toward the exit by her arm."

I followed without anything further to say. I waved at Nikko and Seth. No need for anything more because we'd be seeing them again soon. I allowed Vick to grab my arm for guidance. I Donkey-Konged him for a moment and he ran into me instead of forcing me on my way. When he realized he couldn't move me, the light of illumination began to brighten in his head. Vick let me go and I followed Harv and Erin outside.

They walked us around to the shadowed 34th Street side of the building. "Thanks, guys. That's far enough. We're going back inside now."

"You're still not funny, asshole." Harv produced a very wicked looking stiletto knife with seven inch blade. "Maybe if you two beg for your lives we'll let you go."

I broke Harv's wrist in a violent flash of speed so intense his hand dangled on the end of the skin with no attachment to bone before he could move. The stiletto dropped silently toward the ground. I chopped his throat with a side hand strike that nearly decapitated him. Before he could fall I caught the stiletto. With an eye blurring twist I planted the stiletto in Vick's chest. I eased him gasping to the ground next to Harv. After wiping the handle of prints, I put Harv's hand on it. I straightened, surveyed my handy-work, and turned to Erin.

"What do you think, Eerie?"

"I think you are one scary dude, Fangster." Erin took my arm, her hand only shaking slightly. "Do you think they were really going to kill us?"

"I don't know," I answered truthfully. "They're killers and now they won't be killing anyone. Shall we have that coffee now?"

"We're really going to simply walk inside and order a coffee with these two dead bodies lying here?"

I looked back over my two victims. "Why, do you think they'd mind?"

Erin shrugged. "I guess not. This new paradigm between us is going to take some getting used to."

I walked her around the building to the entrance once again. "Want to discuss it over sex later tonight."

Erin giggled. "If I say no will you compel me, monster?"

"Absolutely not, Eerie. I'll only compel you if you beg me to do it. Maybe it would make it easier for you to spend the night with me again."

"I can't think straight when we're a couple, Jed. You're dangerous. Now that I realize how dangerous, I'm not too sure a continuing affair or marriage is a good idea. Are you in love with me?"

"I've been in love with you since the first time you helped clean me off near the river when I killed the predator." I paused to allow my senses to encompass everything within my range. Arthur's Supper Club's darkened 34$^{th}$ Street side evoked no sense of danger or human presence. "You have thought of marriage and love, huh Eerie? Are you in love with me?"

"I don't know, Jed. Being with you is so intense it overwhelms normal thought. I'm not sure that constitutes love or an addiction."

Now that was funny. "I'm an addiction?"

Erin stroked the side of my face sending chills down my monster spine. "Yes. Interacting with you is like grabbing hold of a live electrical wire: deadly, but impossible to let go of until death."

"Gee... nice word picture." I kissed her, allowing the fierce desire, need, and reaction to her touch flow through me. Erin moaned, gripping me to her in a definite acknowledgement more existed between us than a monster and its keeper.

Erin broke away, gasping breathlessly and pointing her finger at me. "See? You... drive me nuts... and no you can't come over to discuss it with me over sex."

She's so cute, but annoying as hell. "Okay, fine. C'mon. Let's go have our coffee and say hello to the Dots."

"We may as well since I'm already a party to two murders." Erin clasped my hand as she walked beside me. "Here we are... hand in hand from the murder scene. I'm getting to be as sick as you."

"You're not even close. I'll turn you to the dark side yet though."

I waved at Enrique on the way in. We proceeded to the bar, walking over to the Dots. To say they were surprised would be a monstrous understatement. "Hi guys. Vick and Harv told us they won't be joining you two again this evening. If you'd like though, Erin and I could sit down and keep you guys company."

"Get away from us," Nikko ordered.

"If that's how you want to be, then Erin and I will go have our coffee at the bar."

"Wait." Seth wanted to know more in spite of Nikko. "Where are Harv and Vick?"

"They argued about something," Erin replied. "Then they told us they were going around the building to have a private discussion. We didn't wait for them."

We didn't wait for Nikko or Seth to comment on Erin's imaginative reply concerning Harv and Vick. At the bar, we sat near the semi-clothed lady portrait. The bartender, a fashionable lady in her late twenties with worldly smile and grin, sauntered over. Her nametag had Cathy on it.

"Hi, what'll you have?"

"Two coffees with cream and sugar, Cathy." I put a twenty on the bar. "Keep the change."

She liked the tip. Our coffees and additives were brought over promptly. "Thanks. I saw you two being escorted out by Dotsenko's hoods. Usually the people they guide out of the bar don't return. The managers look the other way, but Nikko and his kid cost us business. The cheapskate doesn't tip and expects us peons to treat him like he's royalty. I noticed you two pissed him off. I want to warn you he's as dangerous as they come so it would be to your advantage to steer clear of him and his predator son."

"Predator son, huh?" Interesting. Apparently, the Dots were known by more people than wanted to know them.

Cathy leaned closer to Erin and me. "The kid uses date rape drugs. I saw him do it right here at the bar to a woman he'd talked into having a drink. I knocked over the drink before she had any of it. I apologized profusely, cleaned up, and gave them both their drinks for free. Dipshit was pissed, but I stayed close, keeping a conversation going while serving."

"You took a big risk, Cathy," Erin said. "You're right. We suspect him of other date rapes. I'm with the Sacramento Police. I'm Erin. This is Jed. He's a consultant with the PD."

"I hope you nail his ass." Cathy moved away to do her job.

"See? We're public servants working the will of the people," I told Erin with a grin she smacked lightly with her hand.

"Only in Dhampir land could we be the people's willful hand of justice. I've already admitted I'm on your side in all this. The frustration of being a cop with the criminals coddled and the 'Thin Blue Line' thrown under the bus in a heartbeat has worn me down a bit. I always thought getting my detective's shield would be some kind of cure-all. I've seen the detectives having to wade through more crap from the politicians than we do."

"I try to think of it this way. If people weren't basically good they'd be exploiting the politically correct travesty happening to law enforcement every day. When the media stirs in the race, religion, and wealth cards to any situation, we get the fringe mobs ready for duty. I don't know the answer. It must feel pretty good taking a whack at out of the box justice, huh Eerie?"

"Yes, Fangster, it is." Erin sipped her coffee instead of blurting out a rebuttal statement. "Maybe I shouldn't be a cop. I'm turning into a perversion of the system. Arrest me, Jed. I'm out of control. Oh, wait a minute, you're worse. Do you think the Dots will stay in place as they had planned? Since their minions won't be calling them with updates or mission completed statements, I would imagine they'll be leaving soon, especially since Harv and Vick won't be available for consultation."

I should have thought that through. "You're a day late and a dollar short with that observation Igor. I think you're right. I moved the chess pieces a little too soon. We'll have to finish our coffee and go get in the van until my new buddy Marko brings the Dots to us. We don't want them walking out now. Marko wouldn't know what to do."

"Are you going to let your new friend Marko live?"

"Probably. I don't want to get rid of the limo. I'll have to do some fast moves on the Dots as it is. They are not going to be happy."

"How are you going to do that exactly, Fang?"

"Marko drives next to us. I dive into the back seat. Then I get a taste. They'll be mine in under a minute."

"Scary. Once you have them, what the heck do you do with them? I mean the bodies."

"Elementary, my dear Eerie. I won't have to do anything with them. I'm going to compel them to take a father and son swim in the American River. That way, Marko drives them into position at their direction, lets them off and goes home. We'll stick around and watch for a moment."

"Where do you plan for this to happen?"

"The Sunset Boulevard Bridge. That way we can park underneath along the waterway. It'll work because I'll compel them to hold hands at all times no matter what."

"You are a sick man."

"Yep. It's a relative term to be sick in reference to getting rid of the Dots. Although people think romantically about mobsters as depicted by movies and TV, in real life they're usually date-raping, murdering, extortionists like Nikko and Seth."

"Good point, Fang." Erin stood. "Maybe if we go now they'll take off soon after. Nikko must be getting antsy about where Harv and Vick went. You can bet he's tried to call all the minions he had on the murder trail."

"I believe you're right. Let's say goodbye before we go on stakeout."

Erin sighed. "Of course you would want to do that. Can't you be satisfied with a wave?"

"Where's the fun in that?" I took her hand, gently pulling Erin along with me to where the Dots were morosely sipping their beverages. They did indeed appear to be unhappy with their situation. I noticed both had their mobile phones on the table which they stared at in hopes of news not forthcoming."

They noticed our approach with baleful eyes from Nikko and fearful ones from Seth.

"Erin and I wanted to say goodnight for now. It was real nice running into our favorite father and son duo tonight. I wish I could say we should do it again sometime but I don't think that will be an option in the future. Did you hear from Harv and Vick yet? That wasn't very polite for them to leave you guys hangin' like they did."

"Fuck off!" Nikko sent laser eyed beams of death at me, but alas... for him they didn't work. He stared too long and I had old Nikko right where I wanted him. I smiled as Nikko's facial features shifted into neutral. These added practice sessions in the field using my compelling ability were earning dividends.

"I think in ten minutes you and Seth should call it a night and leave. Don't you, Nikko, old pal?"

Nikko straightened, glanced at Seth, and nodded his head slightly. "Yes. I believe that is a good idea."

Erin gripped my hand harder. I felt the excitement flowing inside her as she added another hand to the grasp. I decided maybe it would be good to snag Seth while I was on a roll. Then all I'd have to do is give them directions when we got outside. I grinned at the suddenly uneasy Erin. I reached down and put my hand on a startled Seth's shoulder. Nikko simply watched with passive interest.

"Look at me, Seth." He did so with only slight hesitation. A short moment later, Seth would never be able to hesitate. "Maybe you guys should leave with us. What do you think, Seth?"

"Uh... sure. That would be fine. Let's leave now, Dad."

"Okay," Nikko agreed. He stood when Seth did.

"Don't forget to leave a big tip, Nikko," I told him. "They have excellent service here."

"Yes, you're right," Nikko agreed, taking out a five dollar bill to put on the table.

"Now Nikko... don't be like that. I think a hundred would be a much better show of appreciation for the attitude you give to these poor servers around here."

"Of course." Nikko took a hundred out and put it with the five. I chuckled as he picked up the five instead of leaving it too. Some things you can't compel out of people.

Enrique was on break or something. His fill in, a tall, early twenties blond, smiled at us, but looked fearful of saying anything to us because of Nikko. I could tell she had probably been confronted in some way by the Dotsenko dynamic duo more than once. Outside the restaurant, we rounded the building, heading toward 34th Street. I smilingly glanced over at Erin when we passed by our first murder scene of the evening since coming to the Supper Club. She shook her head in disapproval or disbelief at what we were doing and had already done. We turned the corner, walking toward where I could see Marko parked the limousine. I stopped my mental captives for their briefing.

"Nikko. You know where the Sunset Boulevard Bridge is, right?"

"Of course." Nikko nodded with a helpful look on his face.

"I think it would be an exceptional adventure for you and Seth to have Marko drive to the middle of the bridge and leave you two there. Tell Marko to go home. He doesn't need to stick around. Then I think you and Seth should climb over the barrier, hold hands, and jump into the river. Doesn't that sound like a great adventure to end the evening with?"

My new buddies looked at each other for a moment with heightened anticipation as if they were imagining how adventurous the jump off the bridge would be. Then Erin jumped in with her plan ending guilt trip of bull shit.

"You've cured them, Jed. C'mon. Tell them to go home and do good from now on. You can't order them to their deaths."

"No… we…we want to," Nikko said. "It sounds incredible to plunge over the barrier into the dark river below."

I hugged Nikko. "That's what I'm talkin' about. This is an adventurer. Seth is just like his Dad too. They can't wait. Step off, Eerie. Quit getting into the way of two action figures like the Dotsenkos."

Erin crossed her arms, turned away, and held stance. "Find a different way, Jed! This…this is too much. They're cured. I don't know how you do this thing but you've snapped something inside their heads. I don't want them murdered."

"Seth and I just want to go for a swim, lady. Mind your own business," Nikko told her.

121

"Yeah, lady," Seth responded. "Dad and I know what we're doing."

Erin turned to me with her no nonsense Igor eyes. This is the reason I never let her help me before. "You can't do this, Jed."

I sighed a bit or whined. I'm not sure which. Then I moved on Nikko for a quick bite, allowing his gangster blood and background flow through me, ending with a quick healing. Seth was next. Nikko's mob boss life did not disturb me as much as Seth's sexual predator stint. I nearly ended him. Erin, sensing from the growls beginning to issue from me unbidden, popped me in the back of the head.

"Jed!"

I grunted and healed Seth reluctantly. I then moved Nikko and Seth next to each other. Great. I get to practice my compelling power trying to heal gangsters who can order the deaths of our family members from behind bars if they snap out of my control. Wonderful test. One thing for sure now – they belonged to me from my bloody taste of their lives. It would be some insurance against a relapse. "Nikko and Seth. Erin here, the bleeding heart, wants me to steer you both out of the darkness. Let's forget about the night swim in the American River. It's cold and dark. I bet you two would feel a delicious sense of relief if Marko drove to the police station where you could turn yourselves in, wouldn't you? After all, you two do owe a debt to society."

"That would be refreshing," Nikko stated happily. "Yes. Let's do that, Seth. I'll explain to the police all aspects of my dirty business. I'm sick of it. I owe a great debt to society. Seth has been a bit out of control. He will feel much better after we serve our time, won't you, son?"

"It will be a chance for me to pay for my many sins," Seth agreed with determination. "Thanks, Jed, for showing us the way."

"My pleasure… I think. I'll walk you over to the limo and have a word with Marko. Stay here, Saint Erin."

I guided my charges over to the limo, opened the rear door for them, and said my goodbyes. "You both are doing a wonderful thing. I'm sure your hearts will be lighter. Confession is good for the soul." Oh barf… I think I just threw up in my mouth a little.

"Thank you, Jed!" The wonder boys gave me a dual outpouring of bliss. I slammed the door and moved on to Marko's window.

"Hello, Marko, my good little minion."

"Hello, Sir."

"There's been a change of plan. Take the Dotsenkos to the police station on Franklin. You know where that one is, don't you, Marko?"

"Yes, Sir, I do. Will you need me anymore after I take the Dotsenkos to the police station?"

"No, Marko. You've done very well tonight. Do only good things from now on. I want you to be a nice man… a man who can be counted on and respected."

"I want that too, Sir. Thank you. Good night."

"Good night, Marko. Drive safely." I waved at the Dots as Marko cruised away. They waved back with big smiles. I rejoined Saint Erin across the street. "We better get the hell out of here before Harv and Vick are discovered in their last embrace."

"You did good tonight, Jed."

"If my influence over them lasts. If not, we'll be in for trouble."

"You're having them surrender with confessions to the police. What more would you have to do?"

"We don't know how long my compelling will last. Did you not think that Nikko could order hits on us from inside prison?"

Erin flashed her all knowing, self congratulatory feature of annoyance – at least to me it was hell of annoying. "After Nikko and Seth confess, they will be targets for everyone they have in their gang connections. Their only chance will be some form of witness protection or minimum secured prison away from any violent inmates. They won't be issuing orders to anyone."

Smartass! "Maybe you're right and maybe Nikko will be so pissed off he'll try to order our families whacked anyhow."

Erin skipped away toward my van singing, 'not going to happen' over and over. The petty seeds of sexual perversity left over from my Seth taste surfaced for a moment. I envisioned Erin in a variety of unclothed situations, none of which were repulsive to me. I had already subjected her to many of them anyway. I discarded the hurtful ones as I regretted for a moment not breaking a few things on Seth before sending him on his way. I followed Erin a few seconds later, warring with myself over the decision to compel or not to compel. At the van, Erin turned to walk into my arms, changing the dynamic of the night.

"You've been a good monster tonight. I believe you deserve a reward."

Oh goody… a reward screw. I bit my tongue, not wanting to shoot my mouth off, thereby dooming myself to an Erin free night. "What did you have in mind besides patting me on the head for not killing two human predators who should be in hell right now?"

"Come over to the house and have a glass of wine with me. I'll order in a pizza or Chinese food if you prefer. We'll talk like in the old days."

My bad. Not even a reward screw. It's lucky I'm on a blood high or I'd be putting sauce on her pizza. I might still get lucky. "I'll have a glass with you. What would you like to talk about? I hope it has nothing to do with joining forces again in the future. You cramped my monster style tonight, Eerie."

"Did not. I acted as your conscience, same as in the past. You knew I was right or you would have killed Nikko and Seth anyway. I think you really changed them, Jed. If what you do really is permanent, that would be awesome."

"Yeah, because having my sense of right and wrong would be a perfect substitute."

"Your sense of right and wrong is a hell of a lot better than Nikko or Seth's." Erin waited for me to open her door, which I did with grandiose gestures of obsequiousness. "Don't pout."

That was uncalled for. She stared at me with her school teacher to pupil admonishing look. I had her in seconds. Erin free night or not, I needed to assert some reminder of power here. I kissed her in full throttle, passionate intensity – lips, tongues, feverish hands, and mind melding Vulcan sexual assault. By the time my kiss ended, Erin's mind went walkabout. She met my gaze with an open mouthed, half lidded entranced state of acknowledgement.

"You... bastard."

Yep. I sure am. "I decided to apply a counterpoint to your 'assuming to know me' stance of ridiculousness. You only have a vague hint of what I'm capable of and I think you know it. Don't worry. If you want me to drop you off without further interaction, it's your call."

125

What I'd done to her warred within Erin's brain for control. "Come have a glass of wine with me. Don't mind swipe me again, Jed."

"Don't act like our third grade teacher when I don't bark like a dog at your command."

"I'll work on it," Erin replied, getting into the van.

"That's all I ask." I still had visions of a 'friends with benefits' night.

That thought died a lingering death as we spotted two black vans in front of her house after a quiet comfortable ride there. Men in black were posturing with hands in plain sight near their vans as if they knew it would be a good idea to let a monster know they came in peace. Interesting. Dangerous territory interrupting a monster's 'friends with benefits' night, but interesting.

"This looks bad, Jed."

"I may have underestimated the powers of observation in the more clandestine institutions of our government. It's obvious they know something. If they knew everything, they would have picked me off from afar with a tranquilizer dart or a .50 caliber round through my head. They must think they have something that will interest me."

Erin grasped my hand. "Maybe you should kill them all and make a run for it. I know you must have a contingency plan in place with a lot of money and resources tied into it."

I did indeed, but my plan did not take into consideration government forces hunting me down in a coordinated effort. This needed to be handled with some careful thought and restraint. "First you want me to spare gangsters' lives and then you want me to whack a bunch of government agents. Let's find out what they want. Do you want in on this Eerie? I'd bet I can get them to leave you out of whatever they're here for."

"I'm in all the way, Jed. You know that."

"I could use your input," I admitted. "Just when we were on the verge of a real hands on collaboration I suddenly become a Men in Black person of interest."

Erin waited until I parked in her driveway. "I can't think of anything else this group could be other than what you suspect. Any thoughts on what to do if this meeting is an intervention?"

"Play along until an opportunity arises would be the smart play unless I'm immediately put into a position where I can't use any of my power. I'm hoping they don't know about my compelling power."

Erin shook her head while opening the van door. "Wishful thinking, Fangster. How much you want to bet it was the head postings at the Capitol Building that busted you?"

"I believe the killer heads statement may have been over the top as you mentioned. I went a couple steps past the overconfidence line on those. Too late for regrets now. I'll have to step up my game. Watch it, copper... I'm going in."

A black guy who looked like a Will Smith clone approached me with a grin which reminded me of the actor's. "Jedidiah Israel Blake. I'm very pleased to make your acquaintance. I'm not going to dance around with you. May we come inside and talk?"

Maybe I could get Erin out of this after all. "This is my friend Erin's house. We could drive to my house in Pollack Pines if you'd like and talk there."

"We know your friend has known about you for a long time as we have so if she doesn't mind, we'd like to talk with you both."

"It's okay, Jed. Come on in, guys." Erin unlocked the door and led the way inside.

"Thank you. I'm Bret Grein, Ms. Constanza." He gestured for the rest of his guys to stay outside. "We know what you can do, Jed. May I call you Jed?"

"Sure." What else could I say? Call me Fang.

"There's no real problem, but we did notice the change in your tactics. The saving of Congressman McRainey and your object lessons in front of the Capitol building required us to speed our planned get acquainted meeting into the here and now." Bret sat down where Erin indicated at her kitchen table. I sat down opposite him.

"I guess it would be stupid to pretend ignorance and tell you I don't know what you're talking about, huh?"

Bret put the satellite uplink notebook on the kitchen table. He simply smiled as he displayed one instance after another of my antics since I was a kid. So much for my extra sensory perception of being followed. They had film on nearly everything and everybody in our lives. I guess there really wasn't any use insulting each other's intelligence. I could tell from some of my late teen interactions on the blood trail they suspected my compelling ability for sure. As Bret stated, there really wasn't any reason to dance around.

"You guys are good."

"You're special, Jed. We wanted to see how you developed. We knew about your Father too. He went on a killing spree in Europe after someone set him free. Aaron represented the only paranormal link to actual vampirism the Company ever found. Your Father was incredibly cunning and intuitive. He alluded all law enforcement agencies during his reawakening rampage. It was a time before 9/11 and Aaron escaped into the United States.

Interpol thought he was a serial killer with a vampire complex. They put us on full alert. The Company didn't find him until just before your Mom killed him. It was unfortunate in many ways because he was a full-fledged vampire, but he was a predator the Company felt they would be unable to deal with. When your Mom became pregnant, we felt it to be the break we needed to observe the only legitimate paranormal event ever studied. Your powers are amazing."

"Is this Company you're referring to the CIA? I'm not thrilled with cute nicknames."

"Yes, but we work with all investigative and law enforcement agencies to facilitate and coordinate overseas intrusions into America. 9/11 enhanced our standing, of course. We operate overseas and within our country. It has taken all our restraint to keep from trying to recruit you earlier. Your stopping the sniper, Mitch Bennett, and subsequent display of information involving him with Bilal Al-Taei, both a Muslim Brotherhood and Isis operative, convinced us the time to recruit you had arrived."

"Recruit him how," Erin asked. "You mean make him a spy?"

"Ah… no – not in the way you mean in terms of a James Bond type. I have a question, Jed. We suspect you can do a number of things, but you've been very low key in dealing with using your powers, so we're not sure of a couple points. Our observations of your helping Erin at crime scenes convinced us you can absorb knowledge from blood. It would be helpful to know how much information you can gain from tasting the blood."

I sat listening to the conversation, contemplating my part in any type of clandestine operation. The possibilities were endless. If what I suspected was true, it might be I could feed at will with protection. The downside would be my constant discarding of evil I absorbed. Having Erin with me would be instrumental in keeping me from the dark side.

"I absorb everything," I admitted.

"Languages too?" Bret's excitement level escalated in a huge leap.

"Yes. I've only been able to do this in a greatly scaled back manner. There may be people unsusceptible to my absorbing power."

"We have Bilal Al-Taei in custody, thanks to you. He tried to flee across the Canadian border earlier today. In custody is a long way from helpful though. Al-Taei could supply us with an incredible amount of information concerning overseas threats developing, including cells already in place here. What do you say to a tryout? I know you don't need money, but you appear to be developing a heightened sense of right and wrong. We know you have a blood lust in spite of being half human. You've been very careful in the past, but the thirst seems to be increasing. Is it because of the power or the euphoria?"

"Both," I admitted. This was proceeding as I had anticipated, and not in a bad way. "I like our talk so far, Bret. Your agency would provide cover for my slaking the blood thirst while providing me with an opportunity to help my country. I like it so far and would be more than willing to take a crack at Al-Taei. If we can establish some parameters I think we can work together."

Bret nodded with his 'Will Smith' smile. "I figured there would be stipulations. You're not stupid. We exist slightly out of any governmental box."

"I think Jed means he wouldn't like sucking on some politician so another entity friendly with your agency gained the upper hand on an election," Erin said. "Would Jed be able to receive concrete information about your interest in any individual so as to avoid being used as someone's personal muckraker?"

"Definitely. He will not be allowed or called on to glean information from anyone other than high priority figures conducting operations against the United States. There would be occasional gangland figures we could become concerned with. What you did with Nikko and Seth Dotsenko was simply amazing."

Damn. These guys were freaky good or I'm going to need every item in my possession or around me checked for electronic devices. I can do that, but what the hell, I'll ask outright. "How have you been able to chart everything I do? That is amazing to me."

"I can understand how disconcerting our knowledge of you, and the intricate details of your life, appear to be. We have satellite capabilities only the most imaginative movies have even scratched the surface of in fiction, let alone reality. We have been using intricate surveillance gear to keep watch over you for a long time. We knew better than to have human beings following you. With your capabilities, I realize you can find all of our electronic tells we've been using. May I suggest leaving them in place so we can continue to monitor and help you? If you suspect we're doing anything hurtful to anyone within your sphere of life, come to me and I will guarantee it will stop. I will make you another promise too. I'll issue a full report on our surveillance activities weekly."

"If Erin will agree to assist me, will it be okay to hire her in as a consultant as well?"

"Of course. We were hoping Officer Constanza would consent to such a job offer. It was the main reason I stopped here to see you." Bret paused. "Uh... this may seem a rather unorthodox first trial, but we have Al-Taei in the back of our van. Would you be comfortable having a go at him now? I admit I can't stand the sight of the arrogant prick. I'd like to water-board him until he grew gills. Unfortunately, we're not allowed to touch these murdering bastards. We have to be better than them and somehow win the terrorist war with our hands figuratively tied behind our backs. Can you help tonight, Jed?"

"I'd love to. I had planned on hunting him down anyway because I figured he'd take another shot at Congressman McRainey. Does anyone know you have him? I mean how official was the capture?"

"It was done discreetly because we didn't want to tip off anyone in his network." Bret grinned at me. "What did you have in mind, Jed?"

"You don't like him anyway. Once I suck him dry I'll know everything he does. If you can make him disappear, I'll finish him off for you."

Bret chuckled, pointing his finger at me. "Hold that thought. Why not find out what he knows first. Then we can make plans. I pictured you being more reluctant to this recruitment endeavor than you are."

"Jed's a genius," Erin said. "He's already figured out every avenue of compliance and escape, along with his chances of killing you and all your men. He could also own you, body and soul. I believe he's come to the conclusion cooperation is the only logical course."

# Chapter Six

## New Job

Bret's grin dropped from his face. When I didn't correct Erin's perception, he glanced for a moment at the door longingly. Erin, as usual, knew me, at least from the happenings we had shared. I'm certain she noticed the slight smile I wore into the house when Bret left his contingent outside. I measured Bret for a compelling he never dreamed of until now when Erin stated how my mind works. Ah... Bret... the door would be far too late for you, my friend.

"Don't bother looking now, Bret. Erin's right. All of what she said I considered, including making you my own personal sock puppet. You made a mistake coming in here alone; not that having your men with you would have done much good either. I think what Erin wants you to know is you can trust my decision making abilities. If you stay straight with us like you have, no one gets hurt. I know your forces could prevail against me if I'm stupid enough not to help. Let's deal with this in a partnership we both understand. I like you. I respect the way you've made your recruitment move. It is logically my only option. I hate to mention this as an ending remark, but I have all of Mitch Bennett's skills, including his knowledge of clandestine operations. He was a formidable soldier. If he had known he was facing a paranormal monster, Mitch would have blown my head apart from half a mile away."

"Meaning with his skills it would not be a good idea for me to play games with you about the seedier side of secret government organizations, right?"

"That is exactly what I meant. Shall we go talk with Al-Taei? He must be getting restless not knowing how much he's going to help us. He'll feel better once I relieve him of all responsibility concerning his knowledge of threats to our country."

Bret took a deep breath and stood. "Yes. Let's go do that. You are welcome to come along if you'd like, Erin."

"I would like to be part of this all the way," Erin answered, grasping my hand. "One thing you should know though: I can't control Jed. I mistakenly thought I was controlling him. I found out recently that is not the case, nor will it be the case in the future. He and I have decided on a partnership too of sorts. I may be able to influence him as I did tonight with the Dotsenkos, but I have no illusions anymore in connection to what I can do in regard to Jed when he makes a decision. My point in telling you what might have happened if Jed had not arrived at the decision he did was so you know I would not have been able to prevent it. He would have killed you all and presented it to me as a done deal."

Bret saw me smiling at Erin. "I get it now. May I ask one other thing in relation to your abilities? Can you tell when someone lies to you?"

Good question. I nearly always instinctually know when someone is lying to me if I'm concentrating on what they're saying. "I would have to say yes with reservations. I haven't practiced my concentration on truth or lies with people. I feel as if I could. I'll work on that aspect so I know in the future. I didn't sense you were lying in what you outlined to me. Was I mistaken?"

"No. I was afraid to lie to you," Bret admitted. "I didn't know if you could tell or not. I would appreciate it if you let me know if that is a phase of your powers you can implement. I could use you witnessing some of the meetings I've had with my own superiors. You would of course have say over what you told me."

"Sounds reasonable. I hope everything you've told me is on the level, Bret. It has the ring of truth. At least you believe it to be true. A lot has happened in the past few weeks. Did you know about Gronsky?"

"Not until you moved on him. We didn't foresee his attacking Erin in her house like he did. We did see him leave the house in a suitcase. That was Gronsky, wasn't it?"

"Yep." I guess that caper wasn't a secret either. "Anton carved his last human being. The reason I brought him up is I didn't feed on him because I avoid demons like Gronsky. I can dismiss their inner workings pretty fast but I'm not always able to get rid of the barf factor for a couple days."

"You did the world a favor with Gronsky. We don't even know the number of victims he was responsible for. Will you act on one if we bring him or her to you?"

"With pleasure. The more I practice, the faster I've gotten with shedding evil characteristics." We left the house. Bret's MIB pals looked relieved to see him. At the van housing Bilal Al-Taei, I readied myself for the task at hand. The more prepared I was, the shorter my evil aftermath dregs lasted. "What information are you suspecting in particular Al-Taei has?"

"We think the cell he's tied in with plans a major attack on some facility in the area, either with great loss of life or maximum sabotage or both, depending on the target status."

The moment Bret opened the rear doors, the muffled sounds coming from the bound and gagged man sitting against the van wall grew in energy, complete with frantic shuffling around.

"Do you mind if I observe, Jed?"

I motioned for Bret to follow us in. "You know all the facts so watching them happen in person won't add much to your oversight burden. Hello there Billy boy."

After greeting Al-Taei while propping him against the van wall I grabbed his jaw in a bone crushing grip. He refused to look at me so I began crushing his upper shoulders. His eyes widened in shock. He was mine, but for me to know everything Bret would want, I needed to feed on Al-Taei's blood. I allowed my fangs to extend so Bret could see them. I sunk them into my now pliable Al-Taei's neck, drinking in the essence of everything he had ever been in his life. He spoke Arabic, Farsi, and French in addition to English. I also knew why Al-Taei was anxious to leave the area. Erin grabbed my arm as I nearly finished him off. I healed his neck after reluctantly pulling away.

"That was an eye-opening experience," Bret said. "Your eyes are again black because of the feeding. Did you cull everything from him we'd hoped for?"

"And then some. We have to go now. There are trucks only forty minutes from leaving a warehouse on District Court in the warehouse district. They're loaded with enough explosives to level Cal State Sacramento which is where they'll be headed. The drivers have all the correct credentials to be allowed inside the security area. These are suicide bombers. They don't plan on coming back. They will drive the trucks directly into the college complex and detonate the explosives. I have an idea, but we have to get there before they leave."

"Let's go! I'll drive. Tell me your idea on the way." Bret spoke into his com unit, getting his men moving to follow us. Bret took out his own satellite uplink laptop, used his access to get Erin into the state of the art tech as she sat on the rear seat. He didn't say anything until we were on our way to the warehouse. "Okay, Jed, I'm listenin'. Please tell me you have some way to fix this without someone detonating trucks full of explosives."

"If we get there before they load up, Jed will super-speed them. They won't have a chance to do much of anything," Erin explained for me.

She was irritatingly completely correct. "I can get them, Bret. I can't take a chance on them warning each other or detonating the explosives when they know I'm there to stop the bombing."

"I don't care what you do. Smash the bastards so they can't do shit. That works for me. I don't want any accidents. We'll let you out far enough from the District Court address for you to make any approach you want to."

Erin used Bret's laptop to get us actual real time satellite data on the street view to study. "Stop at District Court on South Watt and let Jed out. He can make the approach from there."

Erin grabbed my shoulder. "Look Jed. There they are with only a short time delay."

I memorized the details of what she showed me as to where I'd be dropped off and the warehouse where the trucks were parked outside the warehouse, ready to go. "I got it. She's right, Bret. Stop on South Watt a hundred yards before the District Court turnoff. Let me go in, get the situation controlled, and then call you."

"Okay, Jed. Good Lord! I pray to God you can get them. At least if they go off at the warehouse, the damage would be contained."

"Gee… thanks for that, pal. I doubt I could survive an explosion like that, but at least the other damage will be contained."

Erin smacked me in the back of the head. "Man up, Fangster. Move at super-speed and get 'er done. Less whining and more action."

I turned to hold my thumb and forefinger in a clamp like position only a fraction of an inch apart. "You are this close to a compelling that will rock your world, Eerie. By morning you won't know if you're home or in Mystery, Alaska."

"You can't threaten me. I'm a government agent now. I own your butt. Isn't that right, Bret?"

"Can you keep him from sucking all the blood out of me in a few moments whenever he wants to?"

"Uh… no," Erin answered.

"Then no, Erin. You'll be on your own, but I hear Mystery, Alaska is nice in the summer. Play nice and don't get Fang mad at you. You've already pointed out how helpless any immediate action would be within Jed's range of movement." Bret was enjoying Erin's attempt at distraction from block leveling bombs. She was a tough little bugger.

"Never mind. I'll get them," I said. "Don't come near the place until I call you though. If I can't locate them right away, I may have to take them as they approach the trucks."

"That's a bit on the wild side, Jed."

I grinned over at Bret. "Because of your quick actions with Al-Taei, we have a chance to stop these animals from blowing Sac State to kingdom come. It's turning out to be a lot more heroic of a move than you thought. So what? This is what you came to get me for, right?"

Bret shrugged in true Will Smith, MIB form. "You're right. Good luck, Fangster."

"I don't like that name. I already have Erin and my G'ma down for a compelling to stop doing it. Don't make me add you to the list. It won't go well for you. Sometimes compelling is an inexact science."

"Understood."

"Hey... you're not compelling me and that's final. I'll tell your Mom. She'll whup you but good, Fang. If I tell your G'ma you threatened to compel her, all the King's horses and all the King's men wouldn't be able to put Humpty Dumpty Fang back together again."

I folded my arms and leaned back into my seat. It's frustrating as hell being a monster who can be threatened into inaction like a three year old. I remained silent while feeling Erin's smirking gaze at my back. Bret relapsed into all business worry form. I could nearly brush at the tension emanating from him. I understand him having doubts, even after all the surveillance work they'd done with me, but at some point before I left his van he'd need to remember I was betting my life I could stop this. Then we arrived and there was nothing to say other than the usual.

"I'll call you."

I didn't wait around for sloppy goodbyes. I moved at Dhampir speed, wind whistling past my face at a refreshingly chilling pace. I grinned. I was confidently certain I could end this threat without any drama. Remaining on the dark side of the trucks, I moved silently around the trucks. There was no way of knowing if any of the drivers would have remote detonators or not. I didn't need Bret to tell me it was important to know what Al-Taei didn't know: if the trucks would be detonated remotely or not. That meant I needed to keep one of these clowns alive for a small time. It was too much of a gamble to search for them in the warehouse. Waiting for them made more sense. They came out of the warehouse ten minutes later. As if by my command, they walked toward me at the rear of the trucks, probably to either secure, prime, or check their murderous load.

I'll give them this much – they didn't pretend to be anything but what they were, at least in appearance. If someone were to offer a terrorist cliché photo to grace the page of a dictionary, these guys would be in it. Trimmed full chin beards with no mustache, black kufi skull caps, complete with grim glares I could see even in the dark, I momentarily wondered how the hell they ever figured to get past security checkpoints. Then I remembered how the media and our idiot leaders have made the Islamist horde at our country's gate into a sacred protected species. The suicidal practice was a lot like stocking piranha in your swimming pool.

I sped around them to their rear, a blur of movement in the darkness, dropping the one trailing the other three far too hard. His skull caved in under my temple strike. As the second turned, I clotheslined him, forehead high. He hit the pavement still breathing. The third within my target range smashed into the frontrunner by my own directing blow to the center of his face. He died at the same time the force of his hurtling body knocked the leader flat. I plucked the leader to his feet, using side-hand chopping strikes to break bones in his arms and at his knees. I ensured his complete helplessness to do anything but scream. I silenced the screams by sucking the blood from him in a violent flourish of euphoria. I also felt some relief in finding out they were heading to the rear of the trucks in order to set the timers on detonators not yet activated. A woman remained inside the warehouse, her part in this suicidal mission to report instantly on success or failure. I knew where she was. I then smashed the only unneeded survivor's head in with my foot.

Entering the warehouse with full stalking prowess, I found her in a control room environment containing multiple monitors and computer towers. Apparently, they felt their location to be completely safe. Either that or they had the room wired for destruction if triggered by an outside entity once their security protocols were initiated. The woman staring at monitors of the Sac State campus along with frontal video feeds from the trucks' windshields was a vision of concentration. She wore all black clothing, including a black hijab which did not cover her face. Her name was Bashima and she was Bilal Al-Taei's sister.

Bashima muttered a curse in Arabic after moments passed without the trucks starting. When she pushed angrily to her feet, turning toward the door, she found me instead. Bashima screamed, lunging for a switching panel on her main desk. I broke the wrist on the arm she reached with. Yeah, I could have stopped her, had a snack, and owned her butt, but this suicidal cult of murderers were giving us monsters a bad name. Then I taught her a reason for really screaming by letting her see my inner Fangster in full Dhampir form, complete with slowly extended fangs and claws. I backed her shrieking toward the far wall before willing Bashima to expose her neck for my introductory snack. She moaned as I pierced her neck with the utmost deliberate motion, commanding Bashima to remain perfectly still, although her chest heaved in abject terror. I drew out her blood with infinite care, drinking in the fear elixir instead of ravishing the murdering bitch violently. All awareness, fear, and lightness of being faded in streaming intakes of her life's blood. Bashima slid to the floor locked within death's embrace.

I called Bret. He answered almost before the first indication of a connection faded. "Jed?"

"Yep. Jed here. 'Monsters R Us' foiled the dastardly terrorist plot. There were no survivors, but I believe we hit the mother lode of intel. Unfortunately, this cell was run by Al-Taei, and compartmentalized from the Middle East, address unknown. I think you'll like the computer setup intact here, although there is a self-destruct panel to be wary of, the only other danger will have to be handled by whatever bomb squad you have at your beck and call. In other words, you can come on down."

"That's incredible! I'll bring in my team first, assess the situation, and then get whatever help we need to fix this. How many body-bags?"

"Five." It was time to put my next surprise into play. "Do you have a Yala Lantry with you on your team?"

"Yes, he doubles as an interpreter. Why do you ask, and how could you know I have him on my team?"

"He's a traitor. For some reason Bilal didn't know about him, but his sister Bashima did. Would you like me to prove it to you or snack on him for the info?"

"Is there a way to prove it without risking anything?"

"Put him in the warehouse control room with me. I'll outline what panel Bashima reached for to set off the destruct mechanism. If he goes for it instead of guarding against activation, then you'll have your proof."

Bret sighed. "Understood. Let's do it that way first and hope it's a mistake."

"Yeah, because wishin' and hopin' helps all the time."

Erin jogged to me in the control room as Bret entered with Yala Lantry, a fierce looking man of dark complexion and jet black hair. I watched him carefully. When he saw Bashima, he lost it. I didn't need the control panel ploy after all. The blood gathered at her unhealed neck triggered his loving side. It seemed Bashima meant more to him than anyone around them knew. I'd have to taste him to find out whether Bashima recruited Yala or if he was part of a larger traitorous cancer inside Bret's special ops group.

"You bastard!" Yala reached for his weapon after seeing his beloved bloodless Bashima.

Not that it would have done him any good, he should have reached for the weapon first, and skipped my birth proclamation for later. I ran over him, snatching his weapon out of its holster on the way. Yala hit hard and bounced but he'd be okay. Bret was stunned. I believe Yala had Bret fooled for a long time. It amazed me from my youth when I read of our forces being killed by Islamic moles within our military and civilian citizens. In Bret's

142

defense, sometimes women overcome everything within a man. Bashima possibly baited her hook and yanked Yala aboard the traitor train like a big guppy. Let's see for sure. I yanked Yala to his feet for a taste test. I had my fill so after I made sure he was the only mole, I snapped his neck.

"He's the only one, Bret. I think Bashima drew him in. He was in love with her. He's been selling you out for six months. He's told Bashima about me but she never passed the info on because she thought he was nuts. Everything she knows is on those computers, so be careful extracting the data. May I suggest an American of some other descent than Middle East origin? Let me have your phone and I'll note in all the non-financial passwords with access Bashima and Yala knew."

Bret handed me his phone. "Thanks, Jed. This first interaction is huge! With only what we've stopped with your help, I will be able to angle all the leeway we need to make this work in a major way helpful and relevant to all of us."

"You do understand I will confiscate all of their funds, don't you?"

"I noticed you didn't give me any financial passwords. Whatever you confiscate you may do with as you please. If we could direct it back into the possession of the people on our team making ends meet - that would be very nice." Bret delivered his statement on my ability to own everything my victims owned with recognition he couldn't do anything about it even if he wanted to. "Loyalty to God and country does mean a lot to us. Having enough money to ignore bribes in excess of what we earn in a year would go a long way to making sure we can all count on each other."

"Agreed." What do I care? The bad money would continue flowing toward people less worthy than a tuna sandwich. So what? "You want me to put you all on the payroll, huh? What's in it for me? For that kind of payout I should expect high end help. How

143

about you find out exactly what's happening in this land of Al-Taei. Then we'll make a deal as to his illicit goods."

"Done deal. None of this is a deal breaker in my eyes. Grease for the skids works a hell of a lot better than what you've experienced so far with living like paupers at the pleasure of people on the fringes with more money than brains."

"I don't live on the fringes and I eat pleasure puppet managers for breakfast. I don't care in reality if you or your guys get the beaks wet in someone else's bird feeder. What I care about at this time is helping people I care about. Give me the details of this suicidal mission the Al-Taei morons were on. I'll try to delve deeper when I can. I know how important knowing who the ransom claimants must seem to you. To me, they represent all the down-and-outers running scams across America, hoping to be in the top third when the turd world nations take over with their version of perversion."

"You're a little too close to the truth," Bret admitted, "and I don't like it. I'm glad you killed Yala. At least we don't have to air that crappy piece of vetting business for the public. If we had to go through the arrest and charging process, it would have hurt our standings with important congressional backers. I'll have one of my men drive you back to Erin's house. By tomorrow I should have an update for you. I hope this will only be the beginning for us."

"Having a mole inside your crew has to be a bad blow. I hope you can sort out any other problems before they end in disaster," Erin said.

"It will mean a complete investigation into our vetting process accompanied by a reexamination of each member on my team. I won't be ordering you around, Jed. I'll present each case I hope you'll collaborate with me on in a form you'll be able to check and examine. The only exceptions will be highly dangerous and immediate threats like tonight's."

"That's fair enough. I guess Erin and I return to normal everyday life then for the time being, right?"

"Yes. I will certainly be in touch. I would like to request you don't do anymore 'Headhunter' episodes."

"I'll keep your request in mind." The agent driving us to Erin's house kept his mouth shut and a grim look on his face. Bret introduced us to Aiden Soransky. I imagined Aiden's attitude had to do with my handling of Lantry so I didn't try and engage him in conversation. Not so my little Erin canary. I could tell she didn't want to talk in front of him about anything of a personal nature between us, but she was antsy to talk.

"Did you know Lantry very well, Agent Soransky?"

"I didn't know he was a traitor if that's what you're asking. You're a cop. You understand the meaning of having a partner. I'd known Yala a long time. We'd partnered on and off for years on our team. Bret told us what happened when he saw that bitch Bashima. There's not much question she had him as a hell of a lot more than a handler too. Yala selling us out for the past six months changes everything. I'm only now remembering small things he did I didn't question but should have. It would be easy to excuse what he did as crazy love driving him to it. I hate to say it, but I believe she simply triggered his fanaticism."

Interesting take on Yala. "Was Lantry a devote Muslim?"

Aiden nodded his head. "Yeah… he played the whole card whether he was at work or with us in the field, complete with kufi, prayer rug, and beads. The rest of us believed he was on our team working diligently to prove the terrorist business was the work of extremists. I'm not buying that angle ever in the future. I don't give a crap what media propaganda enablers say, along with their Hollywood cohorts' portrayals of misunderstood loyal Muslims. Bullshit! I'll never get fooled again."

145

"I hear you." Erin gripped his shoulder for a moment. "I'll be paying attention in a much more intense way to anything Muslim, from the mosques to the burka wearing nitwits on the street, and especially to their men. Thinking back, I've not questioned a number of things when on duty I should have. I kept my mouth shut while fudging over the incident to the person reporting it, asking them to remain calm, because they were reporting suspicious activity by a Middle Eastern neighbor. I have a group in mind I should have paid more attention to."

This was news to me. If the cops can be hassled into looking the other way with Muslim outrage, then where does that leave the rest of us in these times? "What group are you talking about Eerie?"

"There's a small mosque or masjid or whatever they call it run out of not much more than a house with a gate. They call it the Central Community Masjid if I remember right. The neighbors have complained about it constantly to the point they were shamed in the news. Tony and I got a call about half a dozen bad looking dudes unloading crates from a truck into the so called masjid. The neighbors called it in, but we of course weren't allowed on the premises. The mullah guy running it called in the media before we could even get there. Apparently, he saw the neighbors scoping out his deliveries. Naturally, a film crew came to film little Muslim children playing with their parents in full garb attending a service inside. Tony tried to get the mosque mullah to allow him in for a look around so as to appease tensions with the neighbors. They refused, citing everything from xenophobia to religious persecution. Oh boy, did the news people eat that up."

I remembered Tony and Erin's short TV appearance. "You, two were thrown under the bus for even answering the call. Didn't Tony have to call for his union rep to get the meatheads off his butt?"

146

"Yep. That's the one. We answered a legitimate call and got hosed. Like Aiden says, no more of that crap. Tony and I will find a way to do a more thorough job of checking calls like that. The neighbors who reported the strange stuff were described as Islamo-phobic haters. The calls stopped. I think it was because the people were fed up with being called names for simply reporting a potential dangerous situation."

Aiden passed his phone back to Erin. "If you know the place, note it on my phone, and I'll see if it is mentioned in the computers Jed liberated from Bashima. Maybe Bret can freelance Jed to look into that makeshift mosque."

Erin took the phone, entering in the data, and adding notes describing time and place of the call. She also provided the news agency that did a hit piece on her and Tony for doing their jobs. She handed it back to Aiden. "I hope I'm wrong, because there are a lot of these playhouse type masjid places. I always figured they were simply tax shelters for whomever owned the land. Now I'm wondering if maybe they're being used as arsenals like they do in the Middle East. Are you in, Jed?"

I am so in. "Hell yeah. I saw inside those whackos' minds. They want to kill everyone who doesn't believe as they do. Making it some kind of atrocity to investigate an unusual act at one of these places is a load of crap."

"That's what Tony and I think too. If the more closed and barricaded Christian sects can be called into question, why not the mosques? The Muslims are a lot more interrelated than the Christian sects. The government steamrolled over the Branch Davidians at Waco. The Davidians didn't even have any larger connection to a worldwide terrorist consorting religion guilty of daily atrocities all over the world. You would think with everything going on in the world blanketed under Islam, the so called innocent Muslims in this country would make everything they do visible and above board."

"Instead, they do just the opposite," Aiden added. "We're all in trouble when we can be cowed into not reporting obviously dangerous activity. I'm glad you two are in with us. We need help. We're trying to hunt serial killers, murderers, terrorists, kidnappers, and gangsters while pretending to be politically correct Care Bears. It's ridiculous. No offense, Jed, but we need a monster like you. You may have come along at the perfect time. It would make me feel a little better if I knew how you can even exist, but for now, I don't care. Welcome aboard."

"Thanks. I'm hoping to help without freaking everyone in existence out, especially you guys on Bret's team. I'll help with anything."

Aiden began coming out of his shell. "I read the report on when you and Erin were first in on a rather big cover-up. When you left that predator's body by the stream as kids, didn't you two wonder what happened to the body?"

"Not anymore. I'm thinking back to my rough interactions with bad people. I distinctly remember parts of the body discovery reports were off, as was the conclusion as to how they died. I figured a combination of skill, finesse, and good luck. I'm thinking it was the outfit running your operation covering my ass."

Aiden chuckled. "You would not be mistaken. They still have no idea how you came into being. They've traced your Father back as far as humanly possible. There is no trace to the person who turned him. We have no inkling of anyone else like you either or the existence of any full-fledged vampires."

"What... no werewolves, mummies, or creatures from the black lagoon?"

"Nope. You're all we have, Jed. Frankly, I'm hoping you are the only one. There was some talk about taking your sperm to make others. Common sense finally ruled that out. Someone in the higher echelons asked the golden question: what the hell do we do against a small army of you paranormals. Your secret has been guarded religiously. It was rightly assumed not everyone would fear the chances an army of Dhampirs might rebel, causing instant chaos. Well… anyway… here you are."

Aiden parked next to Erin's driveway. He shook hands with both of us as we left the vehicle. "Have you two talked of children in the future or have I been reading the signs wrong?"

"We're more than friends," Erin answered. "How much more depends a lot on just what you hinted at. Jed and I haven't seriously discussed marriage, let alone having children with his abilities. If he could pass on the Dhampir gene it would make our children targets. I'm not a huge conspiracy freak but I can envision a world where Dhampirs would be hunted down like rabid wolves."

Aiden handed Erin his card. "Call me if you need me. It seems you have an intuitive grasp on what would probably happen as far as consequences. I'll be seeing you."

I handed Aiden a card. "Don't hesitate to call me. I read truth in all you have said. We'll need people we can trust, especially if something happens to Bret. Call me even if you have a personal problem I can help with solving. I'm relieved there aren't any more monsters like me out there that you know of."

Aiden waved my card at me. "Thanks, Jed."

In the next moment Aiden was gone, leaving my buddy Eerie and I alone with our thoughts, desires, and problems. I reached out, stroking her arm. She recoiled as if a snake had struck at her. Gee… that was less than I had hoped for tonight. Maybe all the monster talk had driven the concept into a reality Erin didn't care to face.

"You can never touch me again, you monster! I can see it in your face. You want to make a horde of little monsters to devour the earth!"

"Okay... you had me going there. Have you considered the prospect of having children with me, my dear Eerie?" I moved too fast for her to escape, locking her within my grasp, while dodging knees to the groin and instep stomps. I kissed her with all the blatant need and desire I showed her before. In seconds I didn't need to worry about compelling her. Many moments of intimacy passed in touches, caresses, and melded writhing of bodies so tightly wound as to be one. I then released her in gradual waves of warmth where I only drew away in achingly slow motion until she clung only to my hands, her mouth ajar, and chest heaving.

"God, Jed!" Erin pulled her hands away with a final lurch. "You kill a bunch of people, suck them dry in some cases, and then kiss me like that and I don't even care! I'm as monstrous as you are. Yes, I've thought of what it would mean if we tried to raise a family. It's just one more step of insanity we would have to face."

"Did you ever consider that possibly you think too much? Maybe we should quit fighting about things happening in your imagination and simply make love like a couple of wild animals."

"That's always your solution."

"It works. Why question success. Besides, you told me I deserved a reward for being a bleeding heart, and allowing the Dots to live."

"You're too dangerous. I'll bake you a cake instead for your treat."

"I didn't want to broach this subject, Eerie, but you can't bake or cook. If you want to give me a food item as a treat, buy me a box of chocolates. Don't threaten me with your homemade cake."

Erin took my hand. "I have cake mix and frosting. Come in and help me make a good one."

I can't argue with an offer like that. I get time with Erin. She smells wonderful. Baking a cake smells wonderful, and last but not least, if I don't convince her to make love with me I still get cake. "Okay, but..." Something was wrong. I reversed Erin's grip on my hand, pulling her away from the door.

"Someone's inside," I whispered while drawing her to the side of the door. I made a shushing gesture and concentrated on Erin's house. There were three distinct breathing patterns I could hear once the other noises were filtered out. "We'll have to postpone the bakeoff."

I drew Erin down into a crouch. "They heard us. Their heartbeats quickened along with heightened breathing. "They'll be getting anxious when we don't go inside or talk more. Stay still while I work on that."

Erin nodded her understanding. I stood to the door handle side of the screen. Extending the claws of my right hand, I scratched the screen door's metal frame. I don't use the claws much for anything. They freak me out. When I concentrate on extending them, my hand turns gnarly brownish colored as the claws extend into nearly black pointed constructs, deadly but messy. I know enough about crime scene investigations to know using the claws would not be a tidy way to kill or maim. In this instance, they served me well. I could make the noise sound like the high pitched opening of a rusty metal hinge. I did so with an irritating softness of touch guaranteed to make the blood hum in the veins of those inside. I grinned at Erin who had her hands clamped over her ears accompanied by teeth locked, lips drawn back grimace. My ploy had the desired effect. The doorman couldn't see either of us, but could hear the noise on the screen without seeing its creator. He opened the screen door.

151

I rammed him through the door like a shield which turned out to be a good idea. His buddies shot him with semiauto handguns. I abandoned him the moment I saw where his cohorts took aim from. In seconds, one after the other went down under blows I concentrated on easing before the strikes. I needed to find out if Erin had new villains popping into her life or if this trio made it here under old orders. Once they hit the floor out cold I broke their arms. What can I say? I don't carry restraints and handcuffs. I'm a Dhampir not a camp counselor. Besides, they were only going to live long enough to satisfy my curiosity. They were all Middle Eastern in appearance, so I figured this was Yala trying to reach us from the grave. It was possible he convinced Bashima to put a hit on Erin and me no matter how nuts she thought he was.

"You can come in, Eerie. Close the door behind you."

"It looks like we had some action put on us by someone," Erin said. She walked over next to me. They had shoot to kill orders or they wouldn't have tried to fire through their buddy. What do you think this means?"

"A few loose ends left over from Bashima. I'm going to get the story from one of them now. I'm not real enthused at feeding off another one of these idiots."

Erin drew her weapon. "Go ahead, I'll watch the others."

The two on the floor still breathing hadn't regained consciousness yet, otherwise Erin wouldn't have pulled her piece to watch my back. "No need for the gun. I broke their arms."

"Really? Damn, Jed."

I yanked one off the floor without comment for a quick taste. I was not in a good mood. A few minutes ago, baking a cake and tasting Erin engulfed my thought processes. Now, all I had was a bloody mess on the floor with two more taster's choice

Islamists. I was certain Erin tasted better. "Call Bret. Ask him to send the meat wagon if it's not already gone from my last crime scene. Tell him I'll have confirmation on origin in a few minutes. By the way, they all taste just like chicken."

Erin, my monster in training, had to clamp a hand over her mouth and turn away as she enjoyed my comment a bit too much for her sensibilities. She made the call while I tasted. The blood rush wasn't bad. It soothed some of my annoyance at the interruption. They belonged to Bashima acting as her brother's facilitator, but were resentful at being ordered around by a woman. The only small item of interest was the number of masjids he had visited. Erin's favorite was the most visited one in my Islamist snack's head: the Central Community Masjid near the corner of 47th Street and Folsom Blvd. I dropped my snack and checked out his still living partner – same deal. These two had frequented Central Community Masjid. None of the others I'd tasted had that masjid in their heads. We needed to find out if these guys were locals. That would explain the connection. Erin held her phone in the air when I glanced at her.

"Bret's holding. He wants to talk with you about this."

I snapped the necks of the remaining house visitors before walking over to Erin for the phone. "They belonged to Bashima's crew, but the two alive I tasted confirmed something very interesting – they both were frequent visitors to the Central Community Masjid."

"Damn!" Bret broke in. "That's the place Erin mentioned earlier. I'll be over the moment I get free of here. I'll send Aiden back with a few guys to secure the scene. Does Erin have a place she can stay?"

"I'll take her to my house. Can we leave now?"

"Yes, but do you think it wise to stay at your place. What if Bashima sent a squad to your house too."

"Well... let's consider that from a monster's perspective. Dhampir, remote wooded lot, few neighbors – gee... I don't like their chances. Seriously, we'll be fine. I have a state of the art security system. I'll know if they've been there or are still there unless they're smart enough to take positions in the surrounding woods waiting for our arrival. While I'm not a werewolf, hunting me from the woods is a very bad idea. I may leave Erin at her folks' house though. I'm not sure how many teams this bunch have available for killings."

"Okay, stay in touch, Jed. I'll update you about the identities of the ones at Erin's house as soon as I can. Be careful. They could be resorting to rocket launchers and bombs shortly the way we're handling all of this with kid gloves."

There's a sobering thought. "Will do, Brett."

"I'm going with you. I'll call Mom and do a drive by. Then we'll check your place. It would be a perfect spot for them to create a sniper's nest to deal with you from long range. Do you have a plan for checking your place out?"

"Yep. I'll check my security monitors right now. If they check out, I'll park the van far enough away they won't know anything until I'm into the woods hunting them. Then we'll find out if these guys are afraid of the dark. I'm betting it will be a bad night for the hunters."

"Let's go then. I'll drive." Erin kissed me before we left. Suddenly, I was hoping for our adversaries to stay away for the night.

With Erin driving, I checked my monitors remotely from my laptop. No alarm had been tripped. All video feeds recorded normally and none of my longer range sensors showed signs of touching on anything around my perimeter. It appeared they weren't there. That would be my favorite. I could have a whole contingent in the woods beyond my perimeter though. It was silly to take chances.

"Nothing of note, Eerie. Let me out a couple miles from my house. I'll stay in touch with you. Here." I took out two sets of the communications earwigs from my equipment bag. I handed one set to her. "I won't be talking to you. I'll be hunting. If I find them, I'll probably leave them in the woods. Bret will have his hands full with what he already has. I think I have some muffin mix in the cupboard. We'll make muffins. They smell almost as good as cake."

"Throw in some soup and I'm there," Erin replied. "I think you're thinking of another kind of muffin though."

"Guilty," I admitted. "Who says you can't have your cake and eat it too?"

"For a monster, you're kind of funny."

"For an Igor, I think you're kind of magically delicious."

When we arrived at a distance I felt would be perfect for beginning the hunt without detection, I kissed Erin and slipped out of the van. The woods around my Pollack Pines estate appeared foreboding in the light of a moon sliver barely visible. Not foreboding for me but if human hunters awaited me in my woods, I planned to satisfy all their excitement for the hunt. I knew where they expected me. I also knew from my sniper, Mitch Bennett, where a great nest could be set with an open field of opportunity on an arriving vehicle.

\* \* \*

Outfitted in camouflage, complete with ground tarp and shallow trench, the two man sniper team waited with professional ease. One with night vision range finders and also long range digital binoculars scanned any traffic approaching from either direction. The team had carefully picked a sniper's nest with excellent sighting on the circular driveway rounding the estate front they targeted. They were ordered to take no chances with the target or anyone with him. Their orders were to kill everyone with him, put them in the house, and burn the place down, making it look like a gangland hit.

"When will this Blake arrive, Raiden?" The spotter on the team finished another sweep of the area. "Should we still stay out of contact if no one comes by in the next couple of hours?"

"No calls. Bashima told me Blake would come home tonight. Her contact inside the special task force warned he is some kind of enhanced thing and to not get close to him under any circumstances." The sniper chuckled. "The targets are all indestructible until I have them in my sights. His enhancement will not protect against a .50 caliber hollow point slug when it blows his head apart."

"The college should have been assaulted by now. This will be a glorious night. The statement will be clear. There is no place safe. Isil can strike anywhere, killing their leaders, their parents, and their children. The fools embrace us like long lost brothers. Soon... Sharia will be the law of the land in the next Caliphate."

"It would not be bad to check the news, Saif. Perhaps it is done and everywhere the idiots are running to hide. There is no approach Blake can make where we will not see him. This man must be very dangerous to have everyone he knows killed with him."

"Perhaps it would have been cautious to bring along the rocket launcher." A rustling noise as from something moving incredibly fast through the woods made Saif hesitate. He looked away from his scanning to see his partner lying on his side. A hideous thing with bloody claws pointed at him.

* * *

156

"I have come for you, murderer!" I found these two idiots so easily it wasn't even a good stalking hunt. Then they ran their mouths off nonstop while I approached. I might as well have a little fun as the big bad. "Prepare to die!

The guy I heard named Saif dropped his binoculars while scrambling backwards trying to draw his weapon. My claws raked his arm like razor cutters, opening huge gashes and smashing him to his side. He gripped his arm fearfully. It was plain my appearance evoked all I had hoped for. The blow I struck down his buddy with only rendered him unconscious. I wanted to taste both these bad boys to see if they frequented the same masjid as the other locals at Erin's house.

"What in Allah's name are you?! Be gone, Demon!"

"I am Jedidiah Israel Blake, Destroyer of Worlds!" His world for sure. I drank in the fear so thick I could nearly cut it with my claws.

"I...I am a believer, monster! There is but one God, Allah... and Mohammed is his-"

I ripped him across the face deep enough to tear furrows from his ear to his chin. That shut him up. Then I lifted him gasping for air by the neck, his hands grasping my wrists in an attempt to ease air into his tortured lungs. I drew him inexorably toward my fangs. Knowing what he and his band of psychos had planned for thousands of innocent people in a country stupid enough to allow them inside the borders blunted any semblance of compassion. My fangs pierced his neck. All resistance faded from Saif's features. I knew in an instant my suspicions were correct. Saif was another masjid attendee. I didn't need to waste time on Raiden. They were both participants in an organized network of cells supported by the masjid. All their equipment and weapons came from the supplies stockpiled in a cellar complex beneath the masjid. I twisted Saif's head completely around until it hung by loose skin. I smashed Raiden's skull in since I no longer needed him.

Leaving nothing to chance, I finished my wooded perimeter check with all heightened senses projected outward. Saif believed he and his partner Raiden were the only two here but now was not the time to make those kinds of assumptions. It took only a short time longer to scour my surroundings for any other enemy sign. I grinned thinking of Erin who heard everything during my sniper nest adjustment. The fact she hadn't said anything convinced me she awaited an opening line from me I had no intention of giving her. I was heading her way again when Erin could no longer hold back comment.

"Destroyer of Worlds? Really?"

"I was in the moment. They frequented your favorite masjid. The one named Saif knew of an armory they're hiding in the masjid basement."

"I don't like the sound of that. What are you going to do?"

I waved at her from in front of the van until I had her attention in order not to startle my Igor while entering the vehicle, risking a bullet in the head. "I'm thinking we call Bret, give him the news, and see how he wants to handle it. My thoughts are we visit the masjid tonight. I'll go in and do a complete 'Hulk Smash' on their asses. Then I'll burn the place to the ground as they had planned to do at my place."

Erin sighed. She took out her iPhone. "Yep. That's what I figured. I'll call Bret."

"You talk like I'm some kind of monster."

"Hold that thought." Erin called Bret, explaining my findings to him. She then handed me the phone.

"Hi Bret. Happy Terrorist Eve, buddy."

158

To his credit, Bret was amused. "They have been busy. It fell in our laps. Any government agency hitting the masjid tonight would be castrated as Nazi jack-booted thugs stomping on religious freedom. Would you have an alternative for me I can play off as something else deadly without explosions or extended gun battles?"

I repeated my initial thoughts on the matter I had shared with Erin. Silence on Bret's end for a bit too long. "Too much?"

"I'm thinking."

Wow. If Bret's considering my rather horrific masjid plan, he must logically be even more afraid of the consequences if I didn't do something like I suggested. "I could tone it down some if you'd like."

"Nope. I want you to do it exactly as you described but without the fire. I don't want you to accidentally blow the neighborhood into the next dimension with something stored there. Stop by Erin's house. I'll have some special implements for you to use. Can you gather everything of an informational storage type database there? You're as expert with tech as anyone I have. I will give you as much time as you need even if I have to surround the block with agents."

"Survivors?"

"No prisoners, Jed. That's my vote. I don't expect you'll find any families there. I'll cover anything you do though. If I can move in with body-bags and no other story than what I invent we'll be okay. I have some high tech equipment here you may find useful. Swing by Erin's house. We'll follow you to the masjid as soon as we can."

"I'll be discrete. I can compel anyone remotely innocent, not that I think I'll find any innocents. The only time they trot out the burka women and kids is when the news cameras are rolling.

I'm thinking the only people I find in there will be Isis thugs. They won't be doing much other than plotting how to use the weapons of mass terror in the basement."

"May I say now that monsters are underrated as allies?"

Now that was funny. "We'll swing by and see what goodies you have for us."

Erin heard and drove us toward her house again. "It's a busy night for the war on terror. If Bret doesn't want anything massive done to the masjid, I wonder what the tools are he plans giving us?"

"Something I'm sure he can copy hard drives with at the speed of light or help me not accidentally trigger a deadly explosion. I don't think I'll have time in there for tasting. If Bashima had her stuff trip wired to go off when accessed without permission, you can bet the masjid computers are protected in much the same way. We could use some passwords but the gamble in getting them could be a block destroying catastrophe. What if these clowns have anthrax or some other biological agent with the weapons? My big worry is they have something in the basement armed to blow the whole place if tampered with. I think it best I make the place safe for Bret to move in and experiment on what he finds."

Erin took a deep breath, her features reflecting my own grim outlook. "Gee... that's a sweet take on things, Jed."

We rode in a comfortable silence to her house. She probably thought of bomb scenarios while I thought of impure thoughts concerning my muffin cook-in the Isis idiots cheated me out of so far. Where Erin and erotic thought are concerned I have admittedly tunnel vision. As we neared her house I willed my thought processes toward masjid assaults. If they wired the place to blow if approached, not even I could move fast enough to prevent it. As it turned out, Bret met me with an odd looking gizmo I accepted from him with confusion at first. Then, after checking it over swiftly, I recognized it to be some form of EMP gun.

"Glory be, it's a magnetic pulse weapon." I looked expectantly at Bret. "Can I keep this?"

"I will assign you a prototype if you can get this masjid into our hands without explosions or gun battles spilling into the streets. It will take out anything of an electronic nature including their security systems without affecting the computers inside. It is a prototype, narrow range, very powerful microwave infused beam. It acts like a nuclear reaction would on electronics it is aimed at. If you can use it on anything in their basement weapons armory, it should limit the chances of an accident. I can see by the way you're handling it, you have an intuitive grasp as to how to use it." Bret handed me a micro memory disc and the handy carrying case. "That's the digital manual for it. I also had the latest blueprints for the masjid added to the beginning of the disc. Can I trust you not to use the EMP weapon for nefarious purposes?"

"Can I have an example?" Yeah, my playful side was energized. It had been thwarted from muffins and now must seek other targets.

"Erin's hairdryer," Bret deadpanned.

"Agreed." I handled the EMP gun with a tech nerd's awe of anything electronic, even an electronics killer beam weapon. "I'll feed it, and walk it, and everything, Dad."

"Get out of here. I'll be along shortly. Do you think the sniper team will be okay until morning? I could use everyone on this."

"They won't be going anywhere. I threw their camo tarp over them. I doubt anyone will see Saif and Raiden unless they trip over them in the woods."

# Chapter Seven

## Blood Lust

Erin and I were again on the road to a place on her beat she knew well. I loaded and sped read through the EMP manual, also memorizing the masjid blueprints. The slight smile playing at Erin's lips as she drove convinced me Erin enjoyed the opportunity to watch a past thorn in her side get run over by the karma train. I ran my hand over her upper thigh. She shuddered and slapped at it, only hitting herself while forgetting knowledge of Dhampir speed.

"I'm still thinking of baking muffins."

"Get your head in the game, Jed," Erin admonished. "Can I come along?"

"No. If you don't rule out muffin baking tonight, I'll consider letting you look around the inside of the masjid to appease your vindictive tendencies. I can stay out of anyone's sight, but it would be better for you not to be seen near the masjid. Parking as you did earlier away from my house would be a much more intelligent action in this case than walking around the scene of death I plan to create."

I could tell she knew I was right. She gave in. "You're right. I'll drop you well away from the masjid. There's plenty of cover for you all the way to it on approach... not that you need it. I can't believe Bret would allow you to have an EMP prototype weapon."

"If I know my bureaucrat puppets as I know I do, Bret's giving me an EMP weapon already replaced by a newer more efficient one. This one will do what needs to be done and be a nice addition to my Batmobile."

"It's still remarkable he'd hand you one to keep. I know you, and I'd collect it after the masjid assault."

"You're mean!" I'm with her. I'd collect it from me too.

"Five minutes until I stop. If you have anything to get ready, do it now."

"Listen, Eerie, I'm not jumping out of an airplane. I'm exiting my van. Calm down."

"I believe the moment they suspect anything is wrong, they'll empty the masjid of evidence. We don't know what manner of 'check in procedure' their minions were supposed to follow. They may hear a rumor and blow the whole block to pieces."

Hadn't thought of that. I figured maybe they'd ship the armory out, but with crazies there's no telling what they'll do for sure. "I'll be moving real fast. In any case, I'm ready to go."

"Good."

I didn't want to tell her about another slight problem I would have to deal with when things settled down. The blood lust from tonight's hunting, stalking, and feeding burned through me like lava from a volcanic eruption – not just the blood taste but the essence of the hunt. The fear, terror, and surrender to me rivaled the crack pipe for an addict. At no time in my life had I hunted and fed on so many humans. Their thoughts, deeds, and knowledge rattled through my head in express train style. I grinned at Erin as I jumped out of the van door with a wave. I not only wondered if I could stop, I wondered if I could slow down.

I raced with my new toy to the masjid, taking their eight foot fence in a credible leap near the decorative tree line where I barely touched the pointed tip of one spoke as a guiding reference. Five seconds later two huge dogs ran at me without a warning growl at all, so I gave them mine. I've handled guard dogs before when someone employing them interested me. My low pitched growl in full Dhampir form will bring any animal to a stop. These two were no exceptions. They skidded to a halt in confusion. Then they were mine. I motioned them to lie down which they did immediately. Muslims normally avoided dogs due to their idiotic belief they were unclean animals. It would mean they were possibly using an outside security force or they weren't above using any beast or human to obtain their goal.

The EMP gun worked like a charm. I wasn't too sure of the inside electronics we wanted, but the outside lights and security panel at the door died mysterious deaths as I worked the beam according to the manual instructions. Surprise would be a key factor in my avoidance of Erin's worst case scenario. I decided on a monstrous assault, smashing through the door, luckily as it turned out by going through at an angle. The door slammed inward off its hinges, taking a volley of automatic weapons fire. Then I was amongst them. For the second time in the evening I slashed without mercy, maiming and killing. I left the six bloody bodies strewn across the entranceway, my claws having torn out throats with multiple passes so fast as to seemingly be done by an invisible demon.

I moved through the masjid with demon lust, silent bloody death striking in the dark, screams echoing outward before fading into eternity. Eleven more perished in gruesome merciless fashion, including three women. No one was spared in my deadly journey to the cellar acting as their armory, leaving no one alive. I used the EMP weapon again aimed in broad range down into the basement. The guards in the dark of the cellar shot at shadows. I attacked low from the floor, eviscerating upwards, always moving and maiming, finally with a last pass of death, ripping life from the mutilated. When my rampage ended, the fury of it remained as I walked amongst the weapons, ammo, and explosives. I made one more roof to cellar search for any survivors, this time gathering everything of an electronic storage capacity as I completed the sweep. I placed them in the entryway, no longer interested in info tech gathering.

My call, answered on the first ring by Bret, led to a rather stilted exchange where I described what I had done. "The computer gear is piled near the entrance. I didn't attempt to access any of what is on the hard-drives. This will be a long day's journey into night for you, my friend. They have an armory in the basement of this place. You will need to come here with a team to gather all they have stored and make sure it's done safely. I disturbed nothing in the armory either. I figured your bomb squad would be a better choice for having a first look."

"I have people surrounding your area in place. Finish what you need to. Then leave everything, including the weapons, where they are."

"I have to warn you. It's a mess here. I needed to move quickly because of the remote trigger threat someone could reach." And because I gave into a blood lust so intense, the juice is still boiling through my veins. I didn't even taste a single person, and yet the aftermath of what I'd done satisfied in a way no earlier feeding could compare to. The killings tonight revealed a weakness for taking life I was unaware of until now.

"You and Erin leave. We'll take over from here. Thanks, Jed. I can call you with an update tomorrow. I'll try not to bother you for a while. I sense tonight was a bad one for you."

"The problem with the ability to do this work is that I have a weakness for it."

"Meaning what, Jed?"

"Meaning I may feed without guilt, but I can't allow the hunger and lust for the kill to overpower my will. You were right. This was probably my limit without becoming an uncontrollable monster. I didn't foresee the killing lust. Maybe I should have. I

166

hope you have a team closed mouth enough to arrive on scene here. It ain't pretty."

"Let me worry about that. I have a rock solid group of veteran special-forces guys like Aiden Soransky. They've all done at least two tours in the sand. Lantry was the only non-vet in our group because we needed an interpreter. The rest of my team are familiar with the jackals in action against their own people overseas. They won't feel sorry for the bunch you took out if that's what you're worried about. They also know your sudden introduction into our task force saved thousands of lives in this first trial by fire. I have faith you'll get a grip on your problem, Jed. You have in the past."

Not like this, buckaroo. "Thanks, Bret. Erin and I will be at my house."

"I dispatched a couple guys to collect the sniper team the moment we finished at Erin's house. They found the sniper nest from your description. They'll have the area cleaned by the time you get there, not that you'll be wandering around out in the woods. We'll get what we can from the computers. I know you couldn't take a chance of leaving someone at your back. Can you tell anything from sampling their blood now as you do for Erin on a police crime scene?"

"I'll give it a shot. If I see any images of any importance I'll call you back."

"Okay, Jed. Talk at you in a while." Bret disconnected.

I sampled the blood of each victim after washing at a deep sink in the basement. The images from their victims and cohorts gave me a broader idea of flashed past happenings. Some of it I wish I could have given back. The men were terrorists, trained in Syrian camps. They came from two different training centers. I absorbed images of places nearby and the memories of conversations with their recruiter, Bilal Al-Taei. Those images and snatches of conversation gave me a very good idea of where a couple of authority figures with balls could drone strike the camps into hell. The women were dupes, recruited because of past proven viciousness from Albania. Al-Taei hoped to use their lighter hair and skin to gain access into places where they could leave behind backpack or carrying bag bombs. I could have done without the detailed memories the three had of female genital mutilation their female Islamist village idiots performed on them when they were only kids.

Erin awaited my return anxiously. I hadn't networked with her for fear I might trigger something with our com units. I gave her the details in quick highlights while I used my laptop to figure out where the Syrian training camps were while the visions remained fresh. When I had the two sites narrowed down fairly well I messaged Bret with the files I created. He would have to get someone higher in the food chain to approve a drone mission if a more detailed satellite imaging could find traces of the camps. Closing their passages into our country would be my first priority if I ruled the land. Until I gained control of my dangerous impulse driven thinking, I entertained images of bloody monster rampages at the north and south borders. I shook my head as if I could shudder free of the elation another wild violent night evoked in my subconscious. Erin noticed as she drove away. I could tell her small feeling of vengeance fulfilled missed the satisfaction mark she had anticipated.

"The killings tonight got to you, huh?"

"Not in the way you think," I replied, wondering if I should share anything more. As of now, Erin drove me toward my house. If I overshared she might decide on a motel instead.

"If you thought I figured you loved every second of it you'd be guessing right on my way of thinking."

Interesting. "Really?"

"You forget I've seen your eyes after a killing. Tonight you look ready to bust out of your skin. Is it because of the blood lust?"

"More like a killing lust," I admitted. "Without some extended time working on mobile apps I'll have a difficult time diffusing the rush making my whole body hum."

"You saved possibly a thousand lives or more tonight, Jed. I figured you'd think considering the lives saved would be a pretense for assuaging guilt over what you'd done. Why not do what you always do? Put it behind you. Your Mom would say the same thing. It was a win for everyone but the terrorists."

"I'm not on a guilt trip, Eerie. I'm on a murder high. If Bret had another target I'd race over there to slash the shit out of it. I've never killed like I did tonight. It's flipped a switch inside my head. I'm not launching on a murderous rampage killing on a whim, but the impulse is there without my usual moral compass setting screaming foul in my head."

"Wow. You got it bad. I wonder if it will be days before your eyes return to normal. I'll tell you what. Let's go make muffins together, fool around a little, and see if that helps you down off the ledge."

My first thought was to play the 'murderous rampage' card more often if it gets me more intimate moments with Erin. What can I say? Monster in murder, monster in love. "It sounds inviting. The vivid smell of fresh baking does affect my senses. I washed out all traces of what I'd done before leaving the masjid, but the taste memory will haunt me for a while."

"What do you usually do to wind down off a blood high?"

"I've never had one like this, but I usually work on app projects. Writing code soothes me. I've never told you this before. Maybe you suspected I dabble some in hacking. In actuality I am extremely good at it. I'm wondering if Bret knows. I kept waiting for him to mention it in passing. It may be I'm so good that even with them watching me all this time, I haven't left any trail they could follow. I've never done anything bad. To practice, I pick out the most feared hacker anywhere on the 'Dark Web'. They actually sell their services there."

Erin straightened as we drifted away from my murderous tendencies. "What do you mean when you say you destroy them?"

"I know code. I can write code faster than humans can think. A 'Black-hat' will take the bait when I make a remark challenging to their status on the 'Dark-net' which never gets indexed on the regular internet. The threats they hit me with are very funny. I will assault them much like I did the bad guys in person. I'm so fast, I can literally overwhelm them before they can pull a plug. It helps I own hardware super-computer capability in the range of NASA. I find the little punks and message them with their addresses, telling them either they acknowledge me as their King or I publish their address. It's fun as hell. My handle is Dhampir."

"No shit? So you're doing it as a game?"

"Yeah. It's fun. You can check me out. It's possible Bret didn't care what the hell I'm playing around at online. If he knew I could hack into the Company's database with a worm virus that would destroy the government, he'd probably be a bit more interested. Like I said, I cover my tracks. It may be they don't know about me. Anyway… it's a diversion I use when my head is spinning with too much input."

"Jed! You could bust all kinds of internet thugs preying on old people and novices who don't know any better. We should start doing that together too. You could bust pedophile rings."

"Anonymity is the name of the game, Eerie. Besides, I… uh never mind. Let's forget the hacking business. I'm not sure it would be good for you to know this because you'll get mad I didn't tell you, but here goes. I've already shut down a few things like you mentioned. I found out where they lived and hunted the ringleaders down."

"You killed them?" Erin seemed shocked.

"I can't cure a pedophile. What do you want me to do with them? If I don't kill them, they go out and keep doing what they do and sharing it on the internet for other predators. I can't bring them to the proverbial 'justice' everyone talks about but never does. It's endless anyways. I can't shut down all of them. I get the worst – the ones who dabble in everything of a pedophile's nature, including kidnapping. Did you know on the 'Dark Web' you can barter with one of these assholes to kidnap some little girl or boy through their filters. No cop can reach them through the web. I stalk them. They rarely last a day or two. I hate feeding on them, but if I do, I have to be ready for the backlash of memories. It's not for the faint of heart monster."

"Damn it, Jed, you do a lot of good. I need super powers! Make me into a vampire!"

"Even if I knew how, I wouldn't do it anyway. Have you lost your mind? Do you think this is some kind of TV series like 'Vampire Diaries' or 'Supernatural'? For one thing kiss your day job goodbye. I don't know what the sun does to a real vampire, but if it burns you into ash, I don't have a witch on hand to make you a ring like they do for everyone on the 'Diaries'. It could be you would simply be lethargic like my Dad when Mom staked him, but would you want to take the chance. Although I pray every day, I think we can honestly say I'm more of a demon than an angel. Mom convinced me there were too many wonders of the world for there not to be a creative force behind it all. She also taught me forgiveness for someone who deserves it. I know the bible by heart which is where I've strengthened my moral compass. I'm more of an 'Old Testament' type though. I know for a fact it wouldn't be very Christian to turn you into a vampire which as I said, I can't do anyways."

"I hadn't thought about the sun burning me into a crispy critter. What else can you do? Can you make me into a werewolf or maybe a voodoo princess?"

I enjoyed that line for the next couple miles to my house. Although Erin laughed along with me I'm not sure she didn't mean it in reality about being a vampire. Something else struck me in the head from left field. "Do you have a silver bullet in case you have to put me down, Eerie?"

Silence. Uh oh. "You do have a silver bullet, you little minx!"

"Don't blow a gasket, Fangster. I needed something for a worst case scenario like when Batman hoards a piece of Kryptonite in case Superman grows a pair, ditches that bitch Lois Lane, and porks Wonder Woman."

Oh man, Erin is a treasure when she starts going with her comedy routine. We made it to my house before I could speak, with Erin chuckling at how well I liked her comic book idea. "You're not serious about wanting to be a vampire, are you?"

She didn't speak until the van was parked. "We could be crime fighters together and hunt terrorists. We'd live forever young."

"I think that's a myth. I'm getting older. Maybe only the full blood vamps like my Dad live eternally because of the blood. I don't know how it works. It would be major bad to burn up in sunlight instead of being simply sleepy. Even if I could make you into something, I couldn't make you into a Dhampir. There's a tradeoff I guess. Someone made my Dad, but maybe as you suggested they came from another dimension and they're all dead."

"I know you're right about the tradeoff. I would miss the sun. Besides, someone badass like your Mom comes along and there goes eternal life."

Good point. "Mom really is tough beyond words. Now you know why I never hesitated to tell her everything I did do. She's one of those 'I can't fix it if I don't know what's broken' types. Stay here with the van locked until I do a perimeter check."

"Okay, but exit quick if you think there's a possibility of another sniper. They can't hit you. I know your van's bullet proof so I'm good."

"On it." I went out with Dhampir speed, not slowing until I reached the wooded perimeter of my property.

It didn't take long to ascertain the property no longer hosted any snipers or bushwhackers. I waved to Erin for her to join me as I disabled the alarm system and unlocked the door. I looked forward to muffin making with an erotic flavor of conversation mixed in, leading hopefully to a more physical exploration. She interested me with talk of being made into a vampire. Erin was no shrinking violet, either in unarmed combat or firing weapons. She worked hard at both.

"We're not really making muffins are we, Jed?" Erin followed me inside.

I led the way into the kitchen. "Why not? I'll make some coffee. We'll mix and make some muffins. While they're baking you can tell me more about this penchant you have for being a vampire."

"That does sound good, but the only reason I mentioned the vamp making was I forgot about the sunlight. For some reason I figured if you turned me, I'd be a Dhampir too. That was dumb." Erin knew where everything was in my kitchen. She found the muffin mix while I retrieved the other ingredients both needed and

173

added in for my liking. "Don't you think you'll stay young forever?"

I never gave it a thought but if Erin was interested I saw no reason to hide my thoughts on the subject. "I believe I'm aging but we're so young anyway it would be difficult to really know at this stage. You seem intrigued a lot more with my powers than when we were younger."

"I did a lot of research on mythology. I know in Hollywood they always make Dhampirs more powerful than full-fledged vampires. They never say why exactly. In mythology it's because vampires can't breed except by some mutation in the DNA between the vamp and the lover, or in your Mom's case, the victim. When conception does take place, the baby in almost all cases dies. If they live they're said to be stronger than their sire without any weaknesses. You surprised me with the compelling aspect."

"You've surprised me with the Dhampir DNA mutation theory. It runs the same course as Hollywood but makes more sense in that only a few survive because of a mutating DNA strand. I'm sorry I didn't share the rest with you."

"All the things you suspected would probably have been true. I would have obsessed about the morality in your hunts and wondered constantly whether you were compelling me against my will. We've been together so long I know you would never do that. I rebel against nearly everything you advise, many times putting my life in danger as with Gronsky. Instead of compelling me to obey you allow my stupid mistakes to act as a very vivid teacher. It's damn annoying. I do realize if you were prone to making me take your advice I wouldn't have all those embarrassingly stupid examples like Gronsky of my past errors in judgement."

"If I were prone to compelling you'd be naked every moment we're alone or dancing around in skimpy clothing. The lifesaving advice would be secondary." I put the panned muffins in the oven while taking a slap to the back of my head. "It's not fair to hit me while I have muffins in my hand. At least allow me to have your muffin in my hand when you slap me."

Erin giggled at my private muffin mix of terms. She moved into me as I stepped away from the oven. "I want you to taste my blood, Jed. I want to feel what it's like to have your fangs enter my flesh, coupled with the sensation of you drawing my blood from me. The intensity of the act must generate incredible images if done in an erotic manner with all the incredible images it must generate. You care for me. Do you think the act would be as electrifying as they make it in the movies with the Hollywood vamps and their lovers?"

Get thee behind me, Satan! Good Lord, I would have been less surprised if she had tried to stake me. What the hell do I say to that? C'mon, Fang. Even you aren't that much of a demon. Treat it as momentary madness on her part. Her curiosity factor went around the bend and she's watched too many 'Vampire Diaries' reruns. Now she's awakened the Demon's curiosity factor. Damn it! "Seriously, Erin, that's a horrible idea. When I taste a living human's blood I'm like a demonic succubus. All aspects of their being becomes mine. You get embarrassed when you have to use my bathroom. How the hell do you think you'll react knowing I've absorbed the very essence of your soul?"

Erin folded her arms over chest complete with pouting annoyed look. "Gee, Fang... way to bring me down from a nice moment's erotic thought. I figured I'd have a bloody neck by now. Instead I have a guilt trip about being a wanton vampire whore."

Now that was funny. I put an arm around her shoulders. "No, Erin, I've never considered such a thing in any way, shape, or form. Our arrangement as friends, lovers, combatants, and partners would be changed forever. I can't tell you what it would be like because other than my Mom giving me blood as a baby, I've never tasted a loved one's blood. Most often, my feeling from it is a combination of revulsion at the bad folks' lifestyle and elation from the blood feeding. If you've thought I went around compelling beautiful women for a quick erotic moment the answer is no, I haven't."

"Fair enough," Erin replied, facing me again. "Maybe I want to change our dynamic, especially with this secret government task force we're suddenly part of that's been following you since childhood. That must have been an eye opener for you. Can't you open to me in the same way when tasting my blood?"

"How the hell would I know? I don't let go when I drain a bad guy. I feed. I don't share anything. If you want to try it, I've fed enough I wouldn't be like that vampire on the old TV series 'Moonlight' where the female lead wanted to give the vampire character her blood."

"I remember that one! It was so good." Erin shifted back into vampire meal mode. "Alex O'Loughlin starred as the vamp. He looked at Sophia Myles and agrees but tells her as he begins to feed 'at some point you're going to have to stop me'. It was so sexy! Do me, Fangster!"

"You're nuts." I moved my face near hers, leaning in to brush her lips with mine. "You do understand this isn't a TV show, don't you? When I sip your blood with my fangs you won't even be able to think about stopping me let alone stop me in reality."

Erin moaned, opening her lips to me in a fervently hot coupling my senses joined with the smell of baking muffins and her pheromones, driving me feverishly toward exactly what she wanted. She broke free, sensuously returning my open eyed desirous stare before offering her neck. Enough of this! The demon monster within could sense the pulse at her neck pumping red gold, beckoning to me, throbbing for my attention. While Erin watched me with chest heaving and mouth gasping air in short pants of breath, I extended my fangs in a slow motion reach for her neck's flowing channels. They pierced her skin with deadly accuracy, striking their flowing target as Erin shuddered into climax, gripping me around the neck with a cry of completion. I allowed the sweet nectar of her essence to stream into me.

A furious bloody wave crashed through my skull, carrying a lust so powerful I staggered backwards, ripping Erin off her feet, all pretense of gentleness washed aside in a monstrous agony of need. I was lost. Her skin burned me. Her scent tore my breath away. Her sweating grip around my neck clutched at me with the heat of red hot coils closing around my entire consciousness.

"Jedidiah!" She screamed my name as a prayer in the gathering darkness.

The prayer struck me with icy dagger like sharpness. Reality seeped in cold tendrils of naked steel tautness, plucking me from the fiery brink of murdering the love of my life. I healed her wound with iron will while withdrawing my fangs as I gripped her in an unbreakable grip. Erin heaved within my grasp, lungs filling with desperate panic. I then slowly enfolded her in my arms, holding her gently until she could stand on her own. She looked again into my eyes with an awe struck tenderness I welcomed but didn't understand.

"How…how did you stop, Jed?"

"I don't know. We're never doing that again." I heard the words but the only horrible truth I wanted more than life was to siphon her bloody being until only the husk of her body remained in my arms. I released her and turned to take the muffins out of the oven. They were perfect. They smelled wonderful. The grinning demon inside me stirred happily, knowing he had nearly gained control of me in a nightmarish scene of tragedy. I held the pan in front of Erin with a slight shoulder shrug. "Muffin?"

She started laughing and couldn't stop. I put the pan back on the stove top. I hugged Erin until she was able to stop. "Oh

God... you... nearly killed me. You were right, Jed. This is no game."

"Sit down." I guided her to a chair at the kitchen table. I brought over a plate of muffins, two dishes, napkins, and coffee the way we both liked it, along with a big glass of orange juice for Erin. "Let's eat and sip. You'll need your strength. I don't think I took a dangerous amount from you but drink the juice with your coffee and muffins. You'll be fine."

Erin gripped my hand. "I'm sorry for tempting you into that. You resisted killing me when I thought for sure I was doomed. You filled my mind. My entire perception of life became engulfed by one thought - I wanted you to overwhelm me, own me, absorb me. I wanted to become part of you. Is that how it is when you feed on others?"

"Drink your juice and eat your muffins, Eerie." I didn't look away from her until she began eating and drinking. "I've never experienced anything like that ever. It was the most nightmarish and sensual tidal wave of emotion ever, and is never to be repeated."

A sense of loss flowed over Erin's features I didn't like. "Maybe you could control it the next time. You stopped before going too far this time. We'd both have awareness so we could be prepared. I trust you. This...this feeling is too incredible to resist."

"Sucking you dry is the only thing you could trust me to do." I ate a couple of muffins without speaking or looking at her, sipping coffee while using my peripheral vision to make sure she continued to eat and drink. She did. "Even at this moment devouring you drives every thought in my head. I would never be able to stop. My feeding has a compelling aspect to it. The dregs of my will still haunts you until some time passes. It should fade."

"I don't want it to fade."

Yep. Erin's mine. I would have to entertain and humor her down off the ledge. "Too bad. Think of it as being in thrall to Dracula. You're like my little sock puppet for a while. If you don't behave yourself and start talking sense I'll make you wash my feet with your hair or something."

Erin smiled which was a good sign. "I don't have any impulse to obey your commands Sith Lord Darth Jedidiah. We were never as close as at the moment of joining."

Moment of joining? Oh for God's sake. "The only joining going on was with you and death. You were close to never drawing another breath, fairy princess Erin, thrall of Darth Jedidiah. Get a grip and use your brain. Concentrate. Reality will seep in at a faster pace that way."

"I want you, Jed." After a silence as she matter-of-factly devoured her third muffin and gulped down both orange juice and coffee. "You can still be attracted to me without fanging me, right?"

"You're scaring me, Eerie." I would have sent her home if I could have. How about a drink - a real one since you did okay with your juice and coffee?"

Erin shifted over onto my lap, entwining her arms around my neck. "Don't play hard to get. You're not and you know it. If you're fighting off the temptation to eat me then give in to it in another manner, Darth Jed."

"This is going to be one of those morning after scenes where I get blamed for everything. I can tell. I'm not going to fight you though. The muffins and coffee have soothed my killing impulse. Now, I just want to make you scream."

"Wait!" Erin cried out as I lifted her easily. "What do you mean make me scream?"

"You'll see."

And she did.

* * *

Darth Jedidiah felt a disturbance in the force. I slept lightly because I opened every sense within my psychic tool drawer while resting with Erin. I could go literary, claiming to sleep as the wolf and tiger sleep, but I sleep conscious of every foreign noise, scent, and disturbance in the air surrounding me. I didn't need much rest, especially after the prior day's feeding. I smiled down at Erin who slept like the dead while I moved silently from beside her.

As I reached the front entrance my doorbell sounded. I opened the door because nothing much on earth could move or react faster than me. I startled the hell out of Kelly Lamb, the CSI tech who blamed me for everything from job layoffs to Climate Change. I had jeans and a black t-shirt on and I was in my own house so I didn't understand the overreaction as she stumbled backwards off the steps. Then I remembered my eyes. I'd fed so much it would probably be days before they returned to normal. I squinted as if the light bothered me and stepped back.

"Sorry, Kelly, I have a light sensitivity issue on some days. I wear special shielding contacts. Come in. It's Wednesday morning. Why aren't you headed into work?" I motioned to her to follow me inside which she did, but without replying. I snatched my sunglasses from the entryway table, shoving them into place as I led the way into the kitchen. "I'll make coffee. There's a few muffins left from last night. Sit down and have one. I baked them myself. Would you like some juice."

Kelly sat down, took a bit of muffin and shrugged. "Sure. This is good."

"Thanks." I placed a glass of juice in front of her. Next task was making fresh coffee. I had one of those neat but wasteful cartridge type machines so the coffee didn't take long. Kelly nibbled on her second muffin while I served the coffee. "What brings you here to the enemy of mankind's house? My friends now call me Sith Lord Darth Jed so I don't get many visitors, especially ones who supposedly hate my guts."

"I...I don't hate your guts." Kelly looked like she went sleepless in Sacramento. "I need your help. Everett said you're the best security specialist he's ever seen in addition to your CSI expertise."

"I have a number of interests. Private security is one of them. Do you need advice on a reliable system?" This was odd. Kelly worked for the Sheriff's Department. I built Ev a system from scratch that does everything but scratch his nose at nighttime. He had trouble with a neighborhood gang whose leader took a disliking to Ev. They began trespassing on his property at night, scaring him and his family. I installed a state of the art system, but handled his gang problem a bit differently than he had in mind with alarms and monitors. I hunted the leader down, fed and slashed his throat so I knew the next few in line for leader of the pack. For the next few nights, the gang had problems other than my friend, Everett Zanki. They disbanded after I slashed the fifth one in line's throat.

"I have a stalker," Kelly admitted. "Everett helped me make a report, adding his prestige with the department. I now have increased surveillance with extra checks by patrolling squad cars. I have a security company recommended by some of the guys. The company is terrific about answering calls and is the top rated one in the area on the internet."

"So how can I help?"

"Whoever it is stopped visiting my house on a regular basis. He trips alarms and does things around the house I'm renting but no one can catch him doing it. The security company has caught him on video but he has a high tech scrambler that blurs his

181

face into a glowing bulb. He follows me everywhere. I can feel him. I know how paranoid that sounds but I get this bad feeling of foreboding when he's around. I'm like a shut-in now. I run to my car in the morning and run into the house at night. I go nowhere other than work and home. Do you have any ideas or suggestions? I know I'm going to disappear one day and no one will ever see me again."

"Stalkers are out of my area of expertise." I turned on my inner truth detector the moment I saw Kelly standing outside. She was telling the truth. "I'd like to help. I'm good with high tech gizmos but I'm not sure how much help they would be to you other than if I chipped you."

"Chipped... you mean put a monitoring device in my body?"

"It would set your mind at ease about no one knowing what happens if you did disappear. I know it doesn't mean much in reality if someone does seek to harm you. I would imagine you've heard the best defense is a good offense. Pepper spray, stun-guns, and bullet type weapons all give you confidence when you learn to use them. I would have figured working in CSI on the East Coast and even here, you probably have a good knowledge of protective weapons. Do you have your conceal carry permit. Ev does."

"Damn! I was hoping you'd have something out of the box for me to do. I hadn't thought about the chip thing though. I'm carrying a complete armory of what you mentioned. You're right. I know how to use them. I also know when someone gets the drop on me all the weapons in the world won't do any good. Can you chip me? That would at least give me security in knowing I could be found."

Uh no. "I'm talking about a signal device like your mobile phone has we can place somewhere on you. I have prototypes that are very small I've been developing. On a mobile phone the battery powers the device. Mine are self-powered. The trick is to find a place to put it the stalker won't find immediately. You have long hair. The nape of the neck under your hair would be an excellent place. It can be attached with a special flesh toned tape."

"That's better than nothing. I admit I'm scared. This guy is like a ghost... a foul creeping ghost. You can only imagine how desperate I am to ask for your help."

That's where you're wrong. "I can imagine how tough it was."

Erin walked into the kitchen with a slight wave. I could tell she'd taken a shower and brushed the wrinkles out of her clothing the best she could. "You're Kelly Lamb, right? I met you at the McRainey killing. You're a bitch!"

To her credit, Kelly chuckled and nodded in agreement. "I guess I am. I remember treating you and your partner with my usual arrogant crap when Everett and I arrived at the scene. Could I say I'm sorry and start over?"

Erin shrugged while looking at me questioningly. "Sure, but it really depends on why you're here. I have a shift that starts in an hour. Can I borrow the Chevy, Jed?"

"Of course." I quickly explained Kelly's case, including her fears and misgivings about help ever arriving in time to be of any use. It fired the look of interest in Erin, nearly replacing the flame I noticed when she blushed while looking at me. I then turned to Kelly again. "Erin and I are partners in a few outside enterprises. She helps whenever I need detective type assistance. What do you think of my GPS tracker idea, Erin?"

"It's a good backup idea, but as Kelly pointed out to you, if she's taken, the tracker won't help much unless she's held prisoner. You'd have to trust whoever monitors the device to not leave you hanging either, Kelly. Do you have anyone like that in your life?"

183

"Not at this time."

"Jed will do it," Erin volunteered me without so much as a questioning tone. "He needs to keep track of a prototype device like that anyway. No one would have the expertise or gear to track you reliably. You'll do it, won't you, Jed."

"Do you call him Darth Jed," Kelly asked before I could answer Erin.

Erin smiled. "I invented it. I'm surprised he's shared his new nickname with you so soon."

"I was trying to scare her from my doorstep. It didn't work. I'll do the tracking if you'd like." I stood and made Erin a cup of coffee. There seemed to be a strange dynamic between Kelly and Erin I didn't understand. "C'mon. I'll show you my workshop and the device."

Erin visited my workshop many times. It looks a lot like those supercomputer rooms at NASA in half of the huge space. On the other side of the room every electronics tool and part I even dreamed of needing, hung or was drawered, in plainly labeled categorized cabinets. Tool benches with every conceivable welding outfit, microscope enabled enclosed work station, and Faraday Cages to prevent accidental or deliberate EMP events were neatly organized along the walls. Everything I might need to build the smallest circuit board to a fully operational robot I kept in the most efficient manner possible, ready for action. I owned a huge estate. My workspace encompassed my passions, expertise, and creativity in addition to making me a fortune. Kelly gaped in awe at the well-lighted facility.

"Welcome to the domain of Sith Lord Darth Jedidiah," Erin said. "Whatever you do don't touch anything if you value your life. He always has five to ten experimental projects going at the same time. He makes me wear a hazmat suit when I visit this place. Darth Jed feels benevolent this morning."

184

"You're a real comedian this morning, Eerie. Did you sleep on the wrong side of the bed last night?" I grinned as she blushed bright red. Yeah... I could tell realization of our night together could not be discounted quite as easily as she hoped, especially since I had no intention of allowing her to bury it in smartass remarks.

"I'm fine. Thank you for asking." Erin went with formal denial for all the good it would do her.

I guided Kelly over to a bench near my supercomputer section. I retrieved the prototype self-powered GPS tracker which was smaller than a dime. I put it on a piece of flesh toned surgical tape I cut from a roll on the desk. After placing the tracker in the middle of the tape I turned to Kelly while making a motion for her to turn around. She did and I lifted her hair in the back. I placed the taped tracker barely under her hairline. After allowing her hair to drop back into place, I moved over to my bank of monitors. In moments we were watching Kelly being tracked by the device I activated at the monitor station.

"You're on, Kelly. I can add a video cam with audio to your clothing if you'd like."

"No... this is great. It doesn't feel uncomfortable at all. Are there any side effects?"

I couldn't resist. "Once in place and activated as I've done you become a minion of Darth Jed forever."

She laughed and I willed her to lift her left hand over her head by raising my own. I released her immediately as Kelly nearly freaked out with Erin laughing her ass off. I patted Kelly's shoulder.

"It's a joke. Approximately fifty percent of the population would raise their left arm by suggestion after telling them they were in thrall to a Sith Lord. Such is the power of suggestion," I assured her using a combination of half-truth and fiction. "Nothing will happen to you, even if you sleep with it on."

Kelly appeared relieved she wasn't really in thrall to the Darth Lord Jed which was funny in itself. "How will you know if I'm in trouble?"

The truth is always best in these moments. "I'm not omniscient, nor is my electronic gadget. The only way I could know you might be in trouble is for you to stay in touch with either Erin or I. The GPS tracker can be accessed and monitored from my phone, but I wouldn't know you were in the wrong place at the wrong time unless you report in occasionally."

"Oh... I thought... you know... somehow it could send you a signal my core temp was off or something. Now that I think about it, the sillier it seems by the moment."

Damn, that's not bad. Sometimes geniuses don't always know the capabilities of what they create, or the foresight to realize all potential uses for the creations. My prototype did have a temp sensor built in to it. I designed it to be installed on any high end electronic device so the user would be able to retrieve their property if stolen. It doubled as a temperature safety device to inform the owner if their device was overheating.

"Not so silly," I admitted, accessing another screen where Kelly's skin temperature showed in both wave and digital form. I added some parameters and the monitor began calculating a norm from her readings. "This wouldn't be a perfect application for what you're envisioning because of varying environmental temperatures, but it does add an aspect to our surveillance. I can think of another drawback too. If they use a stun-gun or Taser on you, I'm not sure if the device would survive it. I made it resistant to electronic feedback and surges but the only way we could test it would be to use a stun-gun on you."

"No thanks." Kelly smiled and held out her hand. "Thank you for this, Darth Jed."

I shook her hand and so did Erin. "I hope the police or the security firm can catch your stalker before something like this tracker would be necessary. I need to remind you I don't do this professionally. Erin can probably tell you more about your chances of something like this working or not."

"You're armed and trained, Kel. When you see this guy coming at you, shoot him in the dick and then the head," Erin advised.

"If I see him coming I will do exactly that. Unfortunately, I don't have eyes in the back of my head, nor can I anticipate all the places I can be ambushed. For now I'll rely on what I have. When I need to go somewhere out of the ordinary, I'll text you the address. I know after the way I treated you, this is a real kindness on your part, Jed. Thank you."

"No problem. Keep your eyes open as you've been doing. Stay in lighted areas without shadows when you go out. Check your car's interior before popping into it, okay?"

"Will do."

Erin and I walked Kelly to the door. I gave her a card from my entryway table in case she didn't have my number to text. She left and Erin yanked on my arm. "You're going to hunt down the stalker, aren't you?"

Very good. Erin was starting to get me. It was another blood opportunity with bad guy against good guy, Darth Jed. "Yep. I'll let this ride a couple days while we allow the other clichéd irons in the fire to cool down. I'm betting this weekend could be a perfect hunting time."

"You'll need to be careful of the police and security she already has watching her back. I don't want you getting shot as the stalker. How can I help?"

Keep sleeping with me. "I'll fix an iPad to track my device and me. You can watch that while I'm out stalking the stalker. I figure two nights tops and we'll have him."

"Would this be a good arrest for me?"

I hadn't thought about that. I could hunt, feed, heal, and compel. Erin could make the arrest on the spot and take him in with Kelly's grateful reference. I could always hunt the sucker down later and finish the job if the courts let the stalker go. I liked the input. This new partnership with my old Igor worked well if I didn't taste her again.

"I think it's a great idea. You'll have to be in uniform when you take the stalker into custody. Kelly will accompany you down to the station. Would you like to get Tony in on it too?"

"Tony told me flat out not to get him involved with anymore of my 'ambition launched cluster-fucks'... his words. When you find the stalker, are you going to compel him?"

"So you think there's no way it's a woman, huh?" I'm always curious as to the assumption women don't do anything like stalking.

"Women don't engage in such crude behavior."

"What about the astronaut love triangle where the stalker was a woman?"

"An exception to the rule." Erin waved me off on her way to the kitchen. "That was a great presentation for Kelly. I could tell she was shocked seeing your Darth Jed cave. She doesn't seem too bad as a person now that her life's in danger."

"Funny how that works, isn't it. You're really going to continue zinging me with the Sith Lord reference?"

"You call me Eerie which I've already ordered stopped and been ignored. Besides, you drew it on Kelly."

"As you pointed out, Kelly seems human now that her life's in danger. At the McRainey crime scene I didn't care much for her. It's possible the stalker was affecting her attitude."

"Possibly. I'd give her the benefit of the doubt on that," Erin replied as we entered the kitchen and she put her cup down.

"I noticed an underlying connection between you and Kelly. Anything to that?"

"I was being nice. Plus, I considered the fact we could use someone in the CSI lab owing us. I know you can do anything they do but your results wouldn't be official on anything to do with an official case."

Well thought out, Eerie. "That's good thinking. Want another cup of coffee?"

"I have to be at work shortly. I need a shower, but I'm thinking I better have a couple more muffins and juice for blood replenishment."

"I'll get you the juice. You go ahead and heat some muffins for both of us."

While we were eating, Erin kept a running dialogue of items I needed to check on, including Bill and his daughter, Brett and the MIB's, and last but not least how my Mom felt after telling us about how she dusted my Dad. I kept a running thought about how good it had been with Erin after the blood episode. It surprised me she kept talking while eating but avoiding all reference to our night together. Erin gave me a moment to get a word in when she nearly choked while talking and eating.

189

"You've talked about everything else except our night together. You also haven't mentioned if there are any lingering effects from our blood event."

Erin blushed again as she washed down muffin with juice. "Our lovemaking was super intense because of the blood interlude. I'm not sure how much more I can add other than as we agreed, it was dangerous last night. You were right when you told me the residual urge to have you do it again was probably related to the compelling aspect. This morning I recognize how goofy that idea is. I know without doubt you were going to kill me. Could you feed on Kelly without going postal?"

What? Erin lanced me with that last question. "Why the hell would I want to suck Kelly's blood?"

"I'm curious as to the female aspect if you know the woman. If you nearly ripped my throat out even though you love me, I wonder how it would be with another woman you know."

"I didn't almost rip your throat out. Secondly, last night I sucked the terrorist women, but I didn't have anything like what happened between us. I killed them because of the situation rather than a need to bond with them while doing it. I opened to you as we talked about. It allowed a savage part of me to surface I lost control of with you. That's the reason we can't do it again. The hunger to feed on you again I managed to fight off would resurface. I know it. I'm not experimenting with Kelly. If she found out something I didn't want revealed, I think I could compel her to forget it successfully."

Erin nodded and stood. "I'm going to take a shower. You stay here."

"But Eerie, who will scrub your back? Don't you want to get clean?"

"I'll settle for Eerie clean rather than Dhampir clean, Darth Jed." Erin headed out of the kitchen while finger pointing at me. "Stay Jed."

"Arf," I replied I'm sure with dejection in my tone.

# Chapter Eight

## Stalker

"Really?" Erin shifted slightly in the van while keeping the digital range finders on target. "You picked some butch looking woman so you could screw with me, didn't you? Admit it. Good joke, but I'm not buying it."

I turned the iPad toward her so she could see the movie of Kelly coming out of work late on Friday night. The woman she was watching walk down the street hid behind parked cars, following Kelly with very impressive stealth moves. I didn't think she looked butch. Her brown hair was cut a bit short. She was tall and slender wearing jeans and a black windbreaker. It had only taken me one shadowing of Kelly to spot her stalker. I didn't even have a chance to bring Eerie along to watch the tracker. The woman seemed harmless to me, but she had done damage to Kelly's property and terrorized her. It would be a good collar for Erin.

"Her name's Leslie Sharington. I don't have any idea why she's stalking Kelly other than an unrequited love interest. It's possible Kelly made an enemy of her at some time. I didn't find any connections between the two. Leslie is a native Californian. She grew up in Walnut Creek. They never worked anywhere together, cohabitated, or even spoke to each other that I know of. I figured you wouldn't believe me so I took the video. You'll be able to use it when making your case too."

Erin sat back dejectedly. "I thought this might be a serial killer type long haired male freak with wild eyes or something. What do I get - Suzy Sundance with a rejection complex. Why don't you compel her to stay away from Kelly and call it a day?"

"I haven't had a chance to investigate her personal life yet. I was going to leave that to the police when you arrested her. I didn't know we had to capture Jack the Ripper for it to be an interesting case. Are we going to do this or not?"

Erin shrugged. "I guess so. What do you think her next move is?"

"Kelly's going out with a couple of girlfriends tonight. She called to let me know a couple hours ago. They're going to a bar in Citrus Heights and having dinner together. I'm betting Leslie will be shadowing her tonight. If she does, then Leslie has some way of knowing in advance where Kelly will be. I guess I should have swept Kelly's place for bugs. I guess it doesn't matter. We have her dead to rights."

"You are the best at this stalking stuff. We should build a task force around you. Maybe we could do a lot of business with celebrities, politicians, and public figures who think they're being stalked. You could engineer state of the art tracking gizmos and all kinds of new tech gear in that field. We could consult with the police departments and even the FBI."

"What the hell do I need to start doing all that for? I have more money than God now. What happened to the more likely scenario of Erin Constanza, Detective?"

"I don't know. I could just marry you and live high off the hog for the rest of my life. What the hell do I need with a job where I get shot at and abused daily by people I'm trying to protect? I'm rethinking all my goofy youngest detective ever plans. It won't happen anyway. I'm probably a joke the real detectives laugh at every time they hear my name mentioned."

Uh oh. I think maybe Erin is still fighting off the Darth Jedidiah compelling phase. "You're not thinking clearly, Erin. Let's nail this stalker the way we talked about. You take her in with a grateful Kelly at your side and things at the station will be a lot brighter. You can always marry me and retire from life later if things don't work out. In the meantime I'll give your stalking idea some thought. I may be able to create something more efficient for missing persons and people being stalked. I'll give it serious consideration."

"I guess you're right," Erin conceded. "I'll bring her in. Maybe because one of our own people was being stalked I'll get some credit for ending the problem. Kelly will be grateful as you pointed out. We can use that. I scared you with the marriage comment, didn't I?"

"Nope. I love you. I don't want you saying and doing things because of our blood interlude as you call it. Remember, because of the interlude, I know everything about you. This sudden need to change the basic tenets in your life is not like you. I believe we need to allow some time to pass before we rent a church and minister. Besides, I have an app I've been working on for police to find out all the background on a suspect. It will automatically search for unsolved crimes wherever and whenever they happened in the same general area as the suspect. Leslie would be a great real life sample to try it out on."

"Not bad. You and your app's – it's a wonder you have time for illicit thoughts of me. I was excited to be after a badass stalker, but all I ended up with was a campfire girl with a grudge or the hots for Kelly. It's a letdown. Guide me, Darth Jed."

"I thought it would be a good idea to approach Kelly with the movie and pictures I've taken to see if she knows the woman. Now I'm thinking it might be better to have the woman in custody when she's caught in the act. I'll compel her to tell the truth and we can finally learn what she has against Kelly."

"Sounds good, Darth. I'll hang with you until she makes her move. I like the idea of you compelling her to tell the truth. Otherwise, this would be a tough one to prosecute. She's not messing around as much at Kelly's place. Unless there's an assault of some kind or we arrested her inside Kelly's house, we don't have any proof she's a danger. What do we do next?"

"We're close to your house. We'll go have coffee and tear Leslie's personal life apart."

"I have no objection but why tear her life apart? You already told me you didn't find any direct connections. Like you said, I can bring her in and tear it apart then."

"I know you've been working double shifts and haven't had time to get together with me until now. Bret handled everything under the radar so that excitement is over for now except for the terrorist threads we found. He's dealing with those. That leaves us with some relationship time. Besides, Leslie's personal life could have a skeleton in the closet I haven't uncovered yet. We have to be as thorough as possible so you look good when you take her in."

"Fine," Erin replied tiredly. "Let's get started before the idea of it puts me into a coma."

"I am shocked at your poor attitude, Officer Constanza."

"Blow it out your ears, Darth."

* * *

I grinned inappropriately as Leslie's story unfolded before my eyes in a way I never ever expected. Under her given name she only used one credit card. She acquired it right after high school. While she grew up in Walnut Creek, news articles of the time period recorded cat and dog mutilations happening in and around her neighborhood. After high school she disappeared which explains why I couldn't find any connecting threads between her and Kelly. What didn't disappear were credit card charges on her one and only card listing the Walnut Creek address, but paid online. My app digs deep for purchases and locations. Leslie expected one card paid for online to never give her trouble, especially keeping on the move as she did. Eight unexplained mutilation deaths of women in their early twenties to early thirties in locations at the same time Leslie charged purchases made for a convincing pattern.

The most interesting of the locations in New York placed Leslie very near where Kelly worked in the CSI there. Kelly must have upset Leslie's plans getting fired and moving before Leslie could kill her. The fact Kelly moved to a place so near to Leslie's hometown must have seemed like a devilish signpost. That Leslie had never been a suspect in any of the killings made her following Kelly merely an inconvenience. Leslie put in the time and effort involved to perpetrate the perfect murder/mutilation. She didn't want to do a complete reset. She had become too involved with Kelly to let her go. The change in her routine was the stalking part with vandalism. It seemed as if she were punishing Kelly for the inconvenience. I would have to get special permission, maybe from Bret, to find out what souvenir Leslie took, if any. All of her victims were blondes. I looked over at where Erin flitted through Leslie's only known job under her own name. She worked as a waitress – a perfect occupation for a move around killer. My guess would be Leslie worked near her victims and they were all customers of hers.

"Eerie, bring over Leslie's work address."

"You already know the place. She works at The Rind on L Street."

"Perfecto. Come here. I have some very interesting and disturbing news for you."

Erin trudged over pretending to be on her last legs and fading fast. "I'm so bored I'm thinking of letting you eat me again."

I put her in my seat pointing out how to read the app results on the screen along with the connections it had already made. In minutes Erin launched into a deadly serious study of every killing in relation to Leslie's credit card purchases. She began making notes half way through. When she finished and turned to me her face was flushed. My little bored Erin was excited.

"Oh my God, Jed! Sharington is a real honest to God serial killer. No way is all this a coincidence. I'll go track down restaurants in the area of the murder victims. We'll send out photos of Leslie. If we get hits you may not even need to compel her. How much more time do we have?"

"I figure we'll have to be in position by 8 pm. Check for restaurants with bars. I think Leslie picks high end places catering to professional cliental. Her criteria is blondes. We need to know if she takes souvenirs. I'll call Bret. You stick with the restaurant angle. That's a good one."

"On it." Erin nearly ran to her terminal. It was nice seeing her get emotional about something other than my sucking her blood.

I called Bret and gave him a quick version of what I was doing.

"Give me fifteen minutes, Jed," Bret said. "That is hot. If you two can bust a serial killing spree out of the blue, I can highlight it to our backers as more evidence in a positive light. They're already seeing stars over your first action on our behalf. I'll call you back."

I relaxed in my chair considering the possibilities. The electrifying jolt rushing through me at being allowed another sanctioned blood hunt awakened the predator. I felt my fangs and features begin to change unbidden by me. By the time I realized what was happening, I had leaped to my feet in full Dhampir form.

A moment later Erin smacked me across the face. The fact I didn't block the blow or move illustrated what a shock the change caused.

"What the hell, Darth?! Are you out of your monster mind?"

I stumbled backwards warding her off. "Give me a moment. The hunt being sanctioned by Bret on my call to him threw me into predator mode."

Erin waited but she didn't move away. "It's okay, Jed. We'll work through this. All that blood really did do a number on you. This will have to be filed away as a warning in the future. I know you can control it. You were caught by surprise. This will calm you a bit. I found a restaurant near the killing in Arizona shortly after she disappeared from Walnut Creek. I sent the owner an official query from my Sacramento Police Department contact address with my badge number. She responded immediately, identifying Leslie as Leslie Benning. The owner also remembers the victim as a regular in the restaurant. This is huge. I have to keep on this restaurant angle. Will you be okay?"

No. Even as I admitted that to myself, my features returned to normal including my eyes. "I'll be fine. Stay with the restaurant connection. You're doing great. If you can line up a few more positive ID's, you'll really be set when you frog-march her into the station. Bret will be calling soon. Go on, Erin."

She nodded and returned to her terminal. I sat down with the predator lying only beneath my skin a millimeter away, ready and waiting. Bret called then.

"She scalped them, Jed. The scalpings weren't done in laboratory type form either. According to the FBI reports she yanked their hair like an Apache on the plains, and sliced the souvenir haphazardly but with a razor sharp knife. Everyone thinks it's a male attacker. All the profile bulletins have the assumed serial killer as a man in his late thirties to early fifties, Latino or

Native American, with a grudge because of a rejection or failed relationship with a blonde haired woman. Their profile states he is probably a trucker which would explain the random locations."

I told him about Erin's finding. "We have the right one, Bret."

"Excellent, Jed! We're behind you. Call if you need cover. Have Erin message me everything she uncovers with the restaurant angle. That is brilliant and damning. I hope you can take this Sharington woman like you have planned. I'm glad the CSI worker came to you. How did that happen?"

"Everett Zanki, the head of the CSI department, is a very good friend of mine. He recommended me to her."

"If you ever want to read him in on our connection I would not have an objection if you trust him. I'm sure he's smart enough to know how goofy ever trying to expose you would be to the public at large."

Interesting idea. If there was one person I trusted even more than my Mom trusts the Canelos, it would be Ev. I'd have to watch out he didn't have a stroke rather than worry about him exposing me. "I'll keep that under consideration. It's not needed right now, but maybe at another time it will be. We'll keep you updated. Thanks, Bret."

"No problem." Bret disconnected.

I joined Erin then as she spoke to someone on the phone in her Officer Constanza voice. The conversation definitely involved another confirmation from a former Leslie employer. When she finished with the conversation Erin typed in notes on the restaurant file the call concerned. She glanced at me with a self-satisfied smirk.

"I have three confirmations. Three so far that had the murder victims as customers and Leslie as an employee, all under different names. One Leslie trait rising to the forefront in my calls the three owners agreed upon: Leslie gave them the creeps. One said 'when she looked at me I could almost feel my blood getting cold'. He was the same one who added that her personality changed when interacting with the future murder victim. She became effusive, friendly, and caring when serving the victim. The victim actually wrote a sterling 'Yelp' online review of Leslie when she worked for him."

"She's going to be a great collar if we do this right. Bret sanctioned everything. He'll provide backup if needed too. He would like you to message him over everything you're finding with the restaurant angle."

"I'll do it right away," Erin agreed. "When you say sanction you mean arrest the perp, right? Getting into misunderstandings with MIB's is a bad idea."

I chuckled. "He meant working our plan as I outlined for him with the arrest. Give me half of the ones you haven't checked out yet. I'll research them up to the call and then hand it over to you if I have a promising contact."

Erin nodded. "Can you keep from killing her in your present state, Darth Jed?"

"We'll see soon." Great. Another point I hadn't considered – the inadvertent stranger kill in my heightened monster menace persona. I might say yes now and no...no...no later. "I'm glad you'll be with me tonight. Maybe we should think of something you could bop me with if it looks like I'm going into blood lust madness."

My suggestion made Erin grow quiet for a moment, but with a smile spreading slowly on her face. I hoped she wasn't contemplating anything too drastic. Knowing her though, I could never tell how far she'd go with one of my requests. I once asked her during a sleepover when we were kids to stay awake while I slept for a little while and tell me if she noticed anything weird when I did sleep. Erin noticed my fangs grew and retracted when I lapsed into a deeper sleep so she threw a whole bucket of ice cold water on me. I was in my bed at the time. It cured my subconscious of all notions regarding changes during sleep.

"I'll bring along a golf ball and hit you in the head with it," Erin volunteered with more enthusiasm than I cared for.

The idea wasn't too bad and could probably jar me out of it. "Okay... that sounds good."

\* \* \*

Leslie watched the front of her place of employment with the patience of a hunter. Her quarry avoided her clutches in New York, ruining an entire set of plans Leslie worked weeks on to maneuver into place. Becoming a friendly acquaintance to an arrogant bitch like Kelly sapped the energy from Leslie. She loved prey like Kelly. They sent Leslie into her huntress mode and satisfied a sick need deep inside nothing else came close to touching. Demeaning herself for almost a month every morning when the Kelly bitch came in had nearly driven Leslie to assault her before the preparations were finished. When Kelly had informed Leslie of being laid off and that she would be leaving that afternoon while stopping for her morning coffee, it was a devastating blow.

Politely compassionate with an iron will, Leslie took some comfort in wheedling the fact Kelly would be starting another job near Leslie's birth place out of her prey. Leslie mentioned the fact she grew up in Walnut Creek, very near Sacramento. When Kelly expressed interest Leslie told her she would be visiting her parents there within the next month. Knowing Kelly's habits, Leslie had taken the evening shift at The Rind, hoping to avoid any hard to explain meetings. Her stalking game turned feral as the continued sights of Kelly drove all thoughts of patient entrapment from Leslie's consciousness. When nearly captured in the act by a patrolling police vehicle instilled some reality into Leslie's head, she returned to her proven stalking invisibility with constant wardrobe and feature changes. She stayed away from Kelly's home for the most part except when completely safe.

Tonight was the night. Leslie created a perfect spot for Kelly's torturous demise. Her parents owned a cabin on the way to Lake Tahoe she now had the key to. Leslie called them once or twice a year. When they found out in her last phone call she would be visiting and working in Sacramento, they were ecstatic. So stupid. Her Mom and Dad were just as clueless about the creature they had raised as always. They had covered for her at every opportunity - pet mutilations, mean girl pranks at school leading to suspensions, and vandalism for any supposed slight from the neighbors. At home, Leslie perfected the role of innocence. She nearly threw up at the fuss they made over her, but when asked if she could use the cabin, they had been more than happy to accommodate their precious daughter. Soon, Kelly would be saying good night to her friends. Then, the fun would begin.

At nearly midnight, Kelly emerged from the restaurant bar with her three friends, laughing and chattering away like magpies yapping at each other on a tree branch. *Enjoy yourself bitch! I have the perfect place to show you a great time where I can hear you scream.* Leslie loosened the Taser gun under her windbreaker. She smiled, as much in love with the playacting at this point as the capture. Once incapacitated, Leslie would shove Kelly into Kelly's car, use the hypodermic with Fentanyl, and drive her to the cabin with restraints and gag in place. Leslie waited for Kelly to reach her Honda Accord parked on the street, scanning for any observer. This would be the tricky part when everything she worked for could crash down around her ears and she would be on the run.

"Hey... Kelly!" Leslie waved happily from across the street. "I thought that was you. I'm Connie Stallings from New York... remember?"

As she approached Kelly leisurely, Leslie could see the woman's features relax. "I'm visiting my folks in Walnut Creek and working here at The Rind on the night shift."

"Hi," Kelly replied as she opened her driver's door. "This is weird, huh? Are you working tonight?"

"No, I'm off tonight," Leslie answered pulling out the Taser gun. Then everything went wrong.

A huge blurry shadow encompassed Leslie, one vice like grip on her left shoulder, and another nearly crushing the bones in her wrist. She tried to kick, but was pinned by a leg with the feel of a steel stanchion jamming her lower body against Kelly's Honda. Leslie tried to wrap her finger around the Taser weapon trigger but the wrist bones began to crackle.

* * *

"Don't move any more, Leslie, or I break your wrist," I told her as Erin moved in next to Kelly, snapping pictures of our captured stalker with Taser still in hand and Kelly the obvious target. "You did real well, Kelly."

"That's her... the one stalking me? She...she was so nice to me at the restaurant in New York. I bought coffee there every morning."

Erin, in full uniform, patted her shoulder, guiding Kelly into the Honda driver's seat. "We have her. We'll see you at the station. Did you enter the address on your cell?"

"I have it. Thank you. I'll see you there."

"Okay, Jed, I've got it." Erin took charge of the Taser gun with gloved hands. She leaned to look into Leslie's face. "My associate will turn you. We will be cuffing you, gently if you cooperate, hurtfully if you don't."

I forced the still struggling Leslie around. I calmed her struggling with so little effort, I didn't tip off Kelly as to the force I used. Only Leslie's mewling moans gave any sign she was not having a good time being cuffed. Erin slapped the cuffs into place with her usual expertise. When I eased my pinioning position, Leslie tried to kick Erin. I smashed a side foot blocking kick into her ankle, nearly breaking it. Leslie screamed then. Erin smiled at her, patting Leslie's cheek.

"Don't be a slow learner, girl. Jed will not let you do anything but get yourself hurt." Erin Mirandized Leslie then with deliberate enunciation. "We're taking you over to the van for transport. If you cooperate everything will be easier. Do you understand?"

"Fuck you! I understand I want a lawyer… right now! This is ridiculous. I didn't do anything wrong. I'm a friend of Kelly's from New York!"

"Like hell you are, bitch!" Kelly opened her window to take a shot at Leslie's verbal ranting. "You changed your name and followed me here to kill me. Jed and Erin got you! They knew what you were going to do before you could do it. Now you're going to prison!"

Leslie allowed the innocent lamb look to drop away from her features. In its stead stood the creature raised in Walnut Creek who maimed, tortured, and killed for sport. "You better pray to your stupid God they don't ever let me out, little Kelly! I will make you scream for what you'll think of as an eternity."

I enjoyed Leslie's spew as did Erin. "Thanks, Leslie. Did you get that, Officer Constanza?"

204

"Oh yes I did. Go on, Kelly. We'll be at the precinct shortly. I need to stop by my house, but Jed and I will be at the precinct within the next forty-five minutes."

"Thank you both!" Kelly gave Leslie the finger, closed her window, and drove away.

"When I get free, I'll fix you two for interfering. This was none of your business!"

Erin patted her cheek again. "You are such a joy, Leslie. I believe you'll be saving the taxpayers a lot of money with all the nice things you keep saying. Please do go on. Don't let Jed and I interrupt. We'll play it back for entertainment value later after we supply the police and FBI with a copy."

Leslie turned sullen then as she finally realized through the rage how stupid she'd been. It was obvious Leslie never thought anyone would ever catch her. I could tell the wheels were spinning inside her creature feature mind, searching back over her days since arriving in California as to how we could have found her. I planned to introduce her to something a bit beyond what Leslie thought of as nightmarish. One thing I was sure of – by the time Leslie arrived at the precinct, she would be a somewhat more reformed creature with new purpose in her life.

I helped Leslie into the back of my van with Erin following. As I've explained although my van carried a plethora of equipment, it also was very spacious due to its custom enlarged cab. I sat Leslie down on one of the anchored chairs in front of my monitor bank. The blood lust flowed immediately, fiery and intense. My entire body tingled with anticipation. I didn't care about the images, memories, or putrid life Leslie led until now. I wanted her blood... all of it.

Leslie sensed something amiss finally after being seated with Erin and me grinning at her. Erin's grin originated in a satisfaction with justice. Mine originated in the fact I wanted to drain Leslie like a bottle of ice cold root beer on an August day in the Arizona desert. "I don't know what you two fucks are grinning at. Get me to the cops and get me a damn lawyer! I ain't sayin' shit to either of you."

"You won't have to," Erin told her. "Jed has a way with people. He can practically read their minds. Yep, my partner has a really neat trick you'll be amazed by."

Leslie spit on me. Well... she would have, but I moved my leg well before it reached me. It did hit my carpeted van floor. I didn't like that.

"Unless Gumby here can turn into a defense attorney I don't give a shit if he does card tricks and makes bunnies disappear. Lawyer!"

"You'll like this one, Leslie. Show her Jed."

I changed ever so slowly, finger nails, facial features, black marble eyes, and of course my fangs. As I eased toward Leslie, I allowed my fangs to extend toward her as a venomous viper would in warning off danger, only I was danger. My van sound proofing proved its worth as the Walnut Creek Creature Feature turned into a wailing waif with sound intensity making me fear for my special glass. I clamped a clawed hand over her mouth, anchoring her head in place with her neck exposed, arteries pounding under the skin with their siren call. I pierced her skin in minute increments, the rush of blood flowing in a wondrous symphony, fulfilling the grotesque need screaming from every cell in my body. It nearly obscured the creature's horrific life, memories, and dreams – almost. I released her mouth, grasping her shoulders as I sucked away Leslie's inner being with growing bliss.

"Jed!"

Somewhere, Erin's voice screamed out my name. I vaguely felt her hands slapping at me. Faces in a kaleidoscope of dark nightmare flashed through my head, begging, pleading, and finally screaming for mercy where none was forthcoming. In threaded dreadful streams of elated consciousness I felt Leslie's ghastly happiness as her razor sharp knife brutally slashed the scalps from her victims. I ripped deeper into Leslie's throat with monster zeal. Erin stun-gunned me. It was a mere irritation but persistence paid off as she cried out my name while juicing the crap out of me. I grabbed the gun jammed into my side, forcing it away while healing Leslie's throat. Erin backed off as I released Leslie.

"This isn't working, Jed," Erin gasped. "The lust is too strong."

I rubbed my side where the stun-gun electrode pain faded gradually. "What the hell happened to the golf ball?"

Erin held her stun-gun for my inspection. "This is the same as a million golf balls hitting you all at once. I had to go with stun force proportional to your Darth Jed power."

"So you never did bring a golf ball, did you?" I hated to admit it, but Erin brought along the right tool to keep Leslie alive.

"Nope."

"You stopped me. I guess you're working as a partner."

"What about her?" Erin gestured at my blood donator, the former Walnut Creek Creature.

I glanced down at the lolling headed Leslie. "What about her? We'll get her a juice and cookies at the Quick Stop on the way to the precinct. Did you want to put her on a donor list or something?"

"No, smartass, I was wondering about you compelling her."

"Done deal. She's mine. If they ever let her loose, she'll follow me around like a cocker spaniel puppy. I'll brief her on the confession she'll be making after we get her some juice and cookies."

Erin put her hand alongside my face. "You saw hell on earth in her head, didn't you?"

"Yeah, but I wanted to suck her dry for my own desire. Her blasphemy of a life was secondary on the feeding frenzy. You will be Detective Erin Constanza after this, Eerie. You drive. I'll call Bret to update him on Leslie."

Erin didn't move. "Maybe you better drive. Use your Bluetooth to call Bret. I'll stay with Leslie. You have water back here. I'll get her drinking that."

Disappointment flared which I hid instantly. "You don't trust me?"

"Not even a little bit when it comes to blood. I think I'm shedding my 'in thrall to the Darth Jed' malady. Take the wheel, Darth. You're in thrall now to Darth Eerie."

I planned to regain at least my dignity in this exchange. "I am helping you bring a serial killing maniac to living justice, Darth Eerie. It would be good to remember without me you would never have found her, let alone captured her."

She patted my head. "I realize that, my good little minion. Go now and drive to where we can obtain sustenance for our vicious killer before she gives herself up to the authorities."

I smiled. It was good Erin threw off the hold I had on her in all the exciting thrill of capturing Leslie. I planned to make sure she remembered a few of the more erotic moments from our night together. "I plan on extracting payment for tonight's grand criminal justice event."

"What did you have in mind, lowly minion?"

"I see muffins on the horizon."

Erin blushed. "I'm not letting you feed on me again if you have any notion of that. I wouldn't be safe even with my stun-gun."

"True, but my placing you within my power has nothing to do with feeding on you. I have many loving ways to bend your will to mine."

"Not happening, Darth. Now get in the driver's seat and let's get this freak show on the road. We can't keep Kelly waiting."

"This disrespect will not be forgotten."

"With me, it's already a memory. Get moving. Today, Darth Jed, today!"

I think I growled before Erin stun-gunned me again to keep me moving.

* * *

Erin, Kelly, and I watched with one of the detectives assigned to the case from a two way mirror outside an interrogation room where Leslie proceeded to explain in detail everything she had done. My prep work went exceedingly well. Everything we'd hoped for was now being recounted in a confession. The police incorporated both sound and video to accompany the written confession Leslie already provided them. Leslie and I came to an understanding as to the reasoning for her sudden wish to confess. Leslie explained once Erin caught her in the act, she felt relief and was determined to help the police close the other cases. The cops didn't argue.

Erin presented the case to the detectives, complete with her restaurant and murder victim connecting threads. The four owners she found to corroborate her findings made even an unlikely retraction from Leslie a minor inconvenience. Kelly represented the last step in an open and shut incarceration for Leslie – a live victim with face to face knowledge of Leslie's name changes, restaurant stalking, and lastly a video of an attack on her person by Leslie. Erin couldn't quit smiling. We progressed through hours of explanations until garnering the chief of detective's support. He came in early when informed the Sacramento Police Department was about to close a nationwide serial killer case even the FBI couldn't solve. Then the mayor streaked down to get in line for a media announcement press conference.

"Do you want in on the press announcement, Jed?"

Erin was being polite. She knew my aversion to any public record involving my being filmed. I did have some positive press for my apps with CSI, but I found early on in my wealth gathering it was best to stay in the background. Besides, I would be working on improving both my tracking app and the new stalking app I tested out on Leslie. "Nope. If you would be so kind as to mention my technical assistance with the apps I'm developing, that would be all the publicity I care to have. I have to stay relatively invisible to consult with Bret on cases with you."

"You mean feed on cases, don't you," Erin asked in a whisper.

"Very funny. My help certainly came in handy on this."

"I know... I know. The Chief and Mayor want to meet with me officially after the press conference along with my boss. This looks real good, Jed," Erin continued in a whisper.

"No need to whisper, Constanza." The detective with us named Leroy Sereno grinned over at Erin. "Everyone in the department knows you want a gold shield. After this catch I don't think they can keep you out. Once the Mayor starts dancing happily in front of the media with you, I doubt it would look good for the Chief not to promote you along with your commendation.

210

The press will eat up the youngest detective angle coupled with you being a woman."

"Thank you, Detective Sereno," Erin replied politely while shaking Sereno's outstretched hand. "Jed's tech insights help significantly."

"Call me Lee. Blake's your contact, right Jed?"

"That describes it nicely," I answered. "Erin and I grew up together. She's helped immensely with CSI consultations at murder scenes for my app developments. I supplied the tech help when she suspected Leslie."

"Your storyline fits perfectly. Stick to it, especially until we can make this Sharington case a done deal... both of you."

"Will do," Erin agreed. "Jed and I know what's at stake. After this, Sharington would have an impossible time contradicting her confession."

"That's the way we all feel about it too," Sereno agreed. "I've never seen one of these high profile serial killer cases go down quite like this one, and I've studied them all. This Sharington woman broke new ground with the scalpings. When she gave us the location of the souvenirs stored at her parents' cabin, the only thing that can screw us is a technicality. Because you nailed her with visibility, names, and locations, it's an air tight case. Be warned, there will be a bunch of ambulance chasing defense lawyers getting in line to argue any goofball angle they can create so as to get their names in the news."

"Leslie's refused legal representation," I said. I didn't like lawyers getting involved in anything. I had no experience in what outside pressure would do to my compelling power result, namely Leslie's confession eagerness. "What could a lawyer do to force her to get representation?"

"Petition the court concerning her mental health, claiming she must have been railroaded into confessing," Sereno replied. "I'm not saying it would ever happen or that they would have a snowball's chance in hell of the court granting it after this video confession and souvenirs. Anything is possible in this weirdo legal climate with the justice system turned upside down."

I nodded my understanding while wishing they would let her go. I'd suck her dry and throw her in my special ravine. The negative would be if they tried to pin the case failure on Erin. "Why don't we go get a coffee, Erin? We don't have to stay here, do we, Roy?"

"Nope. Don't go far though. The press conference will happen the moment they finish with her in there."

"We'll be here. Thanks," I assured him.

I led Erin out of the interrogation room. I didn't speak until we obtained coffee in the break room and sat down. "I'm a little worried. I didn't know about lawyers being able to force representation. How about you?"

"I've seen it happen before. They have to prove her mental incompetence to give a confession where she not only revealed where the souvenirs were, but also all the details. No judge in their right mind is going to countermand her confession and evidence. They may be rushing the press conference deal a bit though. I'd like to see them do it in a few days after the dust settles. The lawyers need a family member to authorize the appeal I think. Maybe Leslie's parents are in denial. I guess finding scalps in their cabin wasn't good enough for them."

"I should pay the parents a visit if this appeal was launched by them. I could go to their house with you as if it were an official questioning visit. I'll compel, feed, compel, and they'll dismiss the lawyers – easy finish for a potentially long court case."

"We can't keep fixing cases like that, Darth."

"What if one of those idiot lawyers creates some weirdo technicality like serial killing women who change their names when killing don't get charged?"

Erin enjoyed my pseudo legal filing of ridiculousness. "Not happening. If-"

A commotion with a woman screaming epithets while demanding a bunch of garbled items even I couldn't understand interrupted Erin's denial of parent appeals. We were finished with our coffee. I thought it a temperate decision to remain in the break room. Erin's cop persona ruled though as she felt obligated to be on hand if something threatening was happening in the police station. When we reached the point of interaction, an older version of Leslie stood inside the entrance past the initial check point yelling for whoever was in charge.

"Uh oh. I believe your 'not happening' parental intervention has arrived, Eerie. Let's go back and hide in the break room. The way she's going, they'll have her in a straightjacket shortly. C'mon."

Erin followed me on the break room retreat. With another cup of coffee we waited for the war of words to end. It dragged on, intermingled with official voices ordering her to calm down. It wasn't more than fifteen minutes later, the intercom requested both Erin and I report to the Captain's office. Erin and I had a stare down. She lost.

"Okay... maybe we need the fix in on this one. I don't see how you can do anything inside the Captain's office. We may have to go see them later if they'll open the door to us."

"We better get there before the Captain sends a detail to hunt us down. Do you know Captain Branch well?" I had spoken to Celia Branch a few times with Ev when introducing my app.

She was a medium height redhead with a lean stern face. She never struck me as someone who would take a lot of crap from some loudmouthed civilian.

"Only the usual run ins with her during regular duty. She's short tempered with anyone questioning anything she does, but she's fair. If we get a chance to get a word in edgewise we'll be okay. The Captain must be aware of the evidence stacked against Leslie including her confession."

We reached the Captain's office. I saw Mayor Roy 'Camera Commando' Haines through the glass standing next to Captain Branch. They were listening to a rant I could tell was Leslie's Mom. At least they toned her down a couple of octaves. Erin knocked on the door. Branch signaled her in.

"Are these the cops framing our daughter?"

Captain Branch appeared tired of listening to the woman's ranting, probably having explained the facts numerous times with no effect. "I will try informing you of an important fact you keep ignoring. Your daughter confessed to the crimes, told us where she hid the souvenir scalps, and explained in detail how she did each killing – all on video and audio."

"What about this, Officer Constanza?" Roy decided to pretend he hadn't jacked into the case too soon. He didn't want to look bad at the press conference with parents screaming frame-up.

"As Captain Branch stated, Leslie Sharington confessed to her crimes after I issued a Miranda statement, also on video. We caught her red handed getting ready to use a Taser on her next victim Kelly Lamb, an employee for the Sheriff's Crime Scene Investigation unit. We didn't know about the souvenirs at the cabin until she told us about them. I have four eye witness owners of restaurants she worked at across the country in exactly the location as four of the other murders. The four victims in those cases all frequented the restaurants Leslie worked at. We're contacting restaurants Leslie detailed in her confession. The only reason we found out about any of this was when Kelly Lamb requested help to stop the stalker terrorizing her."

"Thank you," Roy said with an unusually noncommittal voice. "Ms. Sharington, I don't know how much more the police can provide to assure you of the fact they have overwhelming evidence your daughter committed all of these heinous acts. Captain Branch has refrained from showing you the video of your daughter confessing and detailing what she has done at my request. If what we've provided for you isn't enough as yet I'll direct Captain Branch to show you the video confession."

I think Erin's no nonsense outline of events finally put Mayor Roy back thinking about serial killer press conferences. Not so, Leslie's Mom.

"Brain washing! I know what you people can do. You couldn't catch the real killer, so you made one out of my daughter!"

"You're delusional!" Captain Branch had enough. "I'll show you the confession right now along with the video of your daughter caught in the act of terrorizing an employee with the Sheriff's Department. If that's not good enough for you, then I'll have to ask that both of you leave the building and proceed in any way you deem feasible."

Mrs. Sharington leaped to her feet. "C'mon Bert, we're not sitting through a brainwashing demonstration. You'll be hearing from our attorneys!"

Attorneys? Oh boy. It was just as Lee stated. Even confessions are no good anymore. Captain Branch looked relieved as she held the door open for the Sharingtons. The Dad didn't look thrilled with the way their meeting progressed. I suspected he knew his daughter was not the brainwashed angel his wife portrayed. If asked, I'll bet he didn't ignore the pet mutilations around their house. I'd also wager he was relieved when she left the house. I doubt he suspected a killing spree blazed across the country by poor innocent Leslie, but he didn't seem all that much surprised. After the Sharingtons were out of the office and on their way to the door with an officer at their side, Branch turned to Erin.

"Great input, Constanza. If not for the fact the Mom's clearly out of her damn mind, I doubt we'd hear anything more about this except from the citizens commending you and Mr. Blake for taking a vicious predator off the street."

"Thank you, Captain. I appreciate your support."

Branch turned to me. "I'm hoping you can corroborate everything done on a technical basis in this case as an expert if need be at trial. This woman may be whacky enough to force it that far. If there's anything you're not telling us now would be the time, Blake."

"Nothing at all, Captain Branch. Everett Zanki recommended my services as a security specialist to Ms. Lamb. I fitted Kelly with a tracking device at her request because she feared being taken and never heard from again. It enabled Erin to notice our suspect stalker: Leslie Sharington. Erin asked me in on the case at that point to see if I could find any threads connecting Kelly and Leslie using the new app I'm developing for police departments. My app tracked her credit card purchases at specific times across country as she moved and worked from place to place. Erin began the detective work that nailed down the name changes and places of employment, matching them to the murder locales. She then began interviewing restaurant owners. After that it was easy to tip off Kelly and wait for Leslie to make her move."

"Incredible work, you two," Branch complimented us. "The lawyers are bombarding the Sharington parents with visions of suing the city for millions. They'll claim false imprisonment and every other goofball con they can convince them to try."

"We can't disregard the woman's concerns," Mayor Roy remarked. "We must make the public aware we take all charges of police wrongdoing seriously. Otherwise this-"

"Are you joking?" Captain Branch stared at Mayor Roy like he was a messy cow splat in the meadow. "You will do no such thing, Mayor. The last thing in the world we should do is claim we're following imaginary clues leading to imaginary frame ups. Each confirmation of guilt will be announced along with reaffirming Leslie Sharington's video confession. People aren't stupid except when they get fed idiocy from politicians questioning legitimate police work for no other reason than to be on all sides of something at the same time."

Mayor Roy's red face and tightening fists relieved all doubt Branch had nailed him on every point. "See here, Captain... just who the hell do you think you are? We'll handle this the way I see fit."

"No we won't. I'm going to the Chief next to brief him on everything that went down with the parents. I'm taking the video confession, evidence, and our two captors here with me. Then if you try and pull anything in the media to sabotage this case, I'll nail you with the facts, and make you look like a horse's ass. If you don't want anything to do with this case, stay the hell away from the cameras."

He stormed toward the door, actually meaning to run me over on the way or push me aside. Not happening. I Donkey Konged him. Mayor Roy hit into me, bounced, and hit the floor to the amusement of my female companions. I of course helped him to his feet where he had to take a moment before talking.

"How dare you, Blake!"

"How dare I what. You ran into me on your way to the door on purpose," I stated calmly. "You bounced and hit the floor. What exactly did I do?"

"Blake didn't do anything other than stand there," Captain Branch said. "Please go, Mayor. We'll be handling the case. It would be to your advantage if the media approaches you about the case, claim it's an ongoing investigation which it is."

"You've not heard the end of this disrespect, Branch!"

"Throw me under the bus at your peril, Haines. It won't go well for you."

After Mayor Roy stormed out, Captain Branch smiled at us. "I'll call you when I get a meeting scheduled with the Chief. Keep following through on the case facts. I've already informed your partner. Your shift is starting soon. Can you continue working the case from your patrol duties, Erin?"

"Absolutely. I'll keep contacting people having to do with the restaurants and gathering testimony. I'm sorry the lawyers got involved. Jed and I thought this was so airtight with her choosing to confess there would never be any kind of court case other than judgement in the penalty phase."

"That's how it should have been. I'll handle Haines. You took a murderous bitch from hell off the streets. It's our job now to make sure no one undercuts our prosecution of the case. The DA has already looked over the findings and confession. He told me he'll have her in court for arraignment in another couple hours. Keep your phone on. If anyone gives you shit about this call me directly. Blake… we need to get you a badge. I've heard nothing but good things about you from everyone. Would you consider a position where you could be consulted on a full time basis with my command here?"

"If it doesn't take me away from my computer app work I'd be happy to assist the police department in any way I can. I appreciate the opportunities given me in the past to visit crime scenes in order to field test and develop my apps."

"From now on, you will have permission to assist anywhere on any case within my jurisdiction. I want you to continue with your work. I've checked your consulting record. That you have not received one complaint in all the time you've worked the crime scenes allowed speaks for itself. You and Erin work well together. Her partner Tony also speaks well of you. Is it true you own a blood bank too?"

"Uh… yes, that's true. I have many investments in various endeavors." Boy, that blood bank mention came out of the dark.

Captain Branch chuckled. "Sorry. When I did a background check on you today, you were listed as a special consultant for an offshoot of the NSA. Then I saw the blood bank holding. You are definitely diversified, Jed. Can I call you Jed?"

"Of course." Bret must have already put a file document on any official search to cover me. I'd have to be careful around Branch. She was no petunia freshly popping up in the garden.

"What is it you do for the NSA?"

"CSI and tracking apps. I work on research and development much like I do here, Captain."

"Call me Celia. You two get to work. I would like all loose ends in this tied into knots before we have to get into a gunfight with the lawyers."

"Right away," Erin said. "Thanks again. I know taking on the Mayor is not conducive to job security."

"Think nothing of it. I can't stand the sight of that two faced prick. Don't quote me."

"Already forgotten, but enjoyed immensely," Erin said on the way out.

I gave the Captain a wave and followed Erin.

219

"Maybe I won't make the evening news tonight but I'll feel better about not being thrown under the bus before I even get to speak."

"Branch has your back, Eerie. Let's go work on your project before the shift with Tony starts. You must be dead tired by now."

"I took a power nap while we were waiting to hear the Leslie confession. Didn't you notice?"

I remained silent. If I said I noticed she'd want to know how. This was a no win question.

Erin sighed. "I snored, didn't I?"

"Very slight, Eerie… hardly noticeable. I would have woken you if it got loud. Let's get to work since you had your replenishing power nap. I'll do the speeding through data. You stick with the restaurant witness search. That's a hot one."

"Will do, Darth. I loved the way the Captain turned Mayor Roy's water off. I didn't believe any of our people in the department had the brass to do that."

"She's good, no doubt about it. By the way, in case you hadn't noticed she's not someone to spew idle comments around."

"Small doubt about that, Jed. I'll watch my mouth around her."

"Wise decision."

# Chapter Nine

## No Good Deed

I entered the parking garage to go home for some much needed downtime. I didn't envy Erin's shift start; but she seemed so excited about everything I figured the extra energy would wear off into a sleep coma when she got home. Then a limo drove next to me. The driver opened the driver's side window to speak. It was the Dotsenkos' driver, my minion Marko. He stiffly turned toward me. His face, a rather grotesque and swollen road map of what a professional pummeling will do, told a grim story pertaining to his life since I last saw him. A big guy in a dark suit sat next to him with a 9mm automatic in his lap. He looked like Fredo from the Godfather. I recognized the weapon, thanks to my Mitch Bennett dead sniper knowledge, as a Glock.

"Hello there, Marko. I see you're having a bad day."

"Yes Sir. Would you please get in the back, Sir?"

"Why would I do that, my rather beat up little minion?"

The big broken nosed thug next to him leaned around Marko with what he thought I'm sure to be an evil, threatening smile. "Get in, Blake. We have your Grandpa some place safe for now. I can't say how safe it will remain if you don't do as I say."

There would be no downtime now... only blood. "Sure. I'll be glad to ride along with you. Did Nikko and Seth ride along with you today, Marko?"

"They're in the back. I-"

"Shut up, ass-wipe! Get in now, Blake!"

"Right away, Sir. I don't want anything to happen to my Pa." I knew I should have waited a few days before giving the folks an all clear sign. I hope Pa didn't resist. Then he would probably be damaged. Then Erin's good little Dots would be praying for death in the near future.

I opened the back door, ready to move at Dhampir speed. I figured the Dots might have a couple guys ready to cap me right on the spot with automatic weapons. Nikko and Seth smirked at me as if they had solved a puzzle or something. Two other very professional mobsters in neat suits sat in the back with weapons pointed at me. Unfortunately for them, they didn't fire. It wouldn't have done them any good but at least they would have died with fingers on the triggers. I smiled at father and son Dot, giving them a polite wave of greeting as I entered the stretch limo.

"Hi there. How in the world did you two escape the justice system? The police must have loved your confessions. I smell a rat. Tell me all about it."

"My lawyer fixed everything," Nikko replied. "We luckily wakened from the drug trance you had us in before mouthing off about our entire lives to the cops."

"He claimed we were drugged at the restaurant," Seth added with his arrogant snarly tone woofing at me again. "We had not been Mirandized yet so the cops had no choice but to let us go."

"What the hell did you do to us?" Nikko may have remembered who he was, but he obviously didn't remember who I am, or he and Seth would be jetting to the ends of the earth. "What drug did you slip us? The last memory we have is seeing you and your cop girlfriend. You're dead, but I'll let your grand-pappy live depending on what the hell you did to us."

He was lying. I knew that much. Nikko probably planned on killing everyone I ever knew. A guy like him doesn't leave loose ends. I looked toward the front seat. Fredo glared at me with yet another smirk through the observation window separating the driver. That would make things easier and possibly keep my true minion, Marko, alive and well. I needed a driver and to get the soon very messy limo somewhere away from the police station. Then my phone rang. It was Bret. I pressed the accept call pad.

"I'll be happy to cooperate, Nikko. May I answer this call? It's a business associate who may come looking for me if I don't speak to him. You have my grandfather so believe me, I'm not going to do anything stupid."

"Go ahead. Make it fast and be damn careful about what you say."

"I will. Thank you." I put the phone to my face. "Hi Bret. I'm with some associates so maybe we'd better talk later."

"We know the address where your grandfather is being held. We were too late to stop him getting taken without possible injury. Would you like us to get him?"

I smiled. "No, but thanks for asking. Text me the address and we'll get together later."

"Will do. Good luck. Call me when you need cleanup."

"Indeed I will, my friend. Goodbye for now." I turned to Nikko after ending the call. "In answer to your question I didn't use any drug on either of you. I used mind control."

"Mind control? You think I'm playin'? Take us to where grandpa's being held, Marko. We'll tune the old man up a little while in front of dip-shit. Grampy's not going to like you much, kid."

Well now, that's real nice. My minion Marko knows where G'pa was being held. "Hold on for a moment, Marko."

223

I slashed weapon hands in the backseat, carving claws down to the bone in each thug's hand so fast the pain didn't hit them until the weapons fell to the limo floor. I continued forward, the index finger claw of my right hand punching through Fredo's forehead. He pitched into the dashboard as if shot. Marko screeched the limo to a halt. I smacked Nikko and Seth with a couple of bitch slaps that nearly decapitated them. The professionals began to realize through the pain they were in big trouble. I grabbed one by the throat while ripping into the other's neck with gusto. Oh God in heaven I loved every sucking second as I went through one mobster hot blood container to the next. Even their murderous lives seeped through one ear and out the other in flashes of bad deeds they would never commit again. I broke their necks after I finished dining.

"Are you okay, Marko?"

"Yes... Sir," Marko said fearfully glancing back at me. He didn't know what I was but he knew better than to run.

"Take us to where my grandfather is being held. Do you know how many guys are watching him?"

"Two, Sir."

"Good man. Let's go there and make things right. Shove Fredo down under the dash so we don't upset the parking garage personnel."

"Yes Sir." Marko kicked and shoved Fredo down as instructed, maneuvering so as not to get blood all over his suit.

Only then did I check on the Dots as Marko drove out of the parking garage. They both groaned and moaned gradually into consciousness. Their painful journey into eye blinking wakefulness would be nothing in comparison to what I had in mind for them. I patted them into a side by side position on the seat while they held their poor heads in hands. Nikko reached for something so I broke his reaching hand at the wrist. He screamed in pain very un-mobster like. I then relieved them of all their personal items.

"Marko's taking us over to get my grandfather. You're going to hide your nasty broken hand in your pants, Nikko, while you assist me in getting into the house with the least amount of resistance. Do you understand or would you like me to tune-up your other wrist?"

"I…I understand. I need a doctor! My hand… my hand's nearly severed."

By the earnest pain filled look I was getting from Nikko I could tell he was under the mistaken impression I cared. I thought what the hell, I probably didn't need him anyway. I broke his other wrist. I not only evoked a nice scream from Nikko, but Seth also joined in and he hadn't been touched yet.

"You'd better save your breath for sticking those hands into your coat pockets or your eyeballs are next."

Hearing my warning about his eyeballs Nikko began painfully stuffed each crippled hand into his coat pockets with Seth's help. I checked the personal weapons and belongings of each Dotsenko. Between the two of them they had Rolex watches and nearly five thousand dollars in cash. These two traveled flush. I passed the money and Rolex watches over the separator to Marko.

"That's for the damage they did to you Marko."

"Thank you, Sir. I wanted to be good as you suggested but they wouldn't let me."

"I know. They will now though. I could use a guy like you Marko. I know you don't understand what I am yet, but you seem capable of handling it. I could use a good driver that can keep his mouth shut. You would absolutely not be getting into any police trouble or illegal activities."

"May I think it over, Sir? Today has been one of those days if you know what I mean."

I enjoyed his response. Marko was sure right. "Take as much time as you need. No one will be bothering you again."

We arrived at a warehouse in Rancho Cordova on Trade Center Drive. I showed Nikko the same clawed index finger I killed Fredo with. "Which door do we go to, Nikko. Think carefully about how it would feel to have your eyeballs plucked out with one of these before you speak."

"The side door. It's a single door with no windows."

"Marko. Did you drop my grandfather off earlier with his captors?"

"No Sir. The guys who took him brought your grandfather here."

"Park by the side door, Marko. Call them, Nikko. Tell them to bring my grandfather outside to the limo. Make your voice sound calm and collected or I'll tear out the throat it originates from with slow painful precision. Enter the number they're monitoring and hold the phone to daddy's ear so he can hold a conversation. Don't forget I can hear everything."

A few minutes later the side door opened. Two gangster wannabes led my G'pa out the door. He wasn't marked and he had a big smile on his face. I grinned too. He probably pictured in his mind how well kidnappers would do using him as a hostage.

"I'm going to open the door. You sit quietly after you tell them to let him enter the limo. Do so convincingly until I get my grandfather inside or I pluck your left eyeball out and feed it to your son."

I opened the car door, stepped out, and waved at G'pa. Nikko leaned toward the opening. "Let him get in."

The guys with G'pa let him go. "Did they hurt you, G'pa?"

"No Jed. I knew you'd be coming for me. Otherwise I would have taken my shot."

"Sit inside and watch those two for me."

"Glad to." G'pa got in the limo.

I smashed a palm into the guy's forehead on my right, caving it in. The second one I fed on, ripping into his neck before breaking it. I turned to the vehicle. "Hit the trunk release, Marko."

The trunk opened. I deposited the two outside in the trunk, followed by the two thugs on the limo rear floor, and Fredo from the front. It was time for the Dots to go the way of the Dodo, directly to extinction. I fed so well my eyes were black as Nikko's heart. I didn't need any new memories to toss out from either of my Dots. I reached in to snap Nikko's neck while the horrified Seth screamed. I yanked Seth out of the rear, turned his head around in one fluid motion, and deposited him on top of the other corpses. Nikko was next. The limo had a great trunk. I was able to shut it without repositioning or bending any of my new corpses. I called Bret.

"Cleanup on Aisle four."

He chuckled. "We're on our way. I'll have one of my guys drop you at the parking garage. How many?"

"Seven, but they were all bad. The good guy's driving. He's going to work for me. I can use a driver for my Mom and Grandparents who can be trusted. I have something to talk over with you about all the action going on. I'd rather not do it on the phone."

"I'll be on scene in ten minutes. I'll talk to you then," Bret replied.

I returned to the limo. "C'mon, 'Pa, we'll wait out here. A new government friend will arrive shortly to take control of the situation. You too, Marko. Join us. My friend will arrange a ride for us to the parking garage. How did they take you, 'Pa?"

"I stopped at the store. They were following me because the moment I turned the engine off and opened my door they were on me. I was outgunned. I figured it might be connected to what you've been doing so I decided to wait it out. The Dotsenkos are the ones you allowed to live at Erin's request, huh kid?"

"Yep. I have to rethink the compelling aspect as permanent. I don't believe it is in every case. How are you feeling, Marko?"

Marko seemed confused at first. "Oh... you mean am I returning to my gangster ways, that would be no. Did you do the compelling thing on me?"

"I did but you seem to have gotten past my suggestive phase. You resisted Nikko's orders. I would say you've decided on a more positive side of the good and bad equation."

"I'm not going back to my old life. I would like very much to work for you. I've seen some of the things you can do, Sir. Are... are you really a vampire?"

"He's a Dhampir," G'pa answered for me, "half human, half vampire. A vampire sired him with my daughter against her will, but Jed turned out real good. It seems our lives are in an upheaval lately."

"I have someone to ask about the escalating number of events involving me. If I'm not mistaken that small caravan of black vans are here to help us out."

"Jesus... there are really vampires in the world?" Marko scanned the surroundings probably wondering if werewolves and zombies were about to attack. "Is your Dad still around, Sir?"

"No, my Mom staked him. Call me Jed. Easy does it, Marko. Don't try to absorb too much all at once. Stay quiet while I handle these government types. Do whatever they say if they need you to move or something."

"Yes, Sir." Marko kept his hands in plain sight and backed about twenty feet away from the scene.

"I'll join Marko until you're done sorting this out," G'pa said. "I hope these guys have a theory. Maybe you should join the priesthood, kid."

"You're just mean, 'Pa." I watched him inappropriately enjoying his smartass priest comment as he joined Marko. Bret walked next to me.

"I bet you're wondering why you've been skating along these past years without gangsters, government agents, terrorists, and serial killers; but now you're under siege by them, aren't you?"

"Yeah, along with friends and family. You have to admit this one shit-pile after another appears spinning out of control. If you have a theory I'd sure like to hear it."

"I know you're going to find this weird. We've studied you, Jed. When a couple of incidents have happened in the past you were directly tied into where you chose to feed, we expected more events would take place, but nothing happened out of the ordinary."

"Then why do you consider telling me that as being weird?" Bret wasn't making any sense. I thought maybe he considered my more public interaction to be causing an upheaval of supernatural forces. I admit I may have watched too many old 'Buffy the Vampire Slayer' episodes.

He paused as his men took charge of the limo after checking the trunk I pointed to. They decided to drive it away as is to a place more private I imagine. Agent Soransky gave me a little wave as he directed the operation. After the men left with the limo Soransky led a small team inside the warehouse to examine any contents of interest. I had tasted one of the guys. There wasn't anything in the warehouse. I called that fact out to him.

"Thanks, Jed," Aiden called back. "We'll collect their personal effects then and leave."

"We don't think this is the start of a demonic convergence or anything of the sort, Jed," Bret said. "Look at it this way – your expertise is growing to a point where people are noticing you, like your friend Zanki recommending you to Kelly Lamb. Add to it your Mom beginning to be more social and finding the man you helped with his daughter Marilyn. Your sphere of influence is growing. Therefore, your interactions multiply. It's only natural instead of seeking normal solutions to problems you would resort to the paranormal. We've been waiting and depending on it happening. Finally, after all this time, your importance is not lost on the pencil necks in Washington."

The light at the back of my brain began flashing. "You didn't want me thinking you were controlling all this so you could study my reaction. I'm beginning to think your hands off observing was important for me to develop as I did. I would never have done half the things I did already, especially building a worldwide corporation with varied product lines listed by numerous police organizations as essential for their productivity. In other words I'm a novelty of your making."

"You created it all, Jed. We're simply stepping forward in a time of need to back you and hopefully gain your enhanced help to fight off these new dangers cropping up all over the world. Nikko and Seth may seem like small gnats on a pig's ass, but Nikko acted as a conduit for illegal operations enabling many parts of the growing terrorist infrastructure. You brought down Bilal Al-Taei's network through your being at an assassination scene where your CSI expertise was needed. Your enhanced powers enabled you to stop Mitch Bennett, a world class assassin working for some very bad people. It's not a coincidence, Jed. It's a widening of your natural progression. With your wealth and this much appreciated continuing collaboration I believe you'll have your hand in on many more."

Damn, Bret made it all seem natural, even my killing spree these past days. "What's your take on my chances of dropping off G'pa and going home for some alone time?"

"I think since you've killed all known aspects of threat, going home for a quiet period is probably doable. Will Erin be joining you after shift?"

"Maybe. Erin doesn't know how the Leslie Sharington notoriety will haunt her through the day. All she really wants is the gold shield. To get the shield, she knows being in front of a camera will make it happen and watching her mouth of course. Erin will come over if it's possible; but with the complications from the Canelos' situation, nothing in the next few days will be a sure thing."

"Erin will be famous for the immediate future. I have contacts. I've heard the parents want to have you and Erin hanged."

"They've enabled Leslie all these years while keeping their heads in the sand. Everyone around them will be thinking of incidents from Leslie's childhood to torture them with. It will be a circus. It could be a great thing or a complicated mess. It has to be done. Leslie's a legitimate psycho. I've seen your evidence growing every moment. Only a technicality of biblical proportions can mangle that case."

I sighed. "I'll compel them to stay the hell away. It didn't work well with Nikko and Seth, but with Leslie's parents I might do a brain reboot on them."

Bret put a hand on my shoulder... a bad sign in my book. He proved my axiom true when speaking again. "I have another favor to ask. You said you knew Arabic now, right?"

Uh oh. I felt my downtime turning to dust. "Yes... I said that."

Bret chuckled. "Don't be like that. We've heard there will be a protest using the immigrant rights bullshit about how Muslims are all being subjected to harassment perpetrated in front of the Capitol Building tomorrow morning. That's the sacred hunting ground of the infamous 'Headhunter', isn't it? I was wondering if you'd mind practicing your new expertise for languages by mingling amongst the Islamist assholes tomorrow. Maybe you could eavesdrop on something of importance. Your risk of danger is low and we were only informed of the demonstration today."

"Why don't you let me find out who the leaders are? I'll suck them dry and then I won't have to eavesdrop for information, I'll suck it in for a win/win. They'll be dead, and we'll know what their target is."

My rather nonchalant suggestion silenced Bret for a moment. "Uh... there will be a crowd of them, Jed. I don't know how easily you could separate someone of importance so quickly. How would you be able to differentiate between the leaders and followers so fast?"

"I wouldn't." I think I found Bret's possible line in the sand for hired monsters. "You of course are assuming there are Muslims who have our best interests at heart. I've never been into the news that much but I don't remember any ever mentioned. I've heard a few on TV mouth platitudes about concerns over the slave trading, female subjugation and mutilation practitioners, who are responsible for nearly every murderous act going on in the world. I have not seen any of them do anything about their Islamist cave dwelling psychopaths running everything inside their so called religion. I would pluck one out of the crowd, sample him, and move on with new knowledge."

Bret smiled. "You think I'm pussying out because of the question, huh?"

"No, I needed to find out what my rules of engagement are. I also wanted you to know I harbor no illusions concerning the non-assimilating Muslim horde our leaders want to welcome with open arms while the rest of us poor schmuck citizens get murdered and subjugated under Sharia Law."

"You seem to have rock solid opinions about the only terrorist sponsoring religion in the world, Jed. Oh my... do I have to send you to sensitivity training?"

It's nice to hear Bret has a sense of humor. "That won't go well for you."

"I like your idea. Forgive me for not remembering your revelation in reference to being able to gain all knowledge from the person you feed on. I think of your abilities as skills. In reality, you can know everything intuitively from the blood. I will not make that mistake again, Jed. I'm sorry your compelling didn't have a permanent effect on the Dotsenkos. I was very interested in monitoring them if the effect had not dissipated so fast."

I gestured at my new driver. "It's worked on Marko over by G'pa. I don't think my compelling can change someone's nature. If they're absolutely rotten inside, I think my compelling effect will only last hours as in the Dotsenkos' case. If I get a really bad guy, I could try a mind wipe. I've never done one, but I could try it."

Bret nodded. "I would not be averse to you doing so. If you found a subject to experiment on tomorrow morning, it would be quite alright with me."

"I think we have an understanding then. If there's nothing else, I'm going home to await Erin. It will be very entertaining to inform her how well the idea of letting the Dots go free turned out. The guilt trip of getting my G'pa taken, whom Erin knows and loves, will make her think twice about overestimating my power to rehabilitate bad guys. The only reason I was successful with Marko is he wanted something better. Are you picking me up tomorrow or should I drive to the Capitol Building at a certain time?"

"I'll be there but I would prefer you drive over yourself. They have a permit to demonstrate at noon. If you showed an hour early, I'm betting you might find a likely subject for interrogation. I'm certain there should be a few of the leaders briefing their sheep on how to take this thing to the furthest reaches of insanity while pissing off as many people as humanly possible."

"I believe you're right, Bret. See you in the morning."

"Walters over there by the rear SUV is the one driving you and your people to the parking garage. He can drop Marko on the way if you're really serious about him as an employee."

"I am." I collected G'pa and Marko. Walters took Marko to the apartment complex he was staying at. I gave him a card with my personal number and reinforced my offer for employment. He promised to take the offer seriously. G'pa and I drove to Mom's house where everyone was waiting for us. G'ma came out on a dead run to engulf her husband in a mixture of relief, love, and retribution.

"You old goat! Damn it! I told you not to go out. There wasn't a damn thing we couldn't have done without until tomorrow or the next day. You nearly got yourself killed."

"I can't do much about it now," G'pa said. "Jed got me easily. He has a few problems tied into this deal, but the main thing is his compelling doesn't work on the really bad guys for very long. Erin talked him into letting Nikko and Seth go in the police station to confess. They didn't. They won't be a problem any longer, not to George or his daughter either. We're in the clear. He has some 'Men in Black' outfit covering for him too now. They've been watching him since the beginning, because they were tracking Aaron from Europe after Interpol warned he was a suspect in multiple murders overseas."

"Are you coming in, Jed?" Mom looked more than a little stunned at the news her actions were known in regard to my Dad. "Good Lord. Erin's going to go on the biggest guilt trip of all time."

"She'll be glad the lesson was relatively inexpensive this time. I have to take a more radical look at approaching this partnership with her. I can't follow her lead in moral terms blindly anymore. We'll be dealing with some extremely bad people in the future if we keep helping the 'MIB's' G'pa's talking about. I can't stay for any time today, but I'll get together with you all tomorrow night. I have another assignment for tomorrow morning. Marilyn should be able to return to her place tomorrow too. George and Marilyn are still here, right?"

"Yes," Mom answered. "I figured I'd better hear the news before I broke it to them."

"Good idea. I'll update everyone as I find out how this all works in reality. Erin will be with me tonight so I'll explain what's happening tomorrow in relation to our new 'MIB' partnership." I hugged everyone. "We're okay, and I may have an actual government agency working on my behalf. I don't blindly take orders either. So far, I think my handler may be queasier about my involvement than I am."

"You be careful with the blood drive, Jed. I'm worried there's a point somewhere we'll lose you to the blood." Mom stroked my face. "You've always been a good boy. I knew ignoring your vampire half would have to be dealt with some day. Please don't let this sweep you away from us down some bloody river of no return."

"I'm still good, Mom," I lied. "This will give you a laugh. Erin calls me Sith Lord Darth Jedidiah, Darth Jed for short."

"Oh my…" Mom said as my Grandparents enjoyed her discomfiture at my new Erin nickname.

"Chill, Jill," 'Ma told her. "It's catchier than Fang. Damn that Erin for upstaging me."

\* \* \*

I drove into my driveway with trepidation, the cause being Erin's car parked with her sitting on the hood. I didn't need to check any timepiece to know she left her shift early. I know Bret wouldn't have called her, nor would my family. It didn't take Sherlock Holmes to deduce she checked on Nikko and Seth in the system, found out they blew off jail, and then called Bret. She wore the look of the penitent, ready to flog herself to death over a blasphemous act. Erin was ruining my night of haughty enjoyment over being right about the gangsters. She looked so pitiful I lost my mojo. I parked behind her instead of heading to my attached garage structure.

I decided on pretending ignorance. "Hey Eerie, how the hell did you get off shift? No… don't tell me… Tony went into a coma hearing about the heroic Eerie and her serial killer capture, right?"

Erin sighed while approaching me to take my hand. "I checked on Nikko and Seth while putting together the file on Leslie's former employers. I'm so sorry, Jed! I called Bret to warn

236

him about those two escaping the system. He explained you already handled it. How's 'Pa?"

"He's fine. Don't sweat it. We know better now. We can't overestimate my compelling power trying to play God. It doesn't work that way. It's still great in the short term even with hardened criminals like the Dots. G'pa's great – not a mark on him. He relaxed and waited for me to arrive. The Dots are done. Let's put the vehicles in the garage and go have some wine. I'll make you my famous turkey sandwich with onion, tomato, pickle, and cheese, all smothered in rye bread with gobs of mayonnaise. You'll feel better in no time."

Erin smiled. "Sounds good. Thanks, Jed."

* * *

While quietly enjoying our second wine helping we devoured my luncheon turkey super sandwiches. As in the past we also enjoyed a comfortable silence. I could tell the first wine smoothed the wrinkles across Erin's forehead. By the time I delivered on my super sandwich promise she floated along humming one of the songs from a mix disc I had playing through my excellent speaker system. One bite into the sandwich and my Igor was lost. I poured us another wine and sat down to eat my monster munch. Yes, I love people food. It would have been even better with a blood cocktail, but... get thee behind me Satan! I can't think like that. I smiled. At least not until I could get a taste of terrifying Muslim tomorrow morning. I thought of the old cliché I used earlier - 'they taste just like chicken'.

Erin paused with only a little left of her sandwich to take a few sips of wine while frowning at me. "You're grinning like a dog who just ran off into the woods with the family pork roast fresh from the table. What aren't you telling me?"

237

So much for guilty penance. "We have another assignment from Bret, depending on your shift tomorrow, there will be a demonstration Bret-"

"He told me. I have tomorrow off thanks to the files I turned in on nailing Leslie. Do you think she'll recant the testimony like Nikko and Seth did their confessions?"

"Not as soon as they did because I drained her down to coma level before adjusting her mental picture of what she should confess to the police. Eventually, in a day, week, or month, the creature inside her will surface though."

"I have a complete witness backup list arranged for trial if it comes to that. All the restaurant people remembered her and the victims. Some of the owners knew other employees who can testify that she changed serving areas to be with the victims. Captain Branch ordered an immediate tox screen on Leslie to prove we didn't drug her by a third party lab to go along with the one done by our own unit. With the video confession, details, and souvenirs it would take one humongous blunder to set her free. The parents have a team though. There are four lawyers working pro bono on the case because of the notoriety, according to the Captain. By the way, Tony gets an extra day off too thanks to me, so I'm golden with him."

I cleared away the dishes, taking my wine with me while rinsing them for the dishwasher. Erin followed me over to the sink with her wine. She loaded the dishwasher while I rinsed. I didn't interrupt the quiet moment, especially after betraying my anticipation for blood in the morning mission. Erin poured a third glass for us when finished. We went into the living room which is done in seascapes, leather, and polished oak. We sat together on the plush loveseat listening to the music mix.

"I want you to taste me again, Jed." Erin put her wine glass down and gripped my stunned face in between her hands. "I know it's sick or stupid... or whatever. I can't get it out of my head. The

238

feeling was so intense as to be indescribable. I haven't been able to think of anything else when I see you. Even with so much going on around us and the questions you've mentioned Bret might be able to answer, all I care to experience involves feeling your fangs sinking slowly into my neck. The explosion of images shattering all other thought cascading through my head surpassed any other feeling I've ever had."

Okay... I'm screwed. Either I get some damn control or I'm going to kill Erin tonight because I will not be able to resist her appeal. I don't know if sick describes what intrigues Erin, but stupid definitely does. She fired all my monster receptors off at the same time with her request. I decided to try a last ditch attempt at a subject change. I put my hands on her shoulders after setting aside my wine glass. Erin's mouth opened slightly, eyes closing, breathing immediately becoming labored, offering the slender pulsing arc of her neck while slipping the blouse straps off her trembling shoulders. She turned her back to me.

Oh good Lord in heaven help me. "Erin! Don't you want to know what Bret thinks about all these... you know... events happening?"

"Darth!" Erin refused to look at me. "Please... hold my hands. Do it ever so slowly... just as you did it the other night. Don't think. Keep your eyes open, watching my face as you sip from me. Make the moment last without consuming me. Join me... in thought and vision."

She reached back to grasp my hands where they were tentatively doing her bidding. I was lost to her body and soul. Erin's touch electrified me. The feel of anticipation in the air overwhelmed all hesitation. I leaned down to the drumming river of blood beneath her skin, my fangs extending into twin conical needles. They pierced the hot lava of Erin's life. I drew her essence into my mind without taking my eyes away from her flushed face. Erin squeezed my hands, shuddering to hold on while a gasping intake of breath ripped through her. I battled the monster clawing my brain apart, ordering me to grip Erin in a life-force draining interlude of horror. My internal war hinged on what Erin suggested – watching her face while the flash flood of our memories together chained the beast raging for control inside me. I glimpsed the innocent young Erin from the riverbank long ago, peering at me from the darkness. I healed and withdrew from Erin, releasing her numbed hands as I held her to me, humanity slamming back into my head.

She leaned into me, her hands clasping my arms where they held her. "You controlled it, Jed. Did… did you see her?"

"The girl?"

"Yes. I sent her to you. I could sense the razor edge of death hovering over us. Were you close to losing it and killing me?"

"I'd be a liar if I told you I wasn't. You knew it was stupid to do this. This isn't a thrill ride at the amusement park."

Erin broke free, turning to kneel on the couch over my lap with her arms clasped loosely around my shoulders. The hem of her dress rode upwards past thighs and my sanity. She lunged to kiss my slightly bloody mouth, moaning as she writhed with wanton passion, driving all other thought and questions from my mind. Into an all-consuming dark desire not to be denied, we plunged with full knowledge this time of the consequences we ignored.

\* \* \*

First light of day broke the darkness into shadowy streams over Erin's sleeping body. I smiled while stroking her body with my fingertips from shoulder to ankles. She groaned while turning her back so my hand would glide upwards over her. I continued my ministrations with utmost concentration on feather soft touch.

240

Minutes later Erin moved as I hoped, springing up from the mattress with an annoyed gasp into my arms, surrendering to the loving assault I planned.

Much later, I served Erin an omelet and jelly toast with plenty of juice. She drank thirstily as I ordered the whole time I cooked. Although I controlled the intake of her blood, I knew what I did drink would need replenishing. We ate together then in quiet enjoyment, both of us avoiding any dissection of the night's sojourn. My doorbell rang seconds after the motion sensors pinged a visitor's arrival. I noted it was only 9:30 am, and Bret would call before coming. Erin wore only a blue silk robe she kept at my house, but I wore jeans and black t-shirt. I checked the monitor in the kitchen.

"It's a couple of suits," I told Erin.

"Maybe they're Bret's."

"I doubt it. I'll ignore them."

Erin chuckled, coming over to hug me from behind. "I'll go take a shower. We'll have to leave for our Capitol Building demonstration soon anyway. Be polite. Don't make enemies you big blood sucker."

"You're mean."

"You charmed me into a helpless victim last night, seducing me to the dark side against my will, nearly sucking me into an empty husk."

Erin ran for it, forgetting I move faster than she can think. I awaited her at the doorway out of the kitchen in full Dhampir mode, fangs, claws, and attitude. She yelped as I swept her into an unbreakable grip while ravishing her neck with tongue and fang tips. In moments, Erin clasped me to her without restraint but then wiggled for freedom.

241

"Let me go, Jed. Check on your guests!"

I released her. "Okay, but I'm not forgetting that 'seducing you to the dark side' remark, Eerie. You will have to be punished."

She slipped her robe down while moving away. "Oh my, whatever will I do against the Darth Jed of nightmare?"

I pointed at her warningly. "I'll be finding out very soon, Eerie. Mark my words."

"That's big talk from a Fang with mommy issues."

"Cheap shot, Eerie!" I didn't know if she heard me because she made a run for it, knowing I planned to answer the door.

I opened the door for my sharply dressed visitors. "Hi, can I help you?"

"I think we can help you," the taller brown haired suit told me. "My name is Carter Sanders. My associate is Jerrod Lane. We're part of the legal team assembled to defend Leslie Sharington. May we come in and talk with you?"

"Nope. I'll come outside and talk with you for a few minutes. I'm not sure what you could help me with though." I didn't want them to see Erin and I knew enough to say as little as possible to them about the Sharington case. "I work as a consultant for the Sacramento Police Department. I have nothing to share with you about the case. I will not jeopardize a deadly serial killer's trial by blurting details having anything to do with her case. I hope for quick judgement and incarceration of Ms. Sharington after hearing her confession."

"I'm sure you haven't heard but Leslie recanted the confession," Lane said. "She claims you and Officer Erin Constanza drugged or hypnotized her."

I grinned. No way would I comment on that crap. "And I should care about what a confessed murderess claims why?"

"Your computer enhancement apps company could be held liable for your actions in the matter. We plan to bring charges against you in civil court unless you admit to coercing Ms. Sharington into the confession."

I opened the security screen door, stepping onto the large walkway to join my two legal bloodsuckers. Professional courtesy. I scanned the immediate area as if trying to find something. "Okay, where are the cameras. I'm being 'Punked', right? Listen. You two are very cute but I have nothing to say. What in the world would make you think I'd be afraid of having my lawyers go against Sharington's legal jackals in court?"

Lane opened his suitcoat to reveal an automatic handgun at his hip in a fancy holster. "We're not exactly lawyers. Carter and I are the consultants who talk sense with potential witnesses. You're a big tough guy. We don't want any misunderstandings."

I ripped his piece out of the fast draw holster, ejected the clip and cleared the chamber before he could blink. "I don't want any misunderstandings either. How about you, Carter? Would you like to show me your weapon too?"

Lane stared from his confiscated weapon to the holster in stunned disbelief. "How the fuck did you do that? Give me my gun back!"

I handed it back into Jerrod's trembling hand, seeing Carter was no dummy. He stepped away with his hands in the air. He didn't understand what I'd done either, but he didn't want a demo. "Stick the clip in your pocket Jerrod or load the weapon. Either one is fine with me. Did you two think to intimidate me? If so, you're wasting your time."

"This isn't over bigshot," Jerrod told me as the two of them backed away. "Perhaps Officer Constanza can be made to see the error of her ways. After all, she's the official responsible for this miscarriage of justice."

"Take my advice and leave her alone. Threatening police officers in the performance of their duties will land you in prison." Not to mention I'll hunt you all down, rip your heads off and drink from your collars like a cup. "What in the world are you bunch doing all this for. Sharington murdered a bunch of young women. Why in hell would any bunch of ambulance chasers be interested in freeing a confessed serial killer?"

They glanced at each other before Jerrod nodded at Carter. "Mrs. Sharington is the daughter of Senator Clifton Berry."

Well damn, that explains a lot. This is an election year. Berry was already in full campaign mode. His radio commercials and placards were everywhere. Having a serial killer granddaughter would not be an election enhancer. Berry ran on a pro-abortion, pro-illegal immigrant, pro-Middle East refugee, anti-Second Amendment platform. He had even made comments about California needing to adopt a more open policy regarding Sharia Law. Tying him in with Leslie would be so sweet I could taste the sugar.

"Oh my, that's lovely. I can sure understand why Leslie's Mom could bring in the big guns for her serial killer creature from the Black Lagoon. It doesn't explain how coercing witnesses would be a political resume enhancer either."

"The Senator simply wants justice for his granddaughter," Carter claimed with a straight face. "He knows she's being railroaded. What exactly do you have for evidence to prove Leslie did anything wrong?"

Yeah, like I'm going to go over it with you, dummy. "The defense team will get full disclosure well before any trial. What could I tell you that Leslie's actual legal team won't have full access to anyway? The prosecution has to make it all available."

"We'd like to get ahead of the many lies being circulated about Leslie," Jerrod found his voice again. "Senator Berry could be a big help to you, Blake. His favor counts for something, especially to a businessman like yourself."

"First you show me the stick and now the carrot, huh? I don't want the time of day from your Senator Berry. There isn't a single thing he stands for that I believe in. The fact he may take a political nosedive because of Leslie warms my heart. You two run along now. Thanks for letting me know why in the world anyone with even a glimmer of a brain would ever defend Leslie. Do yourselves a favor and ask to hear her taped confession. Even a couple of leg breakers like you two would be shocked."

"We work for Berry," Lane told me, pointing in what he probably thought of as a threatening manner. "Don't do anything stupid. Think about backing away from this. You don't want Carter and me to come visiting in the dark some night."

I started laughing. The thought of these two girl-scouts coming after me in the dark would probably make me laugh out loud inappropriately for the next couple weeks. "Oh... good one... you two gerbils coming after me in the dark. Oh my, what fun we'll have. Please... you both have an open invitation. My advice is to kiss everyone you care about passionately before you leave the house hunting me. Tell the Senator to pay whatever it takes to erase his bloodline. If Leslie's confession and our evidence hold up in court, every true news outlet he doesn't own will get a full helpful outline of Leslie's familial ties to Berry along with what a neat human being she turned out to be."

Lane lost his grip for a moment. "Is the same invitation good for that little tasty treat, Officer Constanza?"

I ran Jerrod over. When I run you over, it's pretty much just like when a car hits you. I smashed him flat and unmoving to my pavement. When I turned to take care of Carter, he was again smartly standing still with hands in the air. "Your buddy's a slow learner, Carter. I hope you have more brains in your head than he does. Otherwise, when the two of you come after Officer Constanza or me, I will make your deaths a passing into hell never seen before. Get Lane on his feet and get the hell off my property. If you see me at any time in the future… run. It may save your life, depending on how I feel that day."

"I…I understand." Carter helped Lane to a sitting position. Jerrod was snoring.

"I got him, Carter." I plucked Lane off the pavement with one hand bunching his suit together, holding him snoozing in the air. "Show me where you're parked."

Carter fumbled with his keys, dropped them, picked them up and dropped them again. He grasped the keys finally while taking a deep breath. He then led me over to a late model BMW and beeped the doors unlocked. I jammed Jerrod into the passenger seat before pointing over the BMW's roof at Carter.

"Don't forget what I said, Carter. Advise Senator Berry to shore up his blasphemous run for a senate seat in the greatest country on earth using some other traitorous trick he's learned over the decades. If he loses, he can still steal money from us dumb-shit taxpayers for the rest of his putrid life. I doubt if Iran or Syria or whatever other sandpit bought him will have poor old Berry eliminated. He'll be fine."

Carter nodded his understanding. He dived into the driver's seat. The BMW squealed around my driveway for the road beyond. Just what I needed: another complication. I always look on the bright side because I planned to feed on all my problems. Hell, I fed on Erin last night and I love her. Darth Jed… you are indeed a monster. Erin awaited me on the other side of the door.

"I watched what happened on the monitor in the kitchen. I hope Senator Berry doesn't have anything to do with funding for Bret's agency task force. Those guys meant business. Intimidation of witnesses is a risky endeavor. They were confident which means Berry thinks he can do anything he wants. Do you think you'll be in trouble for bouncing the Lane guy off the pavement?"

I decided to try out my new philosophy on Erin. "I've decided to feed on all my problems and troubles. It's less complicated and um...um good."

"Very funny. You do realize if feeding on troubles and problems becomes your normal confrontational style you'll wind up on top of a windmill with angry villagers below carrying pitchforks and torches, right?"

"I'll consider your input on the matter. Moderation in all things."

"Get Bret's take on your new problem solving formula. I don't think he will approve." We sat at the kitchen table with coffee. Erin remained silent for a few seconds before going on. "By the way, what exactly did you have in mind for me at the demonstration today? The Sharia Law types believe women should all be in burkas. I don't think they'll like my infiltrating their coven of airheads in normal clothes. It will piss them off. Is that what you had in mind for me?"

I admit I forgot for a moment this is the new America where we have to consider third world cave dweller mentality whenever we try to do anything. "Gee... let me think. We're going to an American state Capitol Building where possible terrorists we don't even know are citizens will be demonstrating their first amendment rights we don't know they deserve. Erin Constanza, an actual United States citizen, worries the Islamist toads may be pissed off because she is a woman walking around on American soil without dressing like a Jawa sand-creature from Star Wars movies. I think I should let you piss them off in that very attractive short dress, feed on a couple of them to find out what they're up to, and call it a day."

Erin sighed. "I thought that might be your mindset for the day in regard to my helping. I imagined a more mundane role where I stayed in your van monitoring and recording while you circulated amongst our suspected mob. I could then caution you if I see or hear you forgetting to act with restraint. I didn't know it was our job to reverse the idiot actions of our Islamic ass-kissers in government who are making it impossible to staunch the flow of fifth column terrorist infiltrators. See... I can play the word games too, Darth. What'll it be?"

She's good. "You're right but I don't have to like it. I'll be set for video and audio. You monitor and record. That way you can check faces too for any known leaders on the terrorist lists and databases. If I locate one or two, I'll try and compel them to follow me somewhere private where I can learn what they have planned."

"Now you're talking like the devil-may-care Dhampir I grew up with. When did you start paying attention to the Islamist/Sharia Law insanity creeping into our lives on the backs of coin operated politicians?"

"I am not blind or stupid to what goes on in the world, Erin. I never mentioned it before because like the rest of our citizens getting screwed, I didn't have a way to fight back. Now I do. We fixed a big gash in our armor with the mosque raid. Thanks to what they found there the idiots who forbade any search of mosques and masjids now have to answer for their stupidity. Our vaunted know-it-all government hacks have to admit the troglodytes from the sand are using their so called religious places as weapons dumps. In any case, I'll be careful today. Don't wait too long if I sink my teeth into a tasty meal from the overseas sand-pits. I might forget what I'm supposed to be doing before you chime in."

"Agreed. This is exciting to be on the front lines against a hidden enemy right here in our country," Erin said. "We have government cover too if a certain Fangster can control his baser instincts."

"I controlled them last night, didn't I?"

Erin blushed and looked away. "It's not fair for you to mention a moment of weakness on my part and beat me over the head with it at every opportunity."

"Oh, so now it's my fault because little Eerie pulls her top down, offers her neck, and claims I have to feed on her again because she can't think of anything else. Is that the new paradigm of our relationship?"

To her credit, Erin giggled. "Good one, Darth. I'll dial back my accusations in reference to your control until I can get a handle on my own. Damn though, it is the kinkiest, most erotic experience ever."

"I'm getting hungry just talking to you. Let's go find some real sand creatures for me to feed on."

"Don't forget your sunglasses, marble eyes."

# Chapter Ten

## Healing Factor

I walked amongst my potential targets an hour before the demonstration began. They were huddled in small enclaves, working over last minute details concerning chants, placards, and speeches to eventually be given once the hoped for media morons arrived. I did the repeated As-Salaam-Alaikum in true humble form, allaying suspicion because I could keep speaking in fluent Arabic. They didn't know what to make of me or what to do with me. I kept moving as if waiting for direction.

"You need to mimic the ones I'm seeing from your cam, Darth," Erin informed me. "Walk around with a belligerent scowl on your face as if you're ready to attack anyone looking at you cross-eyed."

"Thanks for the input, but I think I'm getting a bite. There's a small squad angling towards me. They look like they mean to interrogate me. So far the only phrase I've heard that they plan to bop around on placards is a rip off - 'Muslim Lives Matter' which begs the question."

"Don't say it, infidel."

"To whom? I mean as a Muslim your fellow cave dwellers are responsible for every act of violence and terror in the world. Surely, someone understands there will be people who come to the conclusion maybe we need a lot fewer Muslim lives, and the only matter left of substance is how we accomplish that goal."

"Oh boy," Erin muttered. "I guess you're hearing this, huh Bret?"

"I am indeed," Bret answered, with laughter in his voice. "You'll never guess who arrived while the group approaching you formed. Your favorite Senator Berry talked with them for a moment before they trekked toward you. I think you've been outed, Jed."

"What would you like me to do?"

"The two in the lead are on every watch list in the country. If you could compel them into a private meeting maybe they would follow you somewhere private."

"I'll give it a shot." Six men approached with those stupid looking scowls they've perfected when cutting the throats of bound hostages. I kept my eyes on the leader - a bearded, tight mouthed scumbag with an attitude."

"The one you're staring at is on every list, Jed. He's been implicated in terrorism overseas after being allowed into the country without a thorough vetting during the last suicide attempt by our government," Erin stated.

"I wish I could say Erin's wrong, but that sums it up nicely," Bret added.

"I don't often eat Halal, but when I do, I prefer Islamist nut-bag best," I whispered to the appreciation of my listeners.

"You!" Nut-bag pointed at me with head jutted forward in what he thought was a scary approach. He's so cute. "I have been informed by reliable sources you are a spy, infiltrating a scheduled demonstration that has already been sanctioned. You will leave immediately!"

I started laughing. I couldn't help it. The irony of Islamist shitheads showing in numbers to demonstrate for First Amendment rights while denying an actual citizen his First Amendment right was not lost on me. Then dimwit decided to lay hands on me. I broke them both while stepping away. He screamed and hit the ground.

"Don't interfere, Bret! I need to allow the rest of his buddies to look like they're attacking an unarmed innocent before I break things on them."

Bret sighed as I faced off with the henchmen. "A camera crew's already filming from nearby. I hope you can make this look good, kid."

"Be careful, Darth," Erin said, knowing I was beyond turning away.

I moved slightly, covering myself with hands, arms, and legs, defending while weaving enough to make it look like the desperate dance of a trapped man. My attackers learned hitting me did not feel good at all, especially since I never let them hit anything other than my blocking limbs. When the knives and box cutters made their appearance I had already located the cameras. I also noticed what direction half a dozen capitol police were approaching from.

I began with blocking a box cutter swipe at my face, striking the inside of his wrist with my side hand block. It broke like Juliet's heart upon discovering her dead Romeo, loud and screaming. The knife thrust sailing by near my ribs I struck downward with an elbow, shattering his hand bones as if they were soda crackers. A third sap jutted forward in a fake thrust. His nose bone flattened horribly into his features. I pulled the punch so his head wouldn't detach and roll in the opposite direction. I danced around between my remaining two attackers never letting them get a clean shot at me. Then my maneuvering turned the scene into a Jackie Chan movie as I slipped away from between them as they delivered thrusts low to each other's guts. It was a thing of beauty. The police fumbled through a throng of press and bystanders as I covered my head pretending to be anticipating the next blow. The crowd, mostly working stiffs going to work, began cheering and applauding.

"Oh Jed, that… was beautiful," Erin said.

"What she said," Bret added. "It's perfect. I'll be down in a moment to take the leaders away from the Capitol police. Press charges you poor victim of a brutish assault."

"On it," I replied simply, uncovering for the police. They gawked around at the casualties, trying to figure how I finished an assault by six armed men standing with no perceivable wounds. The attackers, with weapons strewn on the ground around them, were writhing in agony. "I…I want to press charges, officer. I was attacked by these men for no reason. I'm a consultant with the Sacramento Police Department and the FBI. I was asked to monitor the demonstrators because I know Arabic. An agent of the FBI will be meeting me here shortly."

I produced my credentials. The officer looked them over carefully just as Bret joined us with Aiden Soransky at his side. They both had their Homeland Security Special Agent credentials out. "I'm Special Agent Bret Grein, and this is my associate Special Agent Aiden Soransky. We're here to arrest those two ringleaders on the ground. Jedidiah Blake, our consultant on this case, recognized those two as being on numerous wanted lists for terrorism overseas."

The officer was relieved to see Bret. He immediately cooperated with Bret's directions to get the injured men arrested and an Emergency Transport called in for triage treatment of the wounds. In the meantime, other officers took statements from the news crew and bystanders that exactly matched my claim of being attacked. The news crew seemed reluctant because they strayed from their agenda to defend what their cameras actually recorded. If they wished to replay any of it on their news programs their witness statements would have to match. The minor brawl also threw the demonstration squad into disarray. I also noticed Senator

253

Berry fled the scene the moment I didn't get my ass kicked into the next hemisphere. I'll have to find a way to repay the Senator's visit. It would be a great fact finding taste, very possibly revealing a multitude of traitorous acts he was involved in.

It took a while for the emergency medical techs to arrive and patch our poor Islamist assholes. Once that was done, Bret confiscated the two we wanted with us for further questioning and away we went. I rode with Erin, but not before offering to give my two broken terrorists a chance to ride with me. Bret and his crew enjoyed the reaction quite a bit. The ones Senator Berry set on me, Amal al-Banna and Kaul Takfir, dived against Bret's vehicle citing everything from diplomatic immunity to Climate Change in order to avoid going with me. Little did they know I would be the one snacking on their information.

"Let's not get too fancy," Bret said. "Why don't we go to your estate? It's not that far and it's private. We can tell the locals if information is requested that we questioned them in DC, and shipped them for 'Rendition' to Egypt."

"Works for me. Erin and I will speed ahead now. I'll leave my garaging facility open for you to follow. Once inside, the doors close, and we can get busy."

"How are you handling the blood, Jed? I could tell you were having trouble with restraint issues. You did incredibly well in an open confrontation this morning."

"It's a process," I admitted. With the surveillance Bret had on me, I was unsure how many half-truths I could get away with. "I'm better than after the mass bloodletting recently. That was a shock to my system. My control is getting better all the time. I felt the urge to go on a rampage this morning, but the thrill I got from turning the assault into an open arrest with video nearly surpassed the urge."

"Darth is doing real well, Bret," Erin chimed in agreement.

254

"Darth?"

"Oh... sorry Bret... I started calling him Sith Lord Darth Jedidiah or Darth Jed for short after the blood massacre. I thought I mentioned it to you."

Bret and crew were amused with that piece of Erin information for a few moments. "That...that's very good, Erin. We'll have to have a codename for Jed anyway in the future. I'd rather not use the Dhampir one we've been using. We'll change it to simply Darth."

"Simply Darth is not amused. It's bad protocol to allow my minion, Eerie, to disrespect me in front of company. I guess it doesn't matter. Let's go, Officer Constanza, before you blurt out anymore verbal gems."

"Yes, Darth."

\* \* \*

Amal and his buddy Kaul exited Bret's transport van in obvious distress, especially since the first person they saw was me waiting for them with arms folded over chest. Erin shut the garage doors. Amal turned to the smiling Bret with a combination of fear and outrage showing through on his features.

"Why have we been brought here? This is not a detention facility. Take us to the proper authorities. Kaul and I will say nothing until our lawyers are present. We are officially connected to numerous Muslim communities. This is exactly the Islamophobia sweeping the nation we are demonstrating against. Why are we being treated as second class citizens?"

"You two are not citizens," Bret informed Amal. "Did you think we're so stupid we don't know your true identities? We know you both came into the country with false passports. You and your pal have been plotting here and overseas for something big. We want to know what that event is."

"Lawyer!" Amal and Kaul did a chorus line move turning away with their handcuffed hands while reciting their learned mantra when dealing with American authorities after they run out of lies.

They didn't understand at first when Bret and his crew showed such appreciative amusement at the declaration. Bret moved closer to his two unloved captives. "I have good news and bad news for you. We're turning your interrogations over to our associate, Darth Jed. Darth doesn't torture anyone. He doesn't need to. That's the good news. The bad news is when he gets done interrogating the suspects, they are no longer breathing."

Amal smiled. "You Americans. All bluster and threats. Did you think Kaul and I would simply fall on our knees begging for mercy? We are soldiers of jihad. Do not waste your time with these idle words you spew. Even your terrorist prison is a pleasure hotel."

"It must make all of you very angry as young men die overseas in the capture of our brothers, and then they get sent to Guantanamo only to be released for political and money favors by your various Presidents," Kaul added, grinning at his compatriot.

Oh my. This is going to be so good. I watched Erin's mouth tighten and her fists clench. I was relaxed. I knew these two dodos were on their way to Dhampir-ville for a short draining and then straight to the virgins. Bret never lost his smile while listening to his two oh so clever captives. They had the world on a string. I could tell Bret's anticipation made him let the two trolls keep talking so he could enjoy the true ending Amal and Kaul so richly deserved. They finished their light banter back and forth, highlighting their stay at Gitmo with Halal meals, Koran, prayer rug, and prayer beads. Then they would patiently await a future day when one of our leaders decided for a nice big payoff that they

256

had been punished enough. Amal and Kaul would then go free to terrorize the world once again. Bret allowed them their lovely fairytale.

"I'm sorry Kaul. When you entered the United States to act with good old Amal for the purpose of terrorism, you both chose door number one. Darth Jed? Would you please show Amal and Kaul what lies beyond door number one."

Four of Bret's men moved to hold my captured audience in place. Only then did doubt start to show on their faces. I let the whole look flow over my countenance, a nightmarish wave of darkness and despair, for them anyway. I allowed the claws, fangs, and eyes as the last features to fully impact my transformation. The screaming began in earnest within seconds. I cuffed Amal to the floor out cold. I scooped the wailing Kaul off the floor of the garage, pinned him to Bret's SUV, and sucked him dry. He confirmed my initial intuitive feeling Amal was the ringleader. Other than that, he was useless. I cast him aside and plucked Amal off the garage floor with anticipatory indescribable relish. Amal groaned as he reluctantly surfaced into consciousness. He saw my face and screamed. I took no offense. In his position I may have screamed too… but I doubt it.

My fangs sank into his throbbing artery with unleashed violence. Nothing stood between us other than revelation. Yeah, I enjoyed the anticipation of his somehow being able to confront me in an imaginary future inside his head. Such was not the case. Amal folded like a dilapidated lawn chair. His secret scared me though – the monster. Amal had ordered a Sarin gas attack on the Sacramento Amtrak train station to go off during the demonstration. This Capitol Building protest was a ruse to draw first responders and city assets to the publicized Islamic nonsense gathering. I knew who would be doing it and when. We had forty-five minutes to intercept them before they put the dispersal vessels in place. I dropped the lifeless Amal.

"We have to go now, Bret! They're hitting the Sac Amtrak station with Sarin gas. There will be a four man crew changing out fire extinguishers there looking very official. What they're replacing them with are timed release capsules looking exactly like fire extinguishers all in the main train station lobby." I threw the bodies of Amal and Kaul across the garage. "You can clean them later."

Erin kept silent, but followed us through our movements to get Bret's vehicle outside. I closed the garage door. Erin and I entered Bret's transport with his other men. In seconds more we were speeding toward Sacramento. "They'll arrive in a Sanderson Fire Extinguisher and Security service vehicle. It's a Ford dark blue Transit with white lettering."

"This will be close," Bret said. "I don't have assets in the area to handle something like that. The Sheriff's department has hazmat incident capability, but this also would be bomb squad type action. I'll level with you and Erin. Any suggestion would be welcome."

"Amal didn't know the trigger they're using," I told him. "From his knowledge, I'm assuming it will be a process of each capsule being time delay activated as each is set in place. There's no way to know for sure. If we can beat them there, the moment they park, I'll rip the door open and kill everyone inside. Then I think the safest bet would be for me to drive the vehicle to an unpopulated spot. Anyone you get on scene then would be able to contain the threat more easily."

"Jed can head out of the city on Route 5 and stop at the first pretty clear spot," Erin suggested. "Getting to him with the teams needed would then be easy, including helicopter."

"I like it," Bret agreed. "You need a hazmat suit though, Jed. Sarin can be absorbed through the skin as well as the eyes or respiratory system. We have a gas mask back there, but we don't have anything to protect the skin."

258

"I'll have to fasten my windbreaker tightly. We can duct tape my pants at the ankles and wrists wearing double crime scene gloves. With the mask I should be okay."

"This is a bad time to test out your healing factor," Bret said.

No doubt about that. "A lot of lives are at stake and I have the best chance of surviving an accidental release. I was thinking more of testing it out on a gunshot or knife wound, but we don't always get what we want."

"Your eyes are black as coal," Erin said as Aiden handed me a roll of duct tape and the oxygen breathing apparatus. "You're blood infused. That should help."

Erin grabbed my arm as I taped my pants legs. "I'm scared, Jed."

"C'mon, Eerie, buck up." I put an arm around her with a big reassuring smile I didn't feel. "Remember what my Mom calls me: the dark superman. Besides, I may get them all in quick order, drive the van to a secluded spot and then guard it until the bomb and hazmat guys get there. Amal was under the impression the timers would not be set until installed."

Erin sighed. "God help you if he didn't know what they planned for a trigger."

"Five minutes out, Jed," Bret announced from the front. "Best put on the mask now. Sarin dissipates quickly and works best in a closed space. Even if you partially opened windows as you drove along, that would make the Sarin exposure threat much less dangerous."

"That's what I'll do when I'm in motion toward a spot but only if there's an event." I had experience with oxygen breathing apparatus's so it only took me a minute to get the mask on and adjusted.

We entered the Amtrak train station in Sacrament just as Bret predicted. We let Aiden exit to check the inside of the station in case they dropped their guys off with the notion to swing by for retrieval when the installation of the nerve agent ended. He ran back out shaking his head in the negative. I stayed by the door, ready when the Ford Transit drove in. Although the mask felt comfortable, it would hamper any attempt to get information from the van riders. When I tore into the van I'd try for prisoners, but only if I could see empty hands.

"I'll throw them out alive if I can, Brett. Maybe I'll be able to get into their heads for more information later."

"That would be nice if it's feasible." Bret stopped twenty feet beyond the front entrance.

"There it is, Bret," Agent Soransky pointed at the station parking lot entrance as a blue Transit turned into the lot. Aiden moved to take the van side door handle to let me loose when it stopped.

The driver halted nearly five feet behind us to allow for the men inside to unload the fake fire extinguishers. The moment the driver began to open his door, I streaked out the side door of the van Aiden opened for me. I slammed into the driver's door, smashing the man exiting between door and frame. Bones crackled. I sped to the back as the unaware men began to exit. The first man stepping out of the van sailed into the front entrance post. Then I was inside. Unfortunately, the man at the rear standing between me and his other companion shielded his cohort who already held one of the extinguishers. I crashed the man into his buddy full force but I heard a hiss.

"One has begun discharging," I told Bret through my com unit.

I slammed the rear door on the unconscious or dead men in the back. A split second later I dived into the driver's seat, started the Transit, and drove around the parking lot fashioned by an idiot, finally exiting onto the street. I drove toward the Route 5 freeway entrance near the train station, cracking open the windows in the front when I reached a stretch unimpeded by traffic.

"I'm on Route 5 now, Bret. Windows are cracked open slightly. There is definitely gas escaping in the rear. I've turned on the blower full blast with fresh air. The Richards Blvd exit is a bit further. I hear the gas stopping. I'll park in the open area beyond the 520 route marker at the exit. It's relatively in the open. I don't want to chance getting affected and wrecking the Transit."

"Do you feel something now, Jed?"

"Yeah, I do." I was sweating which I rarely do. My chest felt like it was in a vice slowly closing off my air passages. The saliva in my mouth worked overtime, filling faster than I could swallow almost. "Traffic's light although I doubt they could be affected anyway from where I am. I...I'm still running the fan and I've opened the windows fully. I'll... go around to the back and open the door too."

"The hazmat and bomb squads are on their way as we speak."

"You don't sound right, Jed," Erin's voice broke in over Bret's. "How bad are you really?"

I made it to the rear door not wanting to speak before I stumbled my way back there and wrenched it open. I knew if my healing factor was worth a damn the oxygen from the breathing apparatus would kick it into gear. Everything turned into grainy shadows of varying consistency. I pulled open the rear hatch door. I then sat down in the doorway after confirming the dead eye stare into eternity from my two terrorists. They weren't going anywhere. I gazed out at the traffic approaching and passing. Vaguely as I began gasping slightly I saw an array of red flashing lights approaching and heard Erin's panicked voice screaming my name – at least it sounded like screaming. I smiled, remembering our night together before hell got dumped over our heads.

"I...I feel real good, Eerie. I... think you're so... cute." I didn't hear her reply because I slid down off the rear entrance onto the paved surface. It felt better down here but the voices in my ear seemed garbled as I drifted into unconsciousness, my last thought of Erin crying out my name the night before in much different circumstances. Damn... she was cute.

    \* \* \*

"There!" Erin nearly ran over Aiden Soransky trying to get a better look ahead. "Oh God... he...he's not moving... scrunched over on his side. He would never do that... never!"

Aiden grabbed her arms, shaking her slightly. "Focus! We have an army of hazmat and bomb squad units converging on us only minutes behind. They'll do everything they can to help Jed. We'll be on scene until the bomb squad/hazmat crews get control over the canisters. There is absolutely nothing we can do besides die rushing to Jed's side. Even residue from Sarin can kill you. Are you with me, Officer Constanza?!"

Erin's features tightened into determination. "Thanks. I'm good. What do we do now that we're here?"

"We'll observe and then follow our main man to wherever they transfer him," Bret answered from the front. "We don't want them getting too wild with their treatments until we see how his healing factor does. Did you see him toss that first guy? His head is mush but it looks like if Jed's okay he'll be able to suck on the driver."

Erin glanced down at the two bodies at her feet. They had collected the other two participants from where Jed left them. The one thrown into the post stared back at her with open unmoving eyes, his skull caved in. The driver twitched, but the morphine shot they gave him to offset reaction to the numerous cracked ribs, fractured shoulder and arm bones made keeping him sedated a must.

"We need to kill all these assholes!"

Bret grinned back at her. "You're not buying into the 'they just need jobs' spiel, huh?"

"I'm at this time considering a nuclear situation involving every Muslim country in the world. Damn it! Have you seen those wailing women cheering and dancing in the streets? All of them squealing in that high pitched, shrill echo of ecstasy every time something belonging to Western culture gets blown up, maimed, or murdered? I ask you Bret... how the hell do we think in reality we're ever going to change those fucking idiots' minds. How? They're a death culture! They live first to annihilate Israel. Since none of them have the balls to do that they murder and maim across the globe wherever any race of people allow them to get their camel's nose under the edge of the tent! I'm sick of it!"

Bret listened to her with the understanding of every other American citizen wondering why the government acts against the best interests of its citizens constantly and consistently. "I know, Erin. Believe me, I know the frustration and outrage you're feeling. Having you and Jed with us on these corrective measures means a lot to the rest of us. Unfortunately, we have to live within the rules in plain sight. I welcome your input as to how we can use Jed's incredible powers for America's wellbeing. I'm not in a position to change what goes on above my paygrade but we can correct some of the mistakes which will definitely damn us."

Erin stared into Bret's eyes without looking away, trying to determine if he believed what he said. She concluded rightly he did. "Thanks for recruiting us when you did. Jed was very close to drifting past any parameters I could influence him to adhere to. He has a purpose since meeting you. He better damn well survive this."

"From your lips to God's ear," Bret stated. "We need him. The horde is on the attack. That's plain after what we've seen these past days. They have an army of agents checking on the Muslim contingent in the East which I think needs to happen out here on the West Coast. Isis and their other lunes in the religion of death and Sharia think they can make serious attacks of terror in the West without repercussions. The media makes excuses, our leaders claim it's only a few bad apples, and the terrorists go on sapping missions with nerve gas. We're screwed. We need Jed."

"Here come the hazmat guys," Aiden said. "They'll get Jed decontaminated and checked."

Erin watched the careful process as workers in hazmat suits transferred Jed onto a gurney for transport. "I know this will sound unfeeling at the moment but I've been thinking of many situations where Jed's powers will help in addition to terrorist hunting. The obvious serial killer application he already demonstrated heads the list, but think how valuable he would be as a consultant on kidnappings, or nearly any case with suspects we can't beat the truth out of."

"Agreed. I don't plan to limit Jed in his endeavors," Bret replied. "On the other hand I don't want to burn him out on cases where local or federal law enforcement can handle the investigation. I will bring him in on high priority cases, but I will support him in anything the two of you agree merit his talents. Is that fair enough?"

"More than fair if we can keep him alive."

* * *

I awoke in a plastic zippered room, recognizable for purpose by the white everything, and meters hooked to my body

264

measuring everything but fuel level. One oddity I noticed instantly – there were no needles pumping stuff into me. I assumed they would pump electrolytes or saline solution into me like they do on TV. I'll have to feed on a doctor next, if only for knowledge needs. Suddenly, the idea of snacking on surgeons as well as general practitioners would make sense from a wellbeing aspect. I could do triage on our own team, especially if Erin needed emergency medical aid. I sat up, noting I was naked except for a white powder residue all over me. Then I spotted Erin waving at me from outside the clear plastic room. She gave me sign language to indicate she would bring a doctor.

A nurse appeared instead, checked the readings on a panel outside the room, and then opened it. She walked in ahead of Erin with a caution. "Stay here for the moment until I can detect whether your friend is safe to be around."

Erin waved happily again at me as the nurse moved to the monitors around me. I waved back. "Hey, Eerie. How did we do?"

"Very well, Jed. There is one prisoner still alive Bret thought would make you feel much better in no time. We need to clear you out of here first though."

"I'll have to draw some blood. Everything else appears perfectly normal," the nurse said.

She retrieved a blood kit from one of the tables. The blood draw only took moments because I have very well defined veins. Erin was allowed over to kiss me and give me a hug, but the nurse curtailed anything else due to the fact I was only covered by a thin blanket. I guess she figured Erin and I would be in danger of getting biblical right there on the gurney. As I noticed how great Erin looked, I thought maybe the precaution was justified.

"I'll be right back after I get these samples to the lab," my nurse said. "I'll be able to release you if the blood panels look good. You were very lucky, Mr. Blake. What those whackos planned to detonate and spread in the train station was definitely weaponized level Sarin gas."

The nurse left. Erin switched to informative Igor. "Your Mom and everyone want us over there at the house the moment you're released. They were all in the waiting area, but like I told them you were going to be fine from all the monitors' data. They agreed to go home and wait. Bret has everything in control for what was prevented, and how much he'll be able to tell the media. I could tell it pissed him off his bosses don't want any of what's happened released to the public. You can guess why."

Yeah, I could. "Regular American citizens would demand the Muslims in this country choose a side. If they didn't, they'd be watched like non-combatant hostiles and shipped out the moment they did anything suspect. In the meantime there would be rightful harassment of mosques, masjids, or any pro-Islam demonstration. It's coming, Eerie. People are pissed with getting white washed bullshit from their government when they can lose their lives because of it. What did Bret decide?"

"He first wants to get you on your feet. Once we walk out of here, he can put you with your previously knocked out prisoner to replenish yourself and find out everything you can. Bret wants you well which means you drain this bastard, Darth."

There's a shocker. "Damn, Eerie, you're getting an edge. First, it was Jed how could you, and now it's 'eat 'em up, Darth'. I will find out as much as I can from the guy. Count on it. These weasels worry me. They have no conscience. This letting off Sarin gas in a train station to kill everyone - and for what? There has to be an ultimate goal in all of this. I'm seeing only a murderous religion causing havoc around the world with only one goal in mind: domination. Just as Islam means surrender, they mean to put the entire world under their heel. That's the message I extracted from those two Isis toads I played with. I would love to drain any

266

terrorist shithead with all the deeds they aspire to and blasphemous deeds they plan. Bring him on!"

Erin grabbed my hands. "I'm with you no matter what. Seeing you lying by that Sarin van nearly collapsed my heart. I'm committed to this! I love you, Jed!"

I restrained every molecule inside me to keep from tearing sensor hookups from my body while reversing the grip on her hands. "I've always loved you, Erin. I need you now more than ever in our weirdo lives to this point. Everything Bret's said so far has been pure truth gold. I can tell. We'll have to ride the wave. I depend on you for common sense input, baby. Bret would not sell me out. If he ever disappears we're in big trouble. He seems to know his way around the political jungle. I'm hoping that fact keeps him in his position for a long time."

"I guess that means we go see the lone survivor before Mom's house, huh?"

"She'll understand. I'll call her on the way to Bret. Where's he conducting this draining?"

"My house. He's there now. I convinced him it's close, and all my neighbors know I'm a cop. There's less likelihood of anyone questioning anything if I'm walking in and out of my own free will even though the MIB's are there."

"If this Isis crap keeps happening, Bret will have to get an office for his private sessions. I know they kept track of me from the Sacramento FBI office, but doing things the way we do it would be more convenient to have a small sound proofed building with a crematorium."

Erin grinned. "He's working on it. Bret mentioned the need for a new headquarters to work out of completely separate from the FBI offices. He believes the backing our thwarting these latest terrorist gambits has gained would cement a new budget in place for a lot more in operating expenses. Bret thinks we may be able to swing a quick response force to be flown anywhere an imminent terrorist threat can be stopped or a killer or even a kidnapper could be apprehended and then disappear."

Oh my, that sounds like a wicked way for me to allow the blood lust trigger to be satisfied on a regular basis. Erin noticed the desirous cruelty probably spreading over my face. I received the fickle finger of fate waving under my nose. "What?"

"I see the blood hunter rising to the surface, Darth. Remember all the players in this present scene we haven't brought into the light yet. Forget the future feedings. I can tell we're going to have a difficult time keeping you harnessed."

So now I'm a Budweiser Clydesdale reined to a government sled. I don't think so. "What kind of leftovers are you talking about anyway?"

"Did you forget Senator Clifton Berry?"

Shit... I sure did. The gas must have messed with my receptors a little. "Sorry. Yes, I did forget about that jackal. He certainly set the very same terrorists responsible for the Sarin plot on me at the Capitol Building. Please tell me Bret has every agency capable of checking into that asshole burning down his personal and financial life."

"In addition to Berry, you've already met a couple of his palace guard."

"Lane and Sanders?" I laughed inappropriately once again remembering Lane threatening to come after me in the dark. "Seriously, Eerie?"

Erin patted me on the shoulder. "I'm reminding you of our loose pieces in the current puzzle still off the board. Bret's giving us full access to all the national security databases for purposes of pursuit. He knows you're better than anyone he has working for him at this time. He issued an information packet to all national agencies outlining Senator Berry's involvement with suspected Isis terrorists in addition to being related to Leslie. Bret explained Berry's ploy to intimidate witnesses using his leg breakers. He's running into flack from the politico backers on the fence, especially when it means confronting a Senator with as much power as Berry. Luckily, those people aren't read in on your powers."

"I wonder if Bret knows how many people know about me in reality. Your windmill comment wouldn't be so farfetched if anyone with a political agenda can be read in on Bret's task force. You and I both know there are ass-wipes in both congressional houses who shouldn't have security clearance to walk down the hall in a government building."

Erin hugged me. "I know. We have to work on a contingency plan. I wonder if there are any good countries without an extradition treaty with the USA."

"No, unless you want to live in a sandpit or Sub-saharan Africa. You don't have to worry about me, Erin. I have a few properties in very hard to get to places no one knows I own... at least I hope no one knows. After meeting Bret, I'm not sure of anything. In any case, I can get away and get lost until they forget about me."

"They'll never forget, Darth. What about me?"

"I'd take you with me, but you don't even like to go camping."

Erin giggled. "True. My love of the outdoors usually involves going to the park or watching out the car window on the way to Lake Tahoe. I guess I wouldn't make a very good fugitive from justice partner."

"We'll see this through." I quieted as my nurse returned with a smile and a clipboard with papers.

"You've been cleared. Sign these forms where I tell you to and I can release you."

I did as ordered, went to the closet with my ass hanging out, and dressed. Erin and the nurse had already seen me naked so pretending to be bashful was a little childish. When I finished the nurse fetched a wheelchair, another safety procedure in our litigious society. Patients, even Dhampirs, can't walk out of a medical facility. After noticing how far below ground I was in the isolation/decontamination lab, it didn't seem like such a bad idea to get a ride out of the danger zone. When we reached the curb Bret was waiting for us. Annoyingly, a limousine also awaited us, parked behind Bret. Carter Sanders stood near the limousine's hood. He didn't speak and kept his eyes studiously off me. I thanked the nurse. After she walked away with my wheelchair transport Bret shook my hand. He spoke for Carter.

"Senator Berry requested a formal meeting with both you and Erin. I won't pretend to know what he wants to talk with you about other than a cheap attempt at a bribe of some kind. You can testify to his talking with a known terrorist infiltrator and his cohorts. You both know he's related to an accused serial killer of young women. The request came from our political cohorts running my task force's budget. The Senator wanted the meeting. I agreed to ask you to talk with him. It's your choice, Darth."

"Well, isn't this nice, Eerie. I'd like to talk with him. How about you?"

Erin shrugged. "I have no qualms getting into any enclosed space with you, even if it means meeting with a known enemy who wants us dead."

"Please don't kill him, Jed," Bret asked politely.

"I'll try not to but I'm hungry… if you know what I mean."

Bret chuckled. "I have a meal waiting for you after your talk. If the limo leaves with you and Erin, we'll be following closely."

I nodded. Turning, I gripped Erin's hand for our short few steps to the Berry mobile. Carter gripped the door handle to open the rear door for us. "Thanks Carter. I see you took my threat a bit lightly."

"No, I didn't. I'm here against my will, Sir. That you can believe."

"I see you're telling the truth. You get a pass for the time being."

"Thank you," Carter whispered as he opened the door.

Inside the limo sat the ubiquitous Senator Berry smiling at us with three professional looking bodyguards near him. Carter must have explained a few events from our prior meeting because all three bodyguards held weapons in their hands vaguely pointing in our direction. Well, alrighty then. Erin covered her mouth, stifling amusement.

"I'm glad you think this is funny, young lady," The imperious Berry said. "Take my word for it: this meeting will involve national security. You two don't understand the underpinnings of government. Many shades of gray exist in layers between the public and the handful of dedicated men and women."

Erin and I chorused gagging noises at the same time. Our host and his glowering guards didn't take kindly to our reaction to the underpinnings of government. We sat together near the door we came in at. The interior of the limo was luxurious so there was plenty of room to be comfortably separate from Berry, not however far enough away to keep me from killing all four of them before they could get off a shot.

The Senator jabbed a finger in my direction. "I know all about you, Blake."

I smiled. "No you don't. After seeing you in action lately by way of your cohorts, I can tell who Leslie gets her serial killer genes from. I notice Carter must have told you about my weapon confiscation trick. It was a good idea to have your men draw and point before you see me."

"You must think this is all a fun joke. People's lives are at stake."

"The only lives in danger lately got that way because of you, Senator," Erin said.

Berry flushed red at Erin's remark, but leaned away with a wave of his hand. "What will it take to make this go away – all of it?"

"You're kidding," Erin kept digging in. "Is that what this meeting is about? I wish you would have simply phoned this in. We could have told you to eat shit and die without doing this in person."

I did enjoy Erin's line a bit too enthusiastically, but it was a little too much for the Senator. To his credit, he didn't do anything stupid. "Are you done now, Senator?"

"I don't think you two know how much power I wield. It's dangerous to have an enemy like me. Recant the accusations made against Leslie, and keep me out of any terrorist implications. I'll make sure Leslie gets the help she needs. There's no need to make this into a vendetta. You will have a very powerful friend in the Senate."

"We're going to link you to the attempted terrorist Sarin attack on the train station, Senator," I informed him. I wanted to see what his reaction would be. He did not disappoint.

"Are you insane?! You can't accuse a sitting Senator of the United States in a terrorist plot." Senator Berry was again leaning forward as his men shifted uneasily. They knew a government agent awaited our leaving the limo. "What proof do you have? Making wild accusations benefits no one. What do you two want?"

"I don't want to speak for Erin but I'd love to see you in front of a firing squad. A public hanging would be acceptable too."

"Jed speaks for me too. I love the firing squad idea."

"Throw these two idiots out of my limo!" Senator Berry didn't appreciate my candor.

His Praetorian guard reached for us, but I put a stopping hand between us and them. "Please don't do anything dumb. Laying hands on us would be dumb. Erin and I can leave the limo of our own accord. Thanks for the face to face, Senator. We'll be in touch."

Erin opened the limo door. I followed her through it. I believed Berry would come after us, but not in a physical sense. I needed to meet with my lawyers of which I did have a team, and my accountants. All financial avenues would have to be covered. It would not be the first time a government official used the IRS against taxpaying citizens. After that meeting, I could use a snack. I hoped I could get some insight into how deeply the Senator was with the Isis splinter group I wiped out. If he could be linked to the Sarin attack no one in government would defend him. He'd be hung out to dry. Bret looked concerned as the limo sped away.

"I should be thankful the Senator still lives. Is there anything else I should know about the meeting?"

273

"Only that I can't wait to chow down on our surviving Sarin spreader," I told him. "Can Berry block his own arrest if implicated in the Sarin attack?"

"I'm not sure," Bret admitted. "We have him on video meeting a leader of the attack shortly before they launched it. I've learned from past experience though, it's never a good idea to count on government to do the right thing when it comes to their hierarchy. They'll many times abandon soldiers and diplomats under fire but they'll move heaven and earth to protect one of their own slime-ball members."

"Maybe Jed can find enough to dump Berry with the prisoner we have," Erin replied. "Let's go find out. It's nice to be back in my house again although I like Jed's estate. I thought you looked a bit annoyed in the limo, Darth."

"I know the governmental weasels come after their political enemies and businessmen with the IRS. I have to make certain my lawyers and accountants are ready. It also means I'll be hacking into Berry's personal business. Don't worry, Bret. I won't misuse my new access."

"Meaning you'll invade with an invisible presence, right," Bret asked rhetorically as we entered his SUV.

"I will make it so there's no trace I ever clawed around in the Senator's trough."

* * *

My bandaged buddy cringed when he saw me enter the room selected for my question and answer feeding session. Erin used it as a spare bedroom. Our prisoner wobbled around on the chair Bret duct taped him to. The man watching him smiled at me and left. I enjoyed doing my slow change which elicited muffled screams from the prisoner. Yeah, I knew I could hurriedly change, drink him and be done, but where's the fun in that? The shit-head tried with his partners in Islamo-idiocy to set off Sarin gas and kill probably a couple hundred innocent people. I grinned with fangs bared while leaning toward my bulging eyed target.

"No need to speak. I'll know all about you in just a moment." I grasped his head in an unbreakable grip, tilting him painfully to expose his throbbing veined neck. My fangs sank ever so slowly into the well of life below his neck's skin. He quieted with a groan of surrender.

I drained him until he was two quarts low. Then I broke his neck. We had decided no matter what he knew about the Senator we couldn't trust my compelling to work well enough to simply arrest him. He would no sooner get the ball rolling on Berry when his inner murderous cult training regained control, leaving us with an expensive show trial we didn't know we could win. The flood of his training and memories seized my mind for a moment before I could shed the parasitic killer content while retaining the knowledge relevant to our mission. Berry's involvement included not only feeding sensitive classified data, but also positions of our naval ships and destinations. Berry told them where Congressman McRainey's two kids go to school. He also told them the times when McRainey's twins, a ten year old boy and girl, were dropped off and picked up. Suddenly, I wasn't as big a monster as I thought. The train station Sarin attack was the only large scale terrorist action my informant, the recently deceased duct taped Ari Bousaid in the chair, knew about.

It took me nearly ten minutes to shed the rest of Ari's cultist insanity and rage. The information indicating Berry's help with a proposed kidnapping of the McRainey twins stirred a rage having nothing to do with Ari. When I ascertained I could communicate coherently I joined Bret, Aiden, and Erin outside the room. I gave them the Reader's Digest version of what Ari knew along with what was planned for the McRainey kids. Ari knew only rumors that the kidnappings would be done by Western looking light skinned Albanians.

"Jesus..." Bret walked away shaking his head. "Good Lord, we're lucky in one way - because of their Mom's death, the kids surely would be held out of school for a while. What in hell could they accomplish by kidnapping McRainey's kids?"

"When they failed to kill McRainey, the crazy bastards figure the kidnappings would frighten any other congressional representatives on the fence about limiting Middle Eastern immigration," Erin said. "Damn. You'd think killing McRainey's wife would be enough to do that."

"Killing his family fits into their operating procedure," I agreed. "It would crush McRainey along with terrorize his cohorts in congress."

Bret turned to me. "Any idea where we could learn the identities of these Albanians, Jed? My people ripped apart the lives of every single participant we identified in the demonstration, including every computer and communication device they had. No mention of Albanians or kidnappings were anywhere to be found."

"My guess would be someone invisible to the rest of the minions. Someone writes checks for Berry. Let me dive into his financial accounts and records. He's probably feeling the pressure which means he'll open the purse strings for a radio or TV campaign message. If he reaches out to this hidden benefactor I may be able to trace our mystery man."

"That will have to do for the time being," Bret agreed. "See what you can find out. We'll take dead man with us now. Will you two be staying at your estate, Jed?"

I glanced at Erin. She nodded. "Yes. Can you put additional eyes on the McRaineys. They've had enough tragedy."

"Right away. No one gets near those kids. I'll see to it they have protection 24/7 starting immediately. Call me anytime day or night if you run down any leads pointing to this possible boss in charge. He would have to incorporate layers of dummy entities between him and what you believe he's doing. Writing payoff checks to a US Senator can't be done in any direct manner."

"I'll keep that in mind, Bret."

"Thanks for saving all our asses out there, Darth Jed."

"Thanks for joining in on the Erin nickname game, you prick." It was growing on me. "That was a hell of a weekend. At least I know now my healing factor is pretty good."

# Chapter Eleven

## Terrorist Tracks

Erin inspected my eyes before we went into my Mom's house. "Just in case Marilyn is there, I want to see how well you're doing with the black marbles. They're clearing real well. The nurse mentioned your eyes freaking the emergency room doctors when they peeled back your eyelid. I told her you had a weird light reaction like always. Since your vitals checked okay, she didn't mention it again."

"Good. I get sick of wearing sunglasses. Maybe I need to get those contacts with colored lenses. I'm pretty sure Marilyn had every intention of moving into her place again after the death of the Dots."

"It won't work with the contacts. Your black marbles cover too much area to be hidden. I think you're right about Marilyn as I remember." Erin tugged on my sleeve. "The boyfriend George won't care what you look like now that he knows the truth. I hope we can get to work on Senator Berry's financials quickly at your Dr. Frankenstein lab."

"That makes two of us. We can't rush this visit though. I'll clue them in on the investigation and the importance of discovering how deep Berry is in all this. They'll understand how vital it will be to learn the identity of the man signing his checks."

I led the way in the house. They were very glad to see me. George was on hand. He and Mom really did seem to mesh. After the initial greetings I explained Erin and I were on the trail of the man responsible for nearly everything happening out of the terror network. My Mom listened intently, especially when I was going over the dangers involved, and the Senator's threat.

"Your Grandmother has something to add. Go on, Mom. Tell Jed about the free cruise specifics."

"Before I do, Fang, I'm no dummy. I've never fallen for any 'something for nothing' scheme. The guy giving me the spiel sent us a thousand dollar check, saying we actually won a promotional cruise deal because of our travels overseas. We do enter into all those goofy promotion contests on our tours. The check was real. We deposited it. According to the so called agent who contacted me, there would be another five thousand dollars along with tickets for two couples, all expenses paid, to the Caribbean – no strings attached, meaning no sales meetings on timeshares or house flipper cons. We were discussing the trip now, trying to get Jill and George to come along with us. The cruise begins in a week."

"When did you get the money and offer?" I smelled rotten fish.

"Right after the big news stuff about capturing the serial killer. We thought the timing was weird, but Senator Berry's name isn't connected at all, at least not on the papers we have for it. The tickets for the eleven night cruise are legitimate because your G'pa and I signed onto the dashboard online where we could pick activities. It's the Celebrity Caribbean Cruise Line. What do you think is going on?"

"I think it may be a ploy to get all of you somewhere they can capture my whole family together, far away from anywhere I could reach quickly. Cancel it. I'll send you all on any cruise you want to go on after I finish with Senator Berry and these terrorists."

"We want a big luxury cabin with balcony, Fang."

"Yes, G'ma."

"I call him Sith Lord Darth Jedidiah, G'ma," Erin chirped in with a happy smile. "Darth Jed for short."

G'ma loved that one even more hearing Erin say it. She danced around a bit while clapping my little chirpy bird on the back. "Sure... like in Star Wars. Jed told us you nicknamed him with some flair. That's a good one, Eerie!"

"Eerie? You too, G'ma?"

"Would you prefer Whiney, Dear?"

"Uh... no." Erin sighed as chirpy bird got her own beak clipped to much amusement.

"We'll follow the lead you gave us," I told G'ma. "It could really shorten the search if I cross thread your freebie company with anyone dealing with the Senator. We'd like to stay for a while, but I need get back to what Erin has designated as my Dr. Frankenstein lab. With open access from my MIB, I'll be able to trace nearly anything. The inroads into Interpol will help immeasurably for anything going on overseas."

Mom gave me a big hug. "You worried us for the first time, Darth Jed. I'd like you to stay out of the poison gas."

"I think we're getting serious with the invader horde. The Sarin gas attack will awaken a lot of the sandbaggers in DC, along with the enablers and apologists."

"You've always been careful. I know you can sense danger, but these people allowing migration of this murderous flock into the country scare the crap out of me. They don't seem to care they're welcoming a Trojan Horse filled with invaders hell bent on destroying anyone that doesn't believe as they do."

"I'm the last one to defend what's happening, but someone in authority gave Bret enough leeway with a project that must seem like a script for a cheap horror movie."

"Jed knows when he's being lied to," Erin added. "Our contact Bret plans to expand his use of Jed's ability in the DC arena when needed. I've been pessimistic as hell with everything for the last couple years, but Bret makes me believe government policy is turning away from the suicide pact they've been enabling."

"I pray you're right," Mom said, taking George's hand. "You two go on. I hope you can nail Senator Berry and the puppeteer pulling his strings."

"We will, Mom. I'm serious about G'ma's lead. I can sense threads coming together."

"What do you want us to do in the meantime, kid," G'pa asked.

"Keep your heads down for the time being. Check on Erin's folks when you can too."

"I've been calling my Mom a few times a day, but with everything going on lately, I've missed some times when I should have called," Erin said. "If you could add in a couple of calls during the day, I'd really appreciate it."

"Count on it," Mom assured her.

\* \* \*

At Dr. Frankenstein's lab, better known by me as my development lab, I assigned Erin to doing what she was familiar with at work while trying to hone her detective skills – poring through databases for links. The access Bret gave us stunned her. She plugged away, taking it from the beginning. Familiar with police coworkers skimming information, Erin formulated a fixed goal to thread together anything from the multiple databases remotely similar. With each new connection she found, I created a datamining worm to expand worldwide.

It took no more than a couple hours before I joined the shell corporations I hoped to locate as a key. The one fronting the prize cruise G'ma received, called Corporate Cruises, linked to a financial consulting conglomerate making huge fake dividend additions to Senator Berry's portfolio. Once keyed into Erin's threads, my datamining worm struck pay-dirt. My worm burrowed to the bottom of a terrorist shit pile paying into numerous coffers. Those slush funds funneled into enough recognizable Islamic charity names, including mosques and masjids, that the results left very little doubt what they were really up to in my mind. Senator Berry languished atop the pile containing names in authority. I stared at the worm's probability factor's suggested entity at the terror network's heart: a Syrian billionaire philanthropist, Mohammed Drek.

Erin joined me a moment later. "Damn, Darth! Mohammed Drek? The savior of the world according to the media. What the hell do we do with this?"

I grinned at my Igor, rubbing my hands together before working the keyboard with zinging windows flying past at breakneck speed on the monitors in front of me. "The first thing we must do is bring Senator Berry into the light."

"And how do we do that, Sith Lord?"

"We create a charitable organization titled Palestine Surreal Corporation in Burkina Faso." Erin watched while I formed the fake charity using the names of all the Islamic charities listed by my worm as contributors to my Palestine Surreal. Once I established the account the time came for Palestine Surreal's largest contributor to donate a huge portion of his evil holdings into my new fund's wonderfully complex existence.

"Darth Jed... are you..." Erin gasped while watching the ease at which I entered into Senator Berry's holdings everywhere. With all the essentials for slipping into the base architecture of

Clifton's personal and Senatorial networks I hacked into his holdings within seconds. "You... you're stealing his money!"

"I'm insulted you think that Eerie. The Senator is contributing to all of his favorite Islamist charities from which an upstart charity named Palestine Surreal received Clifton's donations within its humble account." Fifteen minutes later all of Clifton's ill-gotten gains became the property of Palestine Surreal. "I can't wait to see how our infamous Senator Berry deals with this crisis. We'll give Bret our complete research, including the proof of threads spiraling from Mohammed Drek to everyone on our suspect list. Once he gets permission to monitor everything Clifton does, I believe Bret will monitor many panicked calls directly linking him without any doubt to a now proven Islamist hidden leader: Mohammed Drek. Then the fun starts."

"You... Sith Lord Darth Jedidiah... are scary good."

"I am indeed, my treasured minion." I called Bret, filling him in on our work while messaging over the files Erin and I created. We kept a few details to ourselves. No need for Bret to know what I planned for Drek until he intimated what his plans were after going over our files.

He called back after studying our lab work. "I'll start proceedings with what you've given me, Jed. I can't poke a single hole into your conclusion. Once I put together a presentation, I will make my case to the people I trust over us. From there, we may be able to get Drek a worldwide rap sheet, making it impossible for him to carry out extensive plots using the shell corporations you've found doing his dirty work. I won't blow smoke up your ass minimizing the difficulty in going after Drek. Do you have plans for him you'd like to share?"

"Not at this time. I'll be happy to await your presentation's success. I don't plan to allow him to hunt our families down or try and lure them into places they can be taken for blackmail. I have money enough to go anywhere he does. As you know, he won't have enough guards to stop me. I know without the proper planning I'm the one who could be designated worldwide as a killer of Saint Drek by Interpol as well as the media."

"Understood. I will contact you the moment I sense where the hierarchy stands on going after Berry. Every phone and network will be monitored when originating from Senator Berry or being received by him no matter what decision is made concerning pursuit of a conviction."

"Thanks. We'll be here." While I talked with Bret, Erin did a provocative exploration of my person as I sat trying to concentrate on Bret's conversation. I reached around to pull her easily onto my lap where I could discover the reason for the enjoyable inspection. "Were you trying to get my attention, young woman?"

Erin gave me a very sensual lap dance for a moment. "It feels as though I've already garnered your attention, Darth. You know what I like."

"If you're referring to the frightening action I do with my fangs I must remind you of the extreme danger. C'mon, Eerie, you're getting to be a Dhampir junky."

She kept moving ever so slowly on my lap while stripping off her blouse. "What's wrong with that? You heal me. No blood, no foul."

"That's not even remotely funny." I gripped her in place, stopping my gyrating provocateur. "I'm not going to do it again."

Erin grabbed my face between her hands, staring straight into my eyes. "You'll do what I say when I say to do it. Understand?"

"I understand you're going through withdrawal. Fight it. I'll make love to you completely, you'll wonder why you ever considered offering your neck for my pleasure."

"You can't duplicate the sensations your fangs provoke in me while you feed. Good Lord, Darth!" Erin twisted to offer her neck after pulling down the bra strap. "You're a Dhampir! Show some control while mind melding with me as before. You stopped. It was incredible and you know it. Afterwards you can make me one of your huge omelets with cheese, plenty of juice and rye toast. Quit playing hard to get!"

"Spoiled brat!" God... I'm weak. My fangs stretched for the beautiful curve of her neck which shivered in anticipation. Erin was right. I loved her so much I'd do anything for her, including gambling with her life.

The moment my needle pointed daggers stabbed gently through her skin, Erin cried out in climax, shuddering so I needed to grip her tightly to keep from ripping into her neck. Erin's essence flooded into my mind and soul once again. All she was or will be I possessed. The seconds stretched into an eternity of intense pleasure so wickedly searing, the moment seemed a threat to burn through my brain. When Erin screamed in an ecstasy beyond anything on earth I recoiled from her, nearly forgetting to heal as I pulled free. She collapsed against me, gasping for breath. I held her with a fierceness born of soul ripping desire. Erin reached with shaking hands to once again frame my face as she stretched against my chest, the back of her head thudding with release against my shoulder. Her hands reached from my face to the back of my neck, clasping around it. She shifted to hold the position, groaning contentedly.

"Oh my... our joining intensifies each time. I should have made you taste me long ago." She released me, twisting around while standing, pointing a warning finger at me. "Don't you dare make a cheap sexual innuendo to ruin the-"

I caught her in my arms. The blood loss combined with her angry leap from my lap to defeat my dear Erin's unfinished threat. I knew it would have been a good one. I walked with her gently towards my kitchen. She wrapped her arms around me weakly with a sigh.

"Am I a quart low, Darth Jed?"

"Nope, but probably a pint, my little Fangster groupie. We'll have to get you some sustenance right away before I abuse you any further."

Erin giggled. "What kind of abuse did you have in mind?"

"A common brand of sexual intensity, but with much more of a messy, writhing melding of mind and body. It will be a bit violent but less dangerous."

"Sounds intriguing."

I smiled at her without a reply. Believe me, my Eerie companion, I will make your after dinner excursion quite intriguing.

* * *

My estate lies within a wooded area of Pollack Pines quite separated from surrounding neighbors or prying eyes. Although as I've explained, my security system combines state of the art HD video, audio, and motion sensing apparatus, I do not rely on it totally. I know every sound inside and outside my house. When a branch crackles in the woods or a squirrel brushes too heavily against a branch I know it. I don't sleep like humans sleep. I rest as the predator in the jungle rests.

Mom witnessed my sense of awareness long ago when two men came calling at 2 am in the morning. I was twelve. My Grandparents were spending a weekend at Lake Tahoe. Although I many times roamed the nights, I normally returned by midnight

286

unless something interested me in my travels. That early morning I rested. I heard the two men approach our house. They broke through the door with a sledge hammer, only to find me waiting. I broke the sledge hammer wielder's neck, swinging his arms before he could release the sledge, smashing his cohort in the temple, caving in his skull. Mom ran down the stairs with shotgun in hand. She grinned at the scene. The police accepted the story we told them because they had no other explanation - we heard the break in and found the two full grown men dead on the floor. The only thing Mom said was if it happened again, I was to take care of the intruders outside the house before they broke something.

I brushed my fingertips across Erin's forehead where she lie entwined in my arms. "Erin?"

Her eyelids fluttered open tiredly. "Hi."

"A crew of men are approaching the house with violence in their hearts. I'm going to take them on the outside of the house."

Erin pointed at her purse. "Bring me my Ruger before you go."

I did as I was told, but reluctantly.

"Oh... get that hurt look off your face," Erin ordered. "I know they don't have an ice cube's chance on a Sac sidewalk in August at noon. The Ruger's so I can shoot you if you wake me before 10 am."

Okay, that was funny. I chose the Terminator line. "I'll be back."

"It better not be before ten."

* * *

The men, dressed in black complete with ninja masks, approached slowly through the woods toward the clearing surrounding my actual estate house. I waited, wondering how they planned to defeat my security system. Then I saw it. One of the men held what appeared to be an electromagnetic pulse weapon. He glanced at his boss who waved him to the side of my front entrance. The leader nodded. I panicked, rushing at the EMP weapon man like a freight train. The force of the collision sent the EMP wielder crashing into a cohort in the path of his flying body. Neither man survived the meeting. I destroyed the weapon before it could be retrieved. The rest of them only saw the results. They didn't see anything of me but a shadowy streak.

I shot by them into the line of woods ringing my estate. Yeah, when you can do what I do, it's a given some predator playing with prey will happen. I wanted to see what my uninvited visitors did. They didn't panic. One hurriedly checked on his two downed companions. He shook his head at the leader who crouched with his other three men, guarding each other's backs while searching the surrounding area for whatever flattened his two dead guys. I didn't want to leave them hangin'. I watched closely. After no follow attack, they stood with weapons still at the ready.

They then fanned out after a few hand signals from their fearless leader. He examined the EMP weapon I broke apart. A few seconds checking it over and he threw it down on the ground with an audible curse. So much for stealth mode – even his men showed some surprise. I welcomed the opportunity by swooping in from the tree line. The man furthest from his group on the left flank turned his silenced Pleter submachine gun on his friends and shot all of them... with my help of course. I chomped him while assisting his final kill bursts. He was nowhere near as tasty as Erin which was a truly sick thought.

After breaking the neck of my shooter, I hurried over to where the leader writhed in horrible pain, clutching his knees. I made sure while guiding my dead-shot helper to only wound his commander. If my hunch proved true we'd have the last cog in the

Senator Berry/Isis connection. No way these guys simply arrived at my home for payback out of the blue. The shooter I bled belonged to an imported cell operating near El Paso. The leader, named Imad Atwa, belonged to the same cell. They had arrived this afternoon by private plane flying into Lodi airport. The plane would be another key if registered to one of the Mohammed Drek front groups. I needed more info before delving into it.

I snatched Atwa from the walkway, tearing into his neck with care not to make the wound so bad as to not be healable. I gorged on his blood feast since I had no other battles to be won, only power and information to be absorbed. To say I overloaded my Dhampir circuits would be an understatement. When engorged with blood my body converts the blood into energy, but also heat. I don't sweat but I can come close to burning off my clothes. I finished with Atwa, healed him and returned to my shooting buddy. I put a round through Atwa's head using the shooter's hands and body. I called Bret from my lab after cooling down outside in the forty degree early morning temperature. I had news and I needed to continue cooling off in the special room I keep my computer towers cooled to fifty degrees in while using the work station inside the room. I also needed to know if he wanted to go public with the bloody scene I created on my doorstep. Bret listened to my description of the scene while watching a video of it I sent him from my security system.

"Leave everything as is, Jed. I'll be over with a legitimate team from Homeland Security in addition to a couple of my guys. From the looks of it, I believe we can play it off as an internal battle that exploded at your estate while they were in the process of assaulting your home. We can follow the leads you accumulated without missing a beat. A targeted news report of a failed terrorist cell attack to the right media outlet would be a boon to Homeland and FBI we'll credit with tracking them down."

"Sounds good. I should be able to trace the plane's owners. Atwa knew the plane's registration and what hangar they used at the Lodi Airport. If one of the dummy corporations Mohammed Drek uses owns the plane and hangar we'll have another golden thread."

"Especially if you find out Senator Berry has used the plane for transportation in his travels," Bret added. "I like it. I'll be there shortly. Excellent work, Darth."

"We need to invent a snappy nickname for you too, my friend."

"How about 'Boss'?"

"How about 'Woodstock'?"

"The yellow bird from the 'Peanuts' comic?" Bret did not sound enthused.

"I sure didn't mean the sixties rock concert."

"It better be 'Boss'. What do you think about hitting the Lodi hangar?"

"Let me grind out the details surrounding the plane used to transport an imported killer Isis cell into Lodi at a corporate hangar possibly tied to Drek. I'll find the flight schedules earmarked for the future and ones from the past. It won't take long to find how many hangars around the country operate under Drek's front group. They could very likely be terrorist cell network points. If a military type team of assassins can be leapfrogged into Lodi to get me at nearly a moment's notice wouldn't you say that could be the worst news of the day, Boss?"

Silence for a moment as Bret mulled my nightmarish logic around in his head. "We'll be there shortly. Yes... you're right. That would be very bad."

He disconnected. It felt as if I cooled down to a dissipation point where I wouldn't scald anyone. Wow, what a rush that energy burn off feels like. I hoped to avoid any questions in the future in reference to how I could drink all the blood I siphon from people without it going anywhere. If my government forces became curious, they might not settle for a few tests. They may think dissection to be the only answer. The other concerns I harbored about government centered on a military aspect. I had no idea how close to cloning people they really were. The thought of my being cloned to create a super soldier army did indeed bother me. All science fiction thought flew out of my head as the beauteous Erin found me while wearing a wisp of a sheer black nightie I forgot I bought and stashed in my drawer to spring on Erin one day. Instead, she sprung it on me, and oh my, that girl looked nice.

"Bret's coming over with a team. God... you look good."

"We've got time to have Dhampir sex like on that show 'True Blood'. Remember when they showed them speeding during sex?"

"I think that was vampire on vampire or it should have been. I'd tear you apart doing that." I gathered her into my arms for a Dhampir quickie at regular speed. "I need to run leads on the gang that just attacked."

"You're still burning bright. I saw you handle those little lambs by the door. You must have put down a couple quarts. That could be an interesting interlude... very hot."

"Agreed. We better stay in the cooling room."

Erin let the nightie fall away. "Agreed."

\* \* \*

Bret and his team policed my murder site with thorough expertise, loading the bodies only an hour after arriving. It was enough time for me to trace the private jet's registration to Ishtar

Financial Corporation, a wholly owned subsidiary of Jonas Shipping Merchant's Fund. Jonas Shipping belonged to Mohammed Drek. More digging exposed Senator Berry's frequent flyer miles traveling on the Ishtar Corporate jet. I made a hard copy for Bret to look over and emailed him the folder with crosschecked steps leading to the conclusions.

Outside as Bret handled the final details of body transfer, digital DNA, pictures and fingerprints, I gave him the report. He looked it over carefully in the early morning light of a new and exciting Dhampir day. I could tell the anticipation had not gone away for nailing Clifton. He let the report drop to his side with a slow headshake.

"The traitorous bastard has been in Drek's pocket for a long damn time. There's no telling how many operations he's compromised. I notice you checked the phone calls on Atwa's burner phone. He was in direct contact with Berry. We've got him, Jed."

"When do you think you'll frog-march him away?"

"Not until we do some extensive research into dates, times, and movements from his personal calendar. I'll make all of this legal because of a terrorist investigation. I can get a blanket warrant for everything Berry owns. The warrant will be an official start. From there we can go after Drek for bribing and using a sitting Senator in acts of attempted murder and terrorism. He'll be public enemy number one on Interpol's hit list. I'd like to hit the private hangar this morning before they know none of their murderers are coming back. I could use you on it."

"I'm in. I can't have this Drek continue trying to murder me. He'll be sending hit teams after all our families. We will eventually run out of luck and skill. Do we ever have any idea where this Drek is? With Berry, he's either in DC or at his Sacramento office. He can't hide. Drek could go into hiding at the first indication we're on to him. Would we be able to find him if that happens?"

Bret shrugged. "I know better than to tell you stories. If a billionaire like Drek goes into hiding anywhere within terrorist lands, we would have to wait until he surfaces."

At least I can envision a different hunt for the future. Bret made it plain with that statement. We have what we have. "We can't let Berry slip through the cracks. I realize if you don't get him all of this will be for nothing. I'll study the great Drek. It may be with enough study I can find a way to locate him without Mohammed knowing he's being tracked."

Bret didn't hide his relief. "Thank you. I know Drek puts all your lives in danger. If we successfully sever all his dealings in the US, we'll have a chance to put him out of business for the time being until we can deal with him."

"Are you hitting the airport hangar now?"

"Yep. I'll let the Homeland team take in our dead guys for disposal. I have my guys here already. We're equipped, especially if we have you along for the initial assault. Follow us there with Erin networking with us. We'll hang back until you can recon the hangar. I'd like to make some arrests on this, but it may not be possible to do so. I understand that. No casualties on our side. I don't give a crap about anything you find inside. I'll be in contact with you. Make your own determination on site. I'll follow your lead."

"On it, Boss."

* * *

Erin parked my Batmobile on the other side of the hangar approach from where Bret and his team positioned for the assault – if an assault was necessary. Erin left the front with me. She would be coordinating with Bret while I did a Dhampir speed recon of the hangar. I opened the back for her to assume position at the monitoring station inside. She grabbed my cheek.

"I had a wonderful night and morning in spite of all the bad guys deciding to pay us a visit. I know the blood fanging I enticed you into again frightens you. What you said about me being a Dhampir junky is probably true. Since there's only one of you it's not really a bad thing is it?"

"It's all fun and games until I lose control and drain you like an Erin smoothie."

"You won't lose control but I have. I can't wait to have you taste me again. Think of it this way, Darth. I'm not playing hard to get any longer. Now go kill some bad guys."

"You're also getting a lot more violently blood thirsty yourself, Eerie."

"That's the price I pay for caring more about you than the terrorist assholes we're hunting. I'll be in your ear on this. You told me already Bret would like arrests. I'll keep reminding you of that. Will there be prisoners?"

"I might say yes now… and no later."

Erin nodded as I began closing the rear hatch. "Understood."

The hangars were spread well apart in the open airport area, bordered by roads, fence, and even crop fields - extremely easy to approach without being seen. At least that would have been true if not for the sentry I saw atop the hangar building as I approached at Dhampir speed, keeping him in sight while weaving around the buildings. Although I can't leap over tall buildings at a single bound, I can leap atop a hangar in the vicinity of a bored guard. I would need a bite so as to get the layout of the inside before my unexpected visit.

The guard watched the main approaches so I positioned myself near where he stood toward the front. My leap consisted of a great takeoff, two hand boost on the roof rim, and a landing only five feet away from his back. He spun toward the noise. By the time he turned my fist was landing at his temple. I luckily pulled the punch enough so as not to cave in his head or launch him over the roof. He carried a Glock 9mm instead of a rifle and never cleared his fast draw holster. Anchoring the guard's shoulders with his unconscious head lolling to the side I fed on my morning Halal meal with great pleasure. I grew more accustomed to the daily blood lust treats every day, probably at a dangerous rate. What rushed through me this time wasn't a satisfied blood appreciation, but the fact Mohammed Drek prepared to use his corporate jet inside the hangar. Oh my... that's just so sweet of him.

"Drek's inside the hangar." I hopped off the roof.

"Uh oh," Erin said.

"What are you... uh oh," Bret echoed Erin's remark as he probably watched me tear the hangar's small door completely off and toss it.

I moved quickly to accomplish my goal. I didn't know how many innocents there were inside the hangar. I didn't care anyway so why give it any thought. You know the old cliché 'sleep with dogs, wake up with fleas'. In this instance that was probably an insult to dogs. I weaved my Dhampir magic amongst the startled hangar occupants with rather haphazard fury. I clotheslined men standing, ran over ones sitting, ripped into the small offices to throw men into walls like rag dolls. I began to think Drek might already be on the corporate jet. He wouldn't be going anywhere because I clotheslined his pilot and copilot during my jaunt around the room. The back office proved my thinking wrong. Drek awaited me with three men, all pointing hand guns at the doorway,

I think because of the commotion and screams I elicited in the main hangar.

They all fired but far too late to hit their speedy Dhampir nemesis. A split second after streaking inside I was amongst them, snapping wrists, slapping faces, and generally working my usual mayhem. Twenty seconds later, three bodies lie strewn around Mohammed and me. He clutched his broken wrist, the one he had been holding a weapon in, rocking with it near his waist from a crouched position. I shoved a chair under him.

"Move in, Boss," I told Bret. "Be careful out there. I didn't stop to check on bad guys so don't take anything for granted with the men lying at different positions in various stages of duress."

"Will do. How's Drek?"

"Alive for now until I find out everything he knows. I need to not be disturbed so I'll leave you to investigate in the main hangar. Prepare any of them you find alive for either transport or for me to dispose of, depending on identity."

"Take your time. We're already at the door," Bret replied.

"Want me to come in, Darth?"

"You can if you want, Eerie," I answered, propping the stunned and still crying Drek against the chair back. I patted Drek's cheek. He was a suave looking devil – long black hair tied at the back of his neck. Drek preferred the dark brooding look with unshaven day old beard, thin dark playboy face, and light gray silk suit with open necked black shirt. Mohammed looked about half a foot shorter than me when he had been standing. "Hi there. Where were you headed this fine morning?"

"I...I need a doctor. My wrist is broken. What is it you want? I will not speak with anyone but the authorities in charge of this outrage! Do you know who I am?"

296

"I sure do. Fine. Let's cut to the chase." I changed into blood sucking mode much to Drek's dismay.

He screamed as my fangs ripped into his neck. Mohammed had traveled to his last mountain. I didn't care about his problems, goals, family or plans for the near future. All of those things would be mine. By the time I finished with him I was steaming with blood burn off. I had big plans for Drek's empire, at least the money portion of it. I figured Bret and I would get along better with our goofy government if I didn't cost them much. After all, why should I fund everything when I had my old pal Mohammed heading for the elephant's graveyard? It would only take me a short time in my lab to transfer everything I could into my Palestine Surreal fund. His head was full of plans to have me wiped off the face of the earth, including everyone who meant anything to me. A nice bonus was the fact I now knew where he kept all his dealings with Senator Berry and the others on his payroll. Drek would be instrumental in bringing down Berry. It was a shame I couldn't have a Berry snack after I burned off Mohammed.

Erin entered, pausing inside the doorway as I finished my Halal treat, dropping his corpse to the floor. "Did you get anything interesting? You're practically glowing. I bet you're a bit hot to the touch, huh?"

"Yeah, I am. It will take us days to go through all the dark corners this asshole had his fingers in. The people list alone he either bought off or blackmailed in this country will blow your mind. The number of lefties and faux conservatives on his tab in government will have a lot of explaining to do when Bret blows the lid off this network. Berry's his kingpin though. He owned Clifton like a pet dog. Drek covered for Berry completely over the decades but kept all the proof if Berry ever got out of hand."

"I guess we'll have time to work it since we won't be fighting for our families' lives," Erin replied. "You only left three alive in the hangar."

"Oh waaahhhh…"

"I figured you'd be touched at the carnage you caused Darth Jedidiah."

"Yes… I'm so ashamed. Can I eat them or are the treats off the table?"

Erin giggled. "I'm getting as bad as you. Anyway, I think Bret wants to keep them for the time being."

I reached down to check on the three bodyguards. They were all alive. Whoopy. I threw one over my shoulder and then dragged the other two. "C'mon Eerie. I have three more goldfish for Bret's pond."

Erin followed me to where Bret watched his team sorting through the hangar and Drek's jet. He grinned and waved as I delivered my three prizes. "These three are still alive. Drek's nearing room temperature in the other room. I know everything. Erin and I will get busy tearing it all down at my lab. Can you keep Drek's body on ice for a while? I'll send the evidence Drek kept on all the dealings with Berry right away so you can move on him, but it would help considerably if I could have a couple days burning through the rest of his manipulations. Once his death is known a lot of his accounts probably have automatic shutdowns on them."

"No problem. If I can go after Berry full bore, that will keep media attention off anything else in the country, especially if you have a bunch of hot items Drek held in reserve." Bret put an arm around my shoulders, but then pulled away. "Damn, boy… you're hot. Is that how you get rid of all the blood?"

"Yeah. My system converts it to energy and then exudes it in the form of heat."

Bret hesitated before replying. "Neat. I know this will sound rather off, but did Drek have an 'enemies list' he used?"

"He had extensive files to be used in any way he wished. There are some big names in all avenues of power. I know you're wondering if I trust you with a list like that. I do. I'm not crazy about the danger of it falling into the wrong hands. What do you think of giving me a name you're having trouble dealing with or becomes a threat to our team? I'll give you what you need to get the situation under control."

"I'm not Hillary Clinton, but I see your point," Bret conceded. "That would be fine. I know you'll give me everything on the people selling out our country. I'll settle for that."

"You got it. Is it okay if Erin and I leave to get started?"

"Sure, Darth. You two take off. Check in with me the moment you get Berry nailed. Send me his stuff right away. He's our number one priority now that his benefactor has been retired for good."

"I'll have that to you by tonight. C'mon Eerie, let's go make music."

* * *

"Can we stop by my house on the way home?"

"Sure. If you're really interested in getting into the Drek business with me, it would be a good idea to bring your weekend bag. You still keep one on hand with your uniform and everything, right?"

"That was my thought, Darth. We can take Route 99 through Sac and head toward your place on 50."

"Gee... thanks for the directions." I think sometimes because I'm a monster, Erin forgets I grew up next to her. I do know my way around the area.

"Sorry. Force of habit. Let's stop at the 7/11 on Folsom and get some wine."

"Okay." That really did sound good. We'd been riding with the AC on to cool the Batmobile. I was still cooking off my Halal meals.

I turned off Route 99 for Folsom Blvd about forty minutes later after a comfortable silence as I cooled to a normal temperature. I no sooner drove into the 7/11 parking lot when a young woman stumbled in front of the Batmobile from the Shell gas station next door, bleeding from the head. I jammed the Batmobile into park, streaking out to catch the woman before she took a header into the pavement. She pointed at a late model Chevy trying to get around a truck at the Shell pumps.

"Car...car jacked. My baby... my baby's inside!"

The burn was on as Erin clutched onto the woman. By the time Mr. Car-jacker reached the exit point onto Folsom Blvd, I reached the driver's window. I smashed through the window, grabbed Mr. Car-jacker and made him fit through the window. Not everything connected to him made it through the window. I tossed him toward Erin while opening the door. He landed on his head thirty or forty feet on the way to the destination. A split second after the toss I jammed on the brake from the driver's seat. The little girl who looked about two in the rear car seat was laughing with her arms waving. We weren't blocking traffic, but I reversed to a spot by the curb and shut off the car. I opened the rear door to retrieve my very amused passenger.

With the little girl in my arms I walked toward where Erin held onto the wounded woman. Erin kept pressure on the bleeding wound with her hand while sitting next to the sobbing Mom. I had to walk by the car-jacker. He was groaning and barking out little screams of pain. He had a handgun in his pants. Although his shoulders were clearly not working thanks to his trip through the driver's window, I kicked him in the head on the way by, ending any need for a trial later. I placed the little girl in her Mom's arms while sirens screamed toward our position from Folsom Blvd. Erin smiled at me.

"I'll get my medical kit." I sped to the Batmobile rear compartment and retrieved my quite complete emergency kit.

By the time the police drove in next to us, I had cleaned the wound with peroxide, and was in the process of holding the bandage in place while Erin added surgical tape to hold it. The woman hugged her bewildered daughter. She was still laughing because I made faces at her while we doctored her mom. Erin showed the arriving police her badge and ID, giving them an abrupt version of what happened. The police inspected the car-jacker, interviewed the few people who had caught glimpses of what happened, and called for the meat wagon. They enjoyed speculating about the car-jacker's trip from the driver's seat to the pavement while we waited for more official arrivals. Luckily, no one saw me dropkick Mr. Car-jacker into eternity. It helped the cops recognized Erin from the serial killer news although they didn't know her personally. A preliminary judgement from the coroner was death by impact with the pavement. A couple hours later we were again on the road with wine.

"We make a good team, Darth. We'll go to your house, find what Bret needs for a Senator Berry frog-march. Then, after we have some wine, I want you to have another taste."

"No! No more tastes, you little Dhampir groupie freak. We'll have some wine after the file's sent to Bret. Then, we'll watch a nice romantic comedy together."

"You'll do what I tell you, when I tell you to do it, Fang!"

I started an angry denial and glanced over to find Erin with her blouse open, neck and breast exposed. "Arrrggghhh!"

"Don't worry, Darth. I'll be gentle."

I tried to speak but managed only another weak, "Arrrggghhh." Such is life in Dhampir land, controlled by an emotional succubus named Erin.


The End

Thank you for purchasing and reading Blood Lust. If you enjoyed the novel, please take a moment and leave a brief review on Amazon and/or Goodreads. Your consideration would be much appreciated. Please visit my Amazon Author's Page if you would like to preview any of my other novels. Thanks again for your support.

Bernard Lee DeLeo


BERNARD'S FACEBOOK GROUP

https://www.facebook.com/groups/BernardLeeDeLeo/

AMAZON AUTHOR'S PAGE (USA)

http://rjpp.ca/BERNARD-DELEO-BOOKS

AMAZON AUTHOR'S PAGE (UK)

http://rjpp.ca/BERNARD-DELEO-UK

Made in the USA
Middletown, DE
24 February 2016